JUST LIKE COMPTON

Academic Edition.

JUST LIKE COMPTON

By Kevon L. Gulley

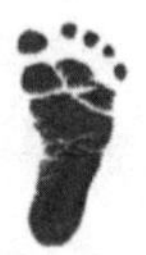

Los Angeles·NewYork·Paris·L'Haiti

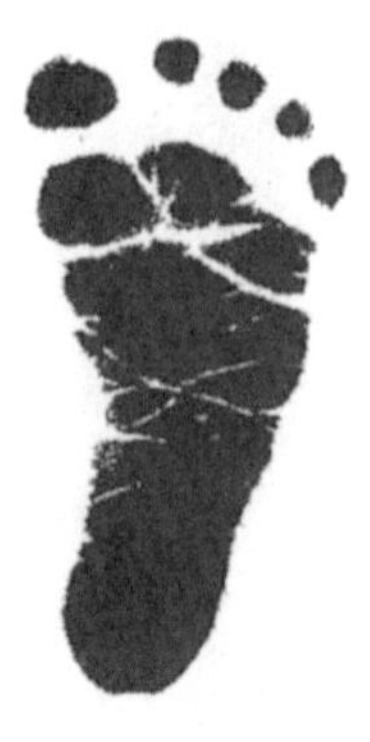

For information:

Coverdesign by Tina Roosen, Photo by Pooh Mayo
Academic Edition. Edited by C. Rhuné Buggage, Kevon Gulley

Soleil Publishing.

justlikecomptonbook@gmail.com

This book is a work of fiction. Names, characters, places and incidents are products of the author's memory, or imagination. Or are used ficticiously. Any resemblance to actual events or locales or persons, living or dead, is entirely coincidental

ISBN-13 9780615494449

For information regarding special discounts for bulk puchases' please contact

Soleil Publishing/REDHANDED FILMS.

This book is dedicated to the streets that raised me,

And to those who betrayed me.

(You know who you are).

For Dannie Lamont Farber,

December 29, 1990 May 24, 2009.

We can still feel you with us when the wind blows.

FOREWARD

JUST LIKE COMPTON does not reflect the lives of the majority of people who reside in Compton. Most people have never seen anyone get shot, they have not robbed banks, nor done a drive-by shooting! **JUST LIKE COMPTON** does, however, depict in vivid imagery the experiences of many young people who have lived in and grown up in Compton and South Los Angeles.

Rather than view **JUST LIKE COMPTON** as another Ghetto thriller, it should be approached as a narrative critique of the consequences of economic injustice, social inequality and limited access to basic rights and social entitlements. **JUST LIKE COMPTON** immerses the reader into the present day realities of those injustices and inconsistencies and inequalities that have bedeviled the African-American and Latino communities for decades.

Referred by a colleague, the author of **JUST LIKE COMPTON**, Kevon Gulley, approached me in early September 2011. He inquired as to the possibilities of me adopting his novel as one of my course texts. I glanced through the book and expressed to Kevon that it was hard for me to see how I could use his novel in my classes. I explained that, unlike my colleague I did not teach English literature, rather I taught Sociology and Political Science. However, I encouraged Kevon to keep writing and promised, after his insistence that I would at least read the book. He was confident and persistent, qualities I felt deserved encouragement so I assured him I would read his work. After a week passed Kevon returned to see me wanting to know what I thought about the book. Having read enough to talk about the story, I still expressed skepticism. As we continued to discuss the possibilities for using it in class, I began to reflect that possibly we could use the novel in a Social Problems class. I shared these thoughts with Kevon. He returned again the following week with a color coded matrix identifying various social problems and the chapters in which they occur throughout the story. Although I had not yet completed reading the book it was then I decided that we would use the book.

The biographical aspect lends legitimacy. It provides an exciting and realistic narrative context for studying social problems related to economic inequity, unemployment, inadequate educational opportunities, delinquency, gender relations, state perpetrated violence, gang violence, cultural dissonance, substance abuse, racism and xenophobia. The story presents these phenomena woven into the lives of the characters; the various scenarios capture the readers' imagination, provoking reflection, analysis and discussion. I believe the story to be very accessible to our students as it unfolds on the streets and in the neighborhoods familiar to us, because this is where we live. The story resonates with the lived experiences and legends of our communities. The book ends with *Lessons Learned,* an epilogue that returns us to the present reality via the personal reflections of the author Kevon Gulley. In order to write about his life Kevon had to reflect upon *"I"*, examine and critique it, in doing so he was able to change the trajectory of his life.

It is my intention that students be able to use the story of **JUST LIKE COMPTON** to develop a sociological perspective to analyze, and have an understanding of the causes and consequences of different social problems, and those elements in society that impact on their personal lives. The use of a narrative instrument and the shared emotions experienced through the story will facilitate an internalization of the academic and analytical aspects of the course.

Dr. Ikaweba Bunting, Ph.D.
Sociology & Political Science
El Camino College/Compton Center

Chapter One

Compton California 2002

The weekend is supposed to be fun… A chance to let it all hang out and be free. "Free." What a word. Instead I'm on the 105 freeway on my way to take my eight year old son home to his crazy ass Moma. The silence is always awkward. And hard. As Lauryn Hill sings slowly in the background about how *it just ain't working*, I alternate between watching the evening traffic in front of me and my son who's sitting next to me, bundled up against the November cold.

"Dad?" he asks, "Are y'all gone argue again?"

This is the part that tears me up inside because the truth is, most likely, and probably. But, instead, I say, "I hope not, but you know how your mom is." That's as far as I'll take it. But I want to say so much more.

Pascal, my son, shrugs his little shoulders and says, "Yeah" And we continue on in silence, with our own thoughts.

My phone began to ring as I got off on the Wilmington Ave exit. The caller I.D. screen read, "Bitch," which meant it was my baby moma and she'd probably been drinking. I answer, "What?" and from the way Pascal looked over at me, he knew who was on the other end.

She asks, "Where y'all at?"

I toss the phone over to my son and say, "It's for you." With an irritated face and a voice still untouched by puberty he said, "Mannn, hi Mom… My Aunties' house, the mall, mostly winter clothes and a Roc a Wear coat, no she didn't come. The Laker's game, they lost by four…."

All these short clipped answers meant one thing. She was grilling my baby about where we went, what we did, and who went with us. He looked at me with his big brown eyes and I laughed and said, "Hey, better you than me." He shook his head and passed me the phone which meant he'd had enough.

I took the phone, said, "Five minutes." and hung it up before she could get another sarcastic word out. I put the phone under my seat next to the other gadget that I kept there. When we pulled into the Taco Bell drive thru I handed my son a $20 bill and said, "Do your stuff." He ordered for himself and his little sister, ol girl's other child. Yeah, I know she's innocent but she and her father are the reasons why I'm a "Weekend Daddy" so I treat them accordingly.

I turned and watched as my son and only child handled the transaction, checked the food, and counted the change all while still wearing his seatbelt. He said, "Thank you" and we headed to his mom's house.

Before we pulled into his mother's apartment complex I stashed my phone in the stash spot behind the glove compartment. My Ex is a L.V.N., but on the weekends, she turns into a damn detective.

I pulled into her parking space and was cheerfully greeted with; "Why you hang up in my mothafuckin' face?"

"Hi Kelis," I say with a plastic smile.

"Hi, my ass, where y'all been?" We both ignored her question and began to unload the clothes I'd bought my son for winter from the Beverly Center. I put a bag in each of her hands, then laid two shoe boxes across her forearms so I couldn't see her face. Before she could say, "Wait," in protest, my son and I walked into her apartment ignoring her as she struggled to reorganize the packages.

I hate her, I really do, but I still love her alot too, and I'm still physically addicted to her. Even after what she did to me. As I walked passed the kitchen where the kids were eating I saw two things I couldn't stand, a pint of Paul Masson and her cousin Pinky.

Pinky is a 17 year old mother of three and a hood rat. She currently has a video of herself getting fucked on the internet and is very proud of it.

"Hey Rowdy."

"Don't call me that!" I said then glanced over my shoulder to make sure my son wasn't listening. He was of course.

"Why you ain't bring me nothing to eat?"

I responded, "You can have some of Kelis'." She made a B-line for the kitchen. I walked back to the front door to watch Kelis Jones, my ex of eight years, diggin through my Camaro looking for any signs of a female I might be dating or something with my address on it.

After coming up empty again, she looked up and gave me the finger, then locked my car and chirped the alarm. I laughed then walked back to the kitchen.

Pinky said, "Kevon ain't no food in here" with a hurt look.

"Man, that sucks huh?" I said.

Much to the kid's amusement. She grabbed the little girl's burrito, took a huge bite, and ran back to the spot on the floor where she was getting her hair braided in 'blue' individuals. I assumed her boyfriend of the month was a Crip. Blue hair? How stupid I thought.

Kelis walked by me and mumbled, "Homo," under her breath.

I said, "Tramp," without moving my lips and our night had officially begun. She went to the living room and I went to the kitchen and stood in the doorway to watch my son finish his dinner.

Pinky asked, "Kevon what happened to that grey Lexus you had?"

Before I could respond Kelis volunteered, "He probably gave it to one of his bitches." Then slurped her drink and spit the ice back into the cup with a smile.

Knowing that got on my nerves. (God I hate her) I said, "Nahh I stopped dealing with bitches after Pascal was born." Again the finger. We do this verbal boxing every Sunday night. It's her way of saying, I miss you and I'm sorry. And my way of saying you fucked up you had your chance.

"Daddy, I'm finished," my son said as he backed away from the table crunching ice cubes in his mouth and rubbing his eyes with the backs of his hands. This is usually when I get ready to leave and when Kelis tries something slick. It's been 1 ½ months since I fucked her and I'm trying to stop. I just can't. Y'all don't understand. She has 42" hips, 38DD titties, and the fact that she's nasty as a mothafucka' keeps me coming back! But on top of all that, it's the way she smells. Her scent. I can't explain it but y'all know what I'm talkin' about!

Anyway, "Shower time kid," I tell my son, then promise him a game of Madden if he hurries. When he took off to get his shower bag his mom and I screamed, "No runnin' in the house!" at the same time. Only this time when she looked, I gave *her* the finger.

When the shower water began to run I drifted towards the back of the house where my son's room was and turned on his bedroom light. Unmade bed, DVD's and video games everywhere, clothes hanging outta the hamper, pajamas still with the underwear in'em like he took them off as one piece. I just laughed and shook my head.

"What's so damn funny?" Kelis asks standing behind me in the hallway.

I waved my hand at the disaster area and said, "He got that from you"

She gave me a fake look of injury and said, "And I got this from yo Moma." And slapped me on the back of my head.

Before she could get away I grabbed her by the ponytail and spun her around. She let out a moan and I brought her close enough to kiss me. "Remember the rules, no touching!" I reminded her.

She smiled and said, "Pull harder," I let go and she said, "Pussy" and walked back down the hallway towards the living room.

As I watched the rhythm of her ass cheeks bounce under her silk pajamas, I knew I had to hurry up and go home.

When Pascal came out of the bathroom I said, "Come're and let me smell you!"

He took off laughing and screaming "Noooo Daddy" because he figures he's too old for that stuff. He's not a baby anymore, but I missed most of those days and I refuse to let him grow up too fast.

When I finally caught him, I picked him up, sniffed his face, and bit his cheek, he giggled and held on for dear life. When I put him down I said, "One game man, then Igotta go. I got work tomorrow."

He said, "Okay," and I left to get a bottle of water.

As I headed towards the kitchen I passed the little girl in the hallway, ignored her like she wasn't even there. When I opened the refrigerator to get a bottle of Dasani I noticed Kelis finishing the last of the few braids which meant I had to hurry up and bounce.

She said," I hope you not all up in my refrigerator like you live here."

I said, "Keep it up and *I'm* filing child support." Not another word, and with good reason. I give her $1,000 a month and buy all of my son's clothes. Child Support would only give her

$376 a month. With that over, I headed back to my son's room to whup his ass in some John Madden 2002.

As we entered the 4th quarter, I heard Pinky leaving and Kelis's foot falls coming towards us on the carpet.

She poked her head in and said, "Triple S time Kiwi." 'Kiwi' was the name she called me in private and triple S meant "Shit, shower, & shave." Translation: she was horny.

I said, "Don't even think about it. I'll be gone before you're done," with a 'so there' look on my face.

She laughed, held up my car keys, and said, "Not without these Boo."

I jumped up and chased her to the bathroom but she beat me there and slammed the door in my face.

I put my forehead against the door, kicked it once and said, "Girl stop playin."

She laughed and started humming the beat to her current favorite song, "Choke me -spank-me-pull my hair!"

Shit! I kicked the door again and tried the door knob. To my surprise, it was unlocked. When I opened the door she was standing with one foot on top of the tub soaping her big ass titties with a body buff. Then she picked up her left titty and pinched the nipple until it got hard. I said, "You think you smart, I ain't coming in there," and slammed the door so hard it bounced back open. She laughed louder and said something perverted but I couldn't hear it all.

The truth is, I could have left if I really wanted to, without my keys. I have OnStar in my Camaro which means I could've called the dealer and had them pop my doors from their satellite. And I have an extra key taped under the hood. But me and my dick knew I wasn't going anywhere.

I walked back to my son's room and noticed he was half sitting and half laying in his bed with the PlayStation remote still in his hand. I put him in his bed properly, then turned off the T.V. and video game and killed the lights.

When I went to look for the little girl I found her asleep in Kelis's bed with an Elmo doll choked in the crook of her arm. To my surprise, I covered her up properly and tucked her in. Man, I was getting soft.

I went back to the living room and sat on the couch to wait for my keys. Time must've passed quickly or I must have been tired because all I remember is waking up to Kelis's voice saying, "You still want your keys?"

When I opened my eyes she was standing in front of me wearing a SpongeBob t-shirt that was way too small. I said, "Nah it's too late."

She left to turn off the lights in the kitchen and those in the hallway, then I heard the sounds of doors closing and knew I had fucked up royally.

When she returned she was carrying a blanket and said, "Scoot over."

I did, and she lay on top of me and covered us both with the blanket. I said, "Whatchu doing?"

She said, "Nothing," then raised the t-shirt over her head and threw it to the side.

The weight of her breasts and the heat from her body was too much. I gave in. I grabbed the two huge globes of her ass and began to rub them and bounce them up and down.

She looked at me and asked, "You miss me?"

I said, "Nope" and turned my head so she could push a thick nipple into my mouth.

She made an, "Ssst," sound and held her titty in front of me so I could flick my tongue and twirl it around her nipple. With my other hand I began to rub up and down between the crack of her ass. When she began to moan and poke her ass out I began to suck and lick her nipple sloppily and she held it up so we could lick it together in a wild frenzy of tongues.

“Unhhh,” she moaned as I bit down on her nipple.

I grabbed a handful of hair, jerked her head towards mine and said, “Rub that pussy”.

I dove in face first….

Chapter Two

Los Angeles California 2002

I awoke to the smell of African Pride hair grease and the feel of someone's head on my chest. Time to go! The clock on the V.C.R read 5:17 a.m. I noticed as I stood to look for my clothes that were scattered everywhere.

I usually get up with the sun anyway. An old habit I've had since my days in prison. In there, everybody has a set program and slacking is dangerous. If the White boys or the Mexicans get up before you do, your ass is grass. I got dressed in yesterday's clothes and walked towards the bathroom.

Without turning to face me she said, "It ain't even 6:00." I said, "I know, call me on your lunch break" and headed down the hall to the bathroom.

After I washed my dick in the sink, I dried it off with one of her "good" towels which I knew would piss her off, then headed to my son's room to see him before I left. With a kiss on his freshly faded head, I left.

When I walked out into the morning cold I stood on the porch for a minute, stretched, and surveyed the street. Yep, same cars that were here last night, so I'm cool I thought, for now. I pushed the automatic start on my keys and listened to my S.S. Camaro come to life. The engine growled as the dual exhaust destroyed the morning quiet.

I walked out the gate and sat in the driver's side then flipped out my Nakamichi 7" in dash T.V. screen to catch the news on FOX 11. The usual, Kobe scored 50 points; roadside bombs kills 30 in Iraq; stocks are down, and a drive-by in Venice killed 2 Hispanic gang members and a little boy. Most likely the Sho'lines and the V-13's still going at it. I shrugged, opened the glove compartment, pushed in the back hinges and got my phone out the stash. Yep, all Camaros '98-2002 have this built in stash spot. It's big enough to hold two 9's or in my case, a 9mm and my Sidekick.

Before I was able to check my messages (all 10 of them) the phone began to ring. At 5:46 a.m.in the morning it could only be one person, Simone. Simone is a 5 foot nothing, 126 pound keg of dynamite. She looked like a midget version of Stacey Dash but with a body like Esther Baxter, her eyes changed colors with her moods. I pushed talk….

"Hey shit head, I have an 8:00 appointment, hurry up!"

I said, "Good morning puppy," she got quiet on her end which meant she was smiling.I call her puppy for 2 reasons: The first: her ass looks like 2 puppies playing under a blanket when she walks, the second, a puppy, is *still* a female dog.

I asked, "Where are your keys to the shop ma?"

"I have my keys, I don't know the alarm code. You shanged it 'member?"

I bust out laughing because she said "Shanged" instead of "changed" with her ever present French accent. The "Fuck you" I got was in perfect English though.

Simone and I are both 3rd generation Creoles, but not like the Louisiana Creoles, *real* Creoles from Haiti. She came to the U.S. when she was six years old but I was born here at Martin Luther King Hospital in Compton, California. And even though I can turn my accent on and off, she can't.

I asked, "Voulez-vous dejeuner? (Do you want breakfast?)" She said, "No, just get me a coffee," then hung up in my face.

In a lot of ways our families were expecting us to produce the 4th generation of Creoles. But I had my son Pascal with somebody else fucking up the plan, and braking Simone's heart. She felt like I had given her baby away, and in a way, I did too.

I pulled into Jordan's Café on 114th and Wilmington Ave and went inside. This is a kind of wild part of town because it's on the Compton and Watts border. It's also close to a hood called P.J. Watts Crips, and these niggas don't like nobody, especially outsiders. I reached in the back seat to get my Red Sox hoodie and put it on to cover the shoulder holster and Beretta 93R I was wearing. At this time of morning there was nobody in the diner except an old couple at a back table and some city workers.

"Can I help you?" Pam the waitress asked as I slid onto a stool at the counter.

"That depends on if you're finally ready to give me some." I said in response. She laughed and said, "Boy, I'm old enough to be yo' moma," but never took her eyes off mine. "I know" I said and looked from her eyes to the abundance of cleavage that was spilling out of her blouse.

She wagged her finger at me then called my order over her shoulder without me having to say a word.

"Chicken and waffle breakfast, 2 extra wings, hash browns fried hard, to go!" Then sashayed off toward the grills, where the cook was doing his thang.

As I read over the menu that I had memorized over the past 20 years I heard the bells on the door jingle signaling that somebody was entering. "Damn cuzz" was the first thing I heard but I smelled the weed as soon as the door opened.

Pam said, "Boy don't smoke that shit in here!"

As I looked over at the old couple shaking their heads, I noticed there were two of them. The one with the scar on his cheek was no more than 17 but obviously the tougher of the two because he said, "Finish outside!" and the older, taller guy did as he was told.

I watched the kid's reflection in the wooden menu board that hung from the ceiling as Pam took his order of "Bacon and eggs." The way he eased onto the seat and adjusted his belt told me he had a gun on him and there was either a conversation, a confrontation, or both coming. I unzipped my sweater and waited...

In the streets of L.A. where having heart will get you famous, but too much heart will get you killed. There are two unwritten rules: #1, respect your surroundings. Especially when you're out of bounds, in another nigga's hood. #2, always use your mental weapons before you use the metal ones.

The blue "P" hat, and "BullSide" t-shirt let me know that he was definitely from the PJ's. "Hey cuzz….."

I turned on the stool softened my eyes, and answered with the universal "safe" word, "What's up *Brotha'*?"

"That's yo' Camaro outside?"

"Yep."

"What color is that?"

"Fire truck red."

He paused to look at my sweater, and the white and red Airmax's I was wearing. "I see you like red huh?"

"Yep."

"Where you from anyway?"

"Compton," I said with a "C" instead of "Bompton," Which would have probably ended the talking and started the shooting.

"$6.85," Pam interrupted as she put my food and Simone's coffee on the counter, looking from me to the kid with the scar.

I gave her a $10 bill and a kiss on the cheek and turned to leave.

"Hey Loc, what you say your name was again?"

"Rowdy," I said as I pushed through the glass door.

When I got outside the other youngster was sitting in a brown cutlass on dented up 20" Dayton's listening to one of Lil' Waynes' thousand mixtapes. When I pulled to the corner he stood up and threw up a "C" with fingers that were so stiff, it looked like it hurt. I shook a non-descript "Peace" sign at him and made the left on Wilmington Ave, headed back to Compton. With a "C".

As I pulled into the parking lot of my barbershop, HEAD UP FADES. I slid into the parking spot next to Simone's pink BMW X5 and saw her sleeping in the passenger seat with her phone clutched in her hand. By now, it's 8:00a.m. and the morning was buzzing with sound of laughing kids on their way to school and parents on their way to work.

"Levez-vous (wake-up)," I said as I knocked on her window.

Simone doesn't jump, it's almost impossible to surprise her. She just rolled down the window, rolled her eyes and reached for the coffee. I gave it to her and opened my shop up for business.

When I sat behind the counter, I put the bags down and took in the scenery of my place of business, 4 barber's chairs, 3 of which I rent out for $200 a week. Two couches and bean bags that I also rent out to Simone for her braiding business (she pays me when she feels like it). My 80" plasma T.V. and surround sound system, (for my Saturday night John Madden tournaments), 2 Arcade games in the corner (My Street Fighter II, and Simone's Mrs. Pac-Man).

There were pictures of various revolutionaries that believed freedom was worth dying and killing for like: Patrice Lumumba, Che Guevara, Kwame Nkrumah, Pedro Campos, and 17 year old Johnathan Jackson. All favorites of mine. Behind every barber chair there are plaques with some of my favorite quotes on them. Behind chair #4, the chair that I cut the kids hair on Fridays for free, the plaque read: "Metal sharpens metal, Man sharpens man."

Simone walked in rubbing her eyes sleepily like a little girl and asked, "Where's the food?" Then parked her green army fatigue skirt in the chair I already had pulled out. She looked at me as she began to take the 2 extra wings off my plate and said, "Shut up, you think you know me, you don't."

I walked around to her side and squeezed the piece of hip and ass that was hanging off the chair and kissed her on the forehead with my greasy chicken lips.

"Ungh boy, stop it!" she said then picked up her phone to read an incoming text message.She looked up as I was dumping my tray in the trash and asked, "Didn't you wear that yesterday?"

I said, "Didn't you wear those *drawlz* yesterday?" with a hearty laugh.

She made a disgusted face and said, "You sound dumb, 'cause I don't even wear panties."And threw a chicken bone at my head.

"Fuck off mannnn," I said in my Katt Williams voice, then headed to the back patio where I kept the blue pit bulls I bred for sale.

Yeah, here at HEAD UP FADES you can get a Taper, some Individuals, buy a Gotti blood lined pit bull, order a Creole dinner (If my Auntie comes to work), and my specialty; Handguns. That's by order and appointments only though. I don't do or keep anything illegal at the shop. For 2 reasons: #1, I'm on parole. And #2, I'm on parole.

As I stepped onto the outside patio the parents of my line of pits began to jump around on their chains and wag their tails in a frenzy. Duchess, the female is all white with brindle patches that look a bluish-grayish color, Duke the male is solid blue. When I walked to the kennel to let the three month old puppies out, all five exploded out of the cage and attacked their parents, their toys, and my damn ankles.

Simone, now standing in the doorway asked, "Which one are you keeping?"

"That bitch in the corner, she's the toughest and she's beautiful." I said with a wink.

She turned away before I could see her blush and said, "My 8:00's here and Chico's on the phone."

I picked up the female puppy (who I had secretly named Simone) who was shaking a miniature soccer ball, then I walked back into the shop. When I saw who Simone's 8:00 appointment was I gritted my teeth. Crystal.

Crystal had gotten arrested 3 times for the same thing and always got out. Her crime partners on the other hand were all upstate doing time.

"Hey, Kevon"

"You wearin' a wire?"

"Fuck you nigga…!" She snarled.

"You wish." I said seriously.

"Whatever." She said.

I put the puppy down hoping she'd go and bite her, then picked up the phone.

"Yo?"

"What's up, cuzzo?"

"Dog this is my business line. If you gone be talkin' reckless use the burn-out phone; and stop callin'me that cuzz shit."

"Man you be on some John Gotti paranoid shit."

"If I'm John Gotti, you must be Sammy the Bull."

"Who?"

"Never mind, call the other phone." Larry, or Chico as he's now called is my god-brother and a Crip from Rollin' 60's. How the last part happened, we have no idea but he's official and has a credit business that's booming. Most of my equipment at the shop came from him.

"Hello."

"Can I speak to John Gotti?"

"Cut the crap fool. Whatchu want, or need?"

"I got a kinda big order for you."

"I only have 4 puppies?"

"They don't want puppies."

"Oh. Who and how big?" I asked interested.

He told me to hold on and I heard him speaking to somebody in the background.

"She wants to meet you."

"She?"

"She wants 10 Glocks and 2 of those fullyBerettas you got."

"That's gone be expensive."

"Trust me, money ain't a problem."

"10 Glocks is 4 racks and 2 Beretta's is 3 racks. Tell her to bring $7,500 to the Food 4 Less on Rosecrans Ave, 3 p.m. At 3:01 I'm leaving."

He relayed the message to the female buyer then came back to the phone.

"What's the extra $500 for?"

"Shipping and handling." I said then hung up the phone. Right after that I shuffled through my phone 'til I found the name I was looking for. 40NHC and pushed send. KD picked up on the first ring.

"Fuck you want Frenchie?" he asked playfully.

KD plays a lot of roles in my life - mentor, big brother, and babysitter of all the hardware. I told him what to bring and to be there 20 minutes early just in case somebody tried to get cute. He said, "Alright," in a bored fashion and we hung up.

KD's a no bullshit type of dude and believes most true answers come from violence. We'd actually met during a riot in New Folsom State Prison. We kinda had a system, every White boy he knocked down I stomped... It was beautiful. After that we stayed in contact and became real close, colors never mattered.

When I got off the phone I noticed 2 of the kids that rent chairs from me walk in with their backpacks and prepare for work. "You're late!" I said to Rodney.To Dannie I said, "Clean that up!" Indicating the newspaper that the puppy had pee'd on.

Then I walked down the hallway to my office. I do okay here. Between 15 to 20 racks a month. Minus supplies and overtures. I pocket ten thousand a month. Most of it is tax free so I can't complain. Not bad for an Ex-con with two strikes huh?

By now it's 10:40 a.m. and I have to go home, change my clothes, and take a shower.

When I walked to the front, Simone askedwithout looking up from her clients head, "Can I use the Camaro today?"

"The last time I let you use my car, when I got it back, it fit in a suitcase."

"Yes, or no?" This was Simone's way of negotiating.

"Okay then, No!" I said and walked towards the door. I don't know who she thought she was talking to like that, *shiiit*!

"Fine, be like that!" she said with an ugly smirk.

When I got outside, there were only two cars in the parking lot, Simone's Jeep and Crystal's Honda Civic. My car was gone. I walked back inside and Simone was holding out her keys to me, smiling her little girl smile. (Damn, I love this girl.)

Simone you gone knock off the Houdini shit. And I want my car back tomorrow! All of it!" Then I turned to leave.

I put this Jeep together for her as a gift when she got out of prison. She took ten years for me. The D.A. tried to turn her but she wouldn't talk. The other nigga sung like Anita Baker and got 3 years suspended. It's strange how there are more loyal women than there are men.

Before I left I poked my head back in and asked,"Ou est ton pistol? (Where is your gun?)"

"Dedans mon sac, et ton? (In my bag and yours?)" I unzipped my sweater and opened the left side she nodded her approval then I walked back into the sunlight of Southern California.

As I drove to my Grandmother's house to trade her girly-ass truck for my Range Rover my phone began to ring. I read the caller ID then pressed talk.

"Sup?"

"Nothing, my booty hurts," she whined.

"Hey, you're the one that kept sayin, harder, harder…"

"Damn, I didn't mean *that* hard," she said and we both began to laugh.

"Hey, you bit me so we're even."

"I did huh?" She giggled. Then she got quiet. I broke the silence by stating the obvious. "You know we shouldn't have done that right?"

"Yeah, I know," she said with a sigh. More silence...

She asks, "Where you going? You driving?"

"To Memom's to get my truck, then home to change my clothes."

"Damn you still ain't changed? Busy morning huh?"

"Don't start." I said then made plans to see her again tonight. We both knew that wouldn't happen but it was fun to pretend.

As I pulled up to the light on Rosecrans Ave and Willowbrook the tolls came down and the lights began to flash indicating that a train was coming. The first thing I did was check the cars directly on the sides of me and the traffic behind me. On my left a fat black lady in a bus driver's uniform was happily murdering a Kelly Price song. To my right, a Paisa in a ten gallon cowboy hat with what looked like a whole damn rooster on the front gave me a gold toothed smile and a thumbs up. Behind me was a string of traffic but no Regals, Cutlasses, or Mexicans with shaved heads which meant no T-Flats.Since that war started there'd been thirty murders in Compton, most of them happening at stoplights.

Before I got locked up and went to the "Y" (Youth Authority), we got along with the Mexican gangs in Compton. But when I got out in 2000, there was a full scaled Race War. Everybody was at it with the Ese gangs close to theirs. Fruit Town versus T-Flats, Leudars Park versus CV70's, Mona Park versus, L36, Santana block versus Willow Street. It was crazy… Now, at every red-light or train, you had to be careful. They say, *"If you stay ready you won't have to get ready."* This proved true in the streets of Compton.

As the train finally showed its ugly rust colored head I laid my head back against the cool leather of the headrest, let out a long breath that I didn't know I had been holding and thought about the events that got me to this point, and the countless mistakes I'd made to get here.

August 1994.

My boy Kili called me and told me he had a proper lick (robbery) for me and to meet him in the projects. I had been doing little bullshit robberies and corner jacks, but I'd been waiting on this call for two weeks. I told my cousin Damion who was also my crimee in my other robberies and he called his homie in Carson that had pistols. The .380 I had didn't even have a firing pin. Thank God I could scare a victim with my accent.The hard part would be getting Simone to let me use her car. Since she'd started working at M&M soul food we hadn't seen a lot of each other. Or should I say, since word got out that I was having a baby.

I walked down Piru Street to her Grandmother's house where she was sitting on the porch.

"No!" she snapped before I could get a word out.

"C'mon Simone don't act like that."

"Act? Nigga this ain't no act!" she said as she put her hand on one of her big hips.

"I need to use your car ma." I said being cautious.

She made a “Humph” sound in her throat then looked at me with cold eyes and said, “Why don’t you use your baby moma’s car?”

There ... it was out.

I said, “I know you’re mad but this is a business trip, and if shit goes right, I’ll pay your car off.”

She looked at me with that same black stare and said, “We’re not done with this baby moma shit, let me get my purse.” After that, we all piled into Simone’s Jetta and headed to the Nickerson Gardens. Twenty minutes later three sixteen year old boys and seventeen year old girl were being given very detailed instructions on how to rob the Washington Mutual Bank on the corner of La Cienega and Wilshire Blvd. in Beverly Hills.

“It’s easy,” Kili said. “All you need is three people and a driver. You walk in, jump over the counters, and hit the three tellers at the end. ‘Cause the first two have bait money, hit the tellers and leave. Fifty seconds tops.”

“No security guards?” I asked.

“Nope, and it’s Beverly Hills so it’s hella’ traffic to get lost in.”

“What’s your cut?” This came from Damion’s friend who I had forgot was even there. With blinding speed Kili reached under the seat of his wheelchair and pulled out a chrome .38 automatic.

“Who is *this* nigga?” He asked, pointing the gun at ol boy. I shrugged my shoulders and thumbed at Damion.

Damion now the center of attention said, “Kili he bool, he goes to Carson High with me”

“Carson? Nigga you from Nachos?” Kili asked as his face started to twist and twitch and I thought, we gone need another person.

“Huh?”

"Naw nigga don't get quiet now. First you was Charlie chatterbox. Are-you-from-nachos? 190, cheese toast, a ricket, a crab?"

It was dead quiet. I looked from the gun to ol boy, then Kili pulled the hammer back. It sounded like somebody ripping open a box.

Simone said, "Let me move before you get this nigga's brains all on me."

Ol' boy said, "No," but it came out like he had a mouthful of popcorn.

"Nuh." 'Kili looked at me and said, "Rowdy, you gone rob somethin' with *this* nigga?"

I said, "Everybody don't have a 'Kill Squad,' Black." Only niggas close to him called him by that name.

"Bad idea champ. He smells too clean." He advised me, then uncocked the hammer and picked up right where he'd left off. "Anyway, each teller has forty G's 'cause it's payday. But if y'all lucky, the Cash Cow will be out, that has over a hunnit' in it." He let that sink in then picked up the gun and turned to ol' boy. "My cut is 10 racks ..." I held my breath and waited for the rest. Akili was easily the craziest bastard I knew but, he was also one of the smartest.

"And y'all owe me a favor..." I *knew* it! He continued, "But we'll talk about that when y'all bring me my money." Then he pushed his wheelchair to the door and went out, ending the meeting. As I was getting in the car I saw Kili in the middle of the street giving the project kids dollar bills for the approaching ice cream truck.

Before I ducked my head in the car he yelled, "Remember what I said," then pointed a long finger at Damion's friend.

When we pulled into the traffic on Imperial Highway I turned around in my seat and asked, "Hey dog what *is* your name?"

He said, “Chris” in a voice much deeper than the one he’d used five minutes ago. After that, we all rode back to Compton in silence. Secretly spending money we didn’t have yet.

Chapter Three

Compton California 1994

"No Simone! You drive and that's it!" We had been having this same argument for about 20 minutes already. We were short one man or a driver and I didn't want to bring in another person. Simone suggested herself and I reluctantly agreed to let her drive. Now she wanted to go "In."

"Pleeeeease." "Hell to the no! If this goes bad, I want you to be able to get away.Your grandmother ain't finna put a spell on my ass."

"Who's gonna watch your back like me huh? Plus you owe me."

I started to say, "I don't owe you shit!" But then it clicked in my head what she was talking about. FUCK! Alright, let's get something understood. You only get to use this once. After this, never again Simone." I said.

Her eyes went from blue to gray and began to light up.

"Promise!"

"I Promise."

She won again, like we both knew she would. With that settled, we continued to plan the minute details. We decided on three people not four which would leave an extra forty grand, and no driver. We'd simply leave the car running on Wilshire Blvd. since it was Beverly Hills and nobody would steal it anyway.

Damion would be waiting in the other G-ride (stolen car) at the gas station on La Cienega and Cadillac, near the 10 freeway. Since we decided that we were going to do it, I mean *really* do it, I'd started reading books about bank robberies and studying how most niggas got caught. I knew about dye packs, homing devices, and bait money already. I learned that if you put mercury (the liquid inside thermometers) on your face the cameras couldn't pick up anything but a glare. I also learned that as soon as we exited the bank we should dump the money in cold water to kill the homing devices and make the dye rise to the top because it's oil based. I explained all this to them, then explained only to Simone that we would only speak French once we entered the bank.

"If they don't know what we said, they can't repeat it to the cops." I said with a wink. We were set to go. And on September 1st 1994, in two weeks, we would put all of our tough and fancy words into action.

"What do you think about ol boy Chris?" I asked Simone as we stepped back out onto the porch.

"I think Kili's right, he's not hood"

"Yeah" I agreed, "He's from Del Amo, them niggas don't have to be in the streets. Their moms and dads are lawyers and doctors. I don't understand it either … I mean, don't get me wrong, every hood got killers but when you have everything already, what's the point?"

"He's doing his part," she reminded me. "He's bringing the guns and one of the cars, but if he tries or does something stupid…"

"I know." I said as we walked back down to my end of Piru Street holding hands.

At 11:45 a.m. on the morning of September 1st, we were sitting outside the Washington Mutual bank, parked on the northwest corner of Wilshire and La Cienega Boulevards. Everybody dressed in green army fatigues, faces covered with mercury, and hands covered with crazy glue to block any fingerprints. Damion, my cousin was parked at the Mobile gas station about seven minutes away on La Cienega and Cadillac. One right turn away from the 10 freeway and our freedom.

Back at the bank I asked, "Y'all ready?"

Chris said, "Y'all for real?" in a small voice.

Simone snapped, “Don’t bitch-up now!” Then opened her car door and got out.

I followed and Chris brought up the rear. When we walked through the double doors, I quickly noticed only six people in various tellers lines, one older looking White man and a little girl I assumed to be his Granddaughter were sitting at the customer service desk.

I turned away from him and screamed, “Tout le monde bas! (Everybody down).” I don’t know if they complied because they all spoke French, or because I had drawn a shiny chrome and black Jennings 9mm. Whatever the case, they listened and got down. Simone and I jumped over the counter and began emptying the teller’s drawers.

Chris who at least had his gun out, was supposed to be watching the door and the floor. We stuck to the plan and only hit the last three drawers as instructed. Then, I noticed the old black lady holding onto what looked like a metal suitcase on wheels. Kili explained this contraption to be the Cash Cow.

I surveyed the floor again and took notice of Chris visibly shaking and sweating profusely. Simone by now was sitting on the counter calm as can be but tense as a nuclear bomb. When I opened the cash cow, I think I pee’d on myself a little bit. I had never seen that much money in my life and immediately began to fill my hefty trash bag with neat stacks of bills. I finished, told the lady that had to be the bank manager, “Merci (thank you)” and looked up.

They say if it *can* go wrong, it *will* go wrong. And as I jumped over the counter, it did… *Very* wrong.

“Grandpa nooo!”

I looked over to where the little girl was and saw the old man (who had to be a cop because of his shooting stance) tell Simone to put the gun down! I raised my gun and pointed it at the old couple laying in the tellers line and screamed, "Tres stupide M'sieu! (very stupid sir)" to the cop.

Chris who was supposed to be watching the floor looked a little sick and green in the face. I thought, this only happens in movies like Diehard and Point Break, but here we were in a Mexican standoff at the lunch hour in Beverly Hills. Everybody had both of their shaky hands filled. Simone and I had a gun pointed and a bag filled with money. The old man had his revolver aimed at Simone, his other hand was rested on the little girl's blond head. Chris was no longer pointing his gun but simply holding it.

"Quoi maintenant? (what now?)"Simone asked sounding irritated.

"Nous allons (we're leaving)." I told her calmly. Then Chris fainted. His body made a meaty smacking sound as he collapsed onto his side. I gave Simone an 'are you surprised?' look and she let out a little laugh, then started to cry.

I was only ten feet from the glass double doors, but Simone was at the third teller near the back of the bank. She looked at the cop who was now patting the crying little girl's head and cooing soft words to her, then looked at me and said, "Quittez-vous (leave)."

I looked at her like she was crazy and said, "Tu es folle? (are you crazy)."

She smiled and said, "En trois (on three)" and began to count. "Une," she said as she wiped tears on her shoulder, "Deux," she said squeezing the handle of her gun.

The cop said, "Oh shit," in a whisper like he understood.

Then without saying, trois, Simone started shooting. So did the cop. So did I. I don't remember too much that happened in the bank after that, except Simone being blown off the counter by one of the cop's bullets, and me hitting him as I fired wildly as I pushed through the double doors.

My face was wet I noticed as I jumped behind the wheel of the Nova. When I wiped it, it came away clear. Tears.

I turned the car into oncoming traffic and headed towards the rendez-vous to meet Damion. All I remember is rocking in the driver's seat as I ran the red light on Pico Boulevard and saying, "Oh God Simone, oh God," over and over. I just kept seeing her fly backwards off the counter as the bullets slammed into her.

When I pulled into the gas station alone I could tell Damion already knew what happened. I grabbed both bags of money and jumped in the trunk as we planned. My cousin made the right turn and got on the 10 freeway East headed home. When the adrenaline and panic of almost being caught began to fade, I cried. Hard painful sobs. I kicked the money away from me, hugged myself and cried. Simone had eagerly traded her life for mines. And I had left her dying in a bank among strangers. Enemies.

As we exited the 105 on Imperial, we did as planned. My cousin took the money with him and I got on the Metro rail and rode it until I had the heart to get off and go home. When I turned onto my block it was about 6 p.m. and I saw Damion and my Grandmother standing at the gate talking to Simone's Grandmother Madame Belleu.

"Madame Belleu…" I started, but was slapped so hard in the face I saw stars. Then she was on me. Beating me and clawing my face. I didn't try to stop her I just said, "Je suis desole (I'm sorry). Je suis desole elle est mort (I'm sorry she's dead)."

"Det? Nobody is det you stupid child!" she said in very broken English. "Simone est dans bastille (Simone is in jail)."

I looked at Damion to confirm what the old lady had just said. He gave me a weak smile and pointed at his shoulder indicating where the bullet had gone.

The robbery had been on the news all day. The reporter said a group of young French terrorist had attempted to rob a bank in broad daylight in Beverly Hills. Two of the robbers were apprehended after a bloody exchange of gunfire with a retired police lieutenant from the Culver City Police department. He was wounded in the exchange along with a seventeen year old terrorist later identified as Simone Belleu. A third suspect was still at large. A large but undisclosed amount of money was taken but later retrieved by the officer. Then they went to live footage outside the bank.

I looked across the couch at my cousin, then burst into laughter. Simone was alive!

Chapter Four

Compton California 2002

Bahhhhhhh Baaaahmm!!I was snatched back to the present by the sounds of seemingly a thousand horns blowing because the dumb-ass in the pink BMW Jeep was holding up traffic.

I waved my hand out the window in an "I'm sorry" gesture and made the right turn on Willowbrook. As I rode down the street headed to downtown Compton, I could still feel the thin spider webs of afterthought about the robbery lurking and knew I wasn't done thinking about it. Sometimes, the memories came gradually like a daddy long legs creeping across my mind. And sometimes they came a lot faster.

When I made the right turn on Burris Ave, my Grandmother's street, I drove passed the house and circled the block to make sure I wasn't being followed. I'm sure there were some niggas that wanted to rob me, and I'm positive the Feds were still waiting for me to make a mistake. I'd moved my Grandmother to this side of Compton, the *good* side, after my Grandfather died and I began to take part in the war with the T-flats.

When I pulled in front of my grandmother's house, I just sat and watched her working in her rose garden. She was the first of my family off the boat from Haiti. Without a doubt the leader of this family, even when my Grandfather was still alive. On the island she came from royal blood and she still held herself in that regard. I loved her. More importantly, I trusted her. She knew all of my hurts and all of my secrets. And she never judged me, even when I came to her bleeding, with a smoking gun in my hand.

She held to the old ways. She'd been in Compton since there had been Whites living there in the 50's and 60's, but she was determined to remain Creole. Her main rule was nobody could speak English in her house except Judge Judy, and the rest of her favorite T.V shows. When I got out of Simone's jeep I could see a smile play at the corners of her mouth and I began to smile myself. She took off her straw hat and gloves and met me at the porch

"Sava mon petit, comment allez vous? (hello little one how are you)," she asks as we embrace and I kissed her on both cheeks.

"Je suis bien, et vous? (I'm fine, and you?)"

"Bien (fine)," was all she said as she lead me up the porch stairs and into the house. Our destination was the kitchen as usual.

While I sat at the oak kitchen table (one of the few things she did allow me to buy for her) she went to the sink to wash her hands.

Avez vous faim? (are you hungry?)" It wasn't a question I noticed as she grabbed a spoon and began to pile Etoufee and dirty rice on a plate. When you came into a Creole household, you came into the kitchen. It was considered the most important room in the house.

While she stood in profile to me at the sink and poured iced tea into a glass, I looked at my grandmother with admiration. Her skin was light enough to be White, but you could tell there was something else in there. Her hair was pulled back into a long silver braid that still shined when the sunlight hit it. But her most impressive feature was her eyes. They were pale gray, sharp and intelligent. And sometimes, they said more than her mouth did. When she sat down next to me she asked about work, Pascal, Simone, and the one and only thing we ever disagreed on; Me going to the island."Je ne veux pas aller (I don't wanna go)."

"Pourquoi pas? (why not?)."

"Pourquoi, ma vie est ici (for what, my life is here)."

"Tu devrais visiter, (you have to visit)."She gave me a hopeful look then took my half eaten plate clicking her tongue as she walked away.

I said, "Merci (thank you)," and went out the side door to the garage where my cars were kept. I own 1 car,a truck and a motorcycle. The car is a candy red 2002 Chevy Camaro, red Coach interior on red, and chrome 21" Alpina's. The truck is a gray 2002 RangeRover. All stock except for the sound system, 3 T.V's, and the PlayStation II. The bike, by far my favorite is a 2002 Suzuki GSXR. Chrome 20's, custom army fatigue paint. The *MovieStar* edition, so it has all the racing parts and stickers. When I put the bike in neutral to let it warm up I saw my Uncle Chris walking up the driveway in his Gas Company uniform.

"What's up nephew?"

"Rien (nothin')," I answered dryly. And watched him go through the kitchen door. When I pulled the bike out of the garage and into the street, my Grandmother was waiting on the porch holding my helmet.

"Wanna ride Memom?" I asked reving the engine. She smiled and shook her head then handed me my helmet. I kissed her noisily on the cheek and got on the bike. When I tapped down to first gear and pulled off I could still see her rubbing the place on her cheek where I had kissed her.

As I made the left on Compton Blvd headed to the 105 freeway I began to feel the familiar freedom that only riding a motorcycle can bring. I won't be so bold to say that it's better than sex, but going 95mph in the carpool lane is pretty fuckin close. I exited the 105 on Sepulveda Blvd where it ends and rode down Sepulveda all the way until I started seeing the few changes that let me know I was leaving the *hood* and entering a place of assumed peace.

First I saw the sign; "Now Entering Westchester." Then my second favorite thing in the world, White people. There are no white people living in Compton. Not one. If you see any white people in Compton, they either work for the police or the Carnival's in town. If I had to do an ethnic breakdown it would read: 45%Mexican, 45% African American, 7% Samoan, and 3% Asian. Westchester was upper middle class and at the present time, had very little crime. I parked the bike in one of my two assigned parking spaces in the underground garage and ran for the elevator as it began to close.

"Hold the door!' I said as I ran with my helmet in my hand. When I got on, I noticed the other occupant of the elevator. She was 5'5, red hair, green eyes and had titties way too big for her small frame. Since she was White I figured they were rented. "Thank you." I said a little out of breath.

"No problem." she said with a lingering look of interest. I looked at her closely now, black spandex halter top that looked like it was being punished by her breasts, matching stretch pants, and a Bally's gym bag. She pushed 5 without me having to ask her and we began the ascent to my floor.

"Whatchu slappin?" I asked, pointing at her Discman

"Huh? I'm sorry."

"What are you listening to?" I rephrased.

'The new 50," she said like it was normal.

"Really?" I said sounding a little surprised.

"You look shocked. What'd you expect me to be listening to? The Dixie Chicks?" she quipped. I laughed, mostly because I felt stupid, but partly because I was caught off guard.

"You ride?" she asked pointing at my helmet.

"Yeah you?"

"Yeah, not bikes though." Again she looked me up and down.

I said, “You look familiar.” I knew it sounded corny but she *did*.

“We’re almost neighbors. I live in 260 and you live in 269” she said knowingly.

“Yep, good ol 69.” I said then looked at the “V” of her crotch and smiled.

DING! The elevators opened. “Ladies first.” I said with a Butler’s wave. She bent slowly at the waist to pick up her gym bag and made sure I got a full view of her ass. Not Buffy, but fat for a White girl.

As she sauntered off the elevator she said, “Bye Mr. 69.”

I said, “68 and I owe you one?”

She stopped, put her key in the lock, then said, “Okay.” and disappeared into her apartment.

Before I could even get to my door I could hear Fifi, my blue pit-bull barking and whining. When I opened the door she almost knocked my helmet out of my hand. “Stop Fiona! You gone get us evicted.” I said as I put my helmet and keys on the counter.

People think I’m crazy to have a big-ass pit-bull living inside a $2,500 a month condo, but she’s litter box trained and is a 24 hour security guard. And, unlike most humans, she’s loyal. I walked to the pantry to refill her bowl and noticed I had 3 messages on my answering machine, I hit play.

Beep: “Daddy it’s Pascal. I have parent-teacher night on Thursday and I have a umm, girlfriend. I think. Call me when you get this.” I pushed save. My kid has a girlfriend, wow!

Beep: “Hey you Carne Asada, Grey Poupon eating mothafucka! Don’t forget the tournament is Saturday night. I want action at my money back. This Capone fool, holla.” I pushed erase.

Beep:” Mr. Dumas this is parole agent Smith, I was calling to let you know that I’d be coming by your job between the hours of 9 and 5, it would be in your best interest to be there.”

Shit!

As I stood at the counter sorting through the mail I saw a letter from my nigga 5fingers from the Black P Stones. I've known him for a long time, the Y.A. days. I told him to get at me if he ever needed anything. To also get at me once a month to let me know how he's doing. I sat down on the brown leather sofa and opened the letter….

Dear Fam,
What's up blood? Long time no speak. How are you and your family? Fine I hope.I'm doing okay except my girl fell off. I got a Dear John letter saying she can't do it no more and since I got life, she movin on. Fuck it blood. What can I do? I probably woulda done the same thing. I got 6 years out of her so I can't complain.My moms and my sister still got me so I'm straight. I guess that's it P.FUNK riderI'll get at you in a minute dog.

SU WHOOP.
LOVE AND RESPECT,

Damn! That could've easily been me. I let out another one of those long breaths I had been holding and headed for the bathroom. When I stepped into the bathroom I noticed Simone's pink toothbrush next to my red one and smiled as I undressed and got under the spray of scalding hot water. After soaping my body twice and rinsing, I just stood under the water and began to once again feel the spiders of the past creep across my conscience.

Compton… 1994

"Count it again!" I told Damion.

"We counted it twice already, $242,000."

"So fuckin' what, count it again!"We sat in the bathroom of our Grandparent's house on the two thousand block of Piru Street in Compton, California and counted $242,000 in cash. I still couldn't believe it. Minus Akili's ten racks and the four racks that got contaminated by the dye packs the three of us would receive almost $73,000 a piece.

We'd already decided Chris wasn't getting shit. He fainted. Fuck'em! He should've had a V8… Simone knew not to call and I knew not to write so we communicated through third parties and always in French. Her Grandmother got her a lawyer and we buried all of the money except the ten racks I'd taken to Akili the day before. He said, "Thank you." The next time I saw him, I was watching his casket being lowered into the ground.

A month had passed since the robbery and I had changed my program completely. I had enrolled in some classes at Cerritos College and was working at the Subway in the Kenneth Hahn shopping center across the street from Martin Luther King hospital, or "Killah' King" as it's called. On Saturday, November 3rd at 8:00 a.m., the phone began to ring. I just knew it was my pregnant girlfriend calling to remind me that we had a prenatal appointment at 12:00 in Lynwood.

When I picked it up the voice in the receiver said, "You have a collect call from (pause) "Pascal" push 5 to accept. I knew it was Simone because Pascal was the name we had picked out for our son when we were kids and expected to be married. When the call was connected I said, "Sava? (what's up?)"

Simone came on and said four words. "Il es dans p.c.(he's in protective custody)," and then she hung up the phone.

I went to the Doctor's appointment as planned, then dropped Kelis off and used her car to go and pick up my check from Subway. When I walked in, Keisha, the super fine assistant manager came rushing towards me and pushed me back outside towards the McDonalds parking lot. We didn't stop til' we got inside McDonalds.

"What did you do?" her face was a mask of concern.

"You trippin' ma, I ain't do shit!"

"Put that on yo' hood."

"Girl, my hood ain't no credit card. What the fuck is wrong with you?" I asked.

She asked, "You *sure* you didn't rob no bank in Beverly Hills? You talk French don't you?" My mouth instantly went dry and the room started to shrink.

"Wha, what?" I asked shedding all my coolness as panic set in.

"Look," she said, "The police came in there during lunch and was showing everybody your picture and asking questions."

"Like what?" I asked, already knowing the answer.

"Do we know you, and where do you hang out? Shit like that."

"Who talked?"

"None of us did, but Sam's Iraninan ass gave them your application so whatever information you put on that paper is exposed."

My mind flashed to a picture of the cops raiding my Grandparent's house, then I stood up, gave Keisha a hug and went to my girlfriend's house to call my Grandmother. I took Imperial to Figueroa, made a left on Fig, and parked by Athens Park. When I walked into the front gate she was standing at the front door rubbing her belly and crying. Her mother was there too. I said,

"What's wrong ma?" She just shook her head, then I heard the sirens.

"Not you?" was all I could say in a hurt voice before her nosey-ass Moma came out the door.

She said, "We gone use that money to take care of this baby. Yo' baby!" And pointed at me disgustedly.

Kelis now hugging herself and crying uncontrollably mouthed the words, "I'm sorry." Then turned and faded into the darkness of the house.

I found out later that the F.B.I. had issued a $20,000 reward for any information leading to my capture, and that Kelis's mom had talked her into giving me up. I loved her and she was the mother of my child, but she had also done to me what Brutus had done to Caesar, and what Judas had done to Jesus. Death would have been easier to accept.

Chapter Five

1994 Beverly Hills/Downey, CA

The court experience was one of the most miserable and most memorable times in my life. The lawyer I had was a nervous old white man that was about to retire from the Public Defender's office (we call them public pretenders), and had forty-six other cases on his case load. He made sure I had all this understood before he opened my file. I knew if this was the guy that was supposed to secure my freedom, I was headed up shit creek without a paddle.

Through the glass partition he explained to me that my case was extremely high profiled and that the evidence was clearly against me. He assured me that I should take the first deal the D.A. offers and end the case as quickly as possible (my hero). When he finally got around to actually reading my file, I took the opportunity to help him along with the facts.

"Here's what they have, nuthin! No gun, no fingerprints, no money and the video surveillance I understand doesn't identify anybody. Pretty easy huh?"

He looked at me through red rimmed eyes and said, "You don't look French?"

I said, "I'm not. I was born at Martin Luther King hospital in Compton, to American parents."

"Do you speak French?"

"Nope."

"The papers said you were a French terrorist," he said sounding disappointed.

"Sorry." I said and he went back to shuffling through the papers in the file.

"Here it is," he said. "The District Attorney's star witness (the fucking cop I thought) is a man named Christopher Daniels. He says you're the ring leader and mastermind behind the entire plot."

"Really?" I asked, "Isn't that the guy that got caught *at* the bank with the girl? And speaking of the girl, what is she saying?"

He shuffled through the file looking for Simone's statement then pulled out a blank piece of paper. "The girl hasn't said a word," again, sounding a bit disappointed."On a more positive note," he said, "Of the eleven witnesses, only one of them picked you out of the six pack photo line-up. Fortunately for you young man, her testimony is inadmissible."

"Really, why?" I asked, hope building in my stomach.

"She's five years old and the jury won't convict you on the word of a toddler."

I blurted, "Okay, so you're telling me that nobody in the bank including the cop has identified me?"

"Christopher Daniels did." he said smugly.

"Fuck Christopher Daniels! He's just trying to save his own ass. Is that how they found me?"

"Christopher Daniels and your baby's mother." Ouch, that let the air out of me.

"Okay so what do we do? And don't tell me none of that take the first deal shit! What're my charges anyway?"

More shuffling, "Robbery, possession of a firearm, attempted murder, discharging a firearm, and twelve counts of false imprisonment".

"Twelve? I thought you said there were only eleven people in the bank"

"Christopher Daniels is no longer a suspect. Now he's the star witness, and a victim."

"Great," I said and sat back in my chair.

This dance went on until the deals became reasonable. They threw out a bunch of the charges and dropped the robbery to attempted robbery because as the media pointed out, all the money had been recovered. This game of chicken continued on for almost eight months. Then on the ninth month we agreed on plea bargains. Simone would receive ten years for attempted murder and various gun charges. I received eight years for attempted robbery and gun charges, and Chris, even though he snitched, got three years for gun possession. I guess the D. A. was mad that they couldn't give any of us life so he snatched the deal back from Chris.

Before the bailiff could usher us back to the holding tank, Mr. Crawford, my lawyer approached me and asked, "Was it worth it?"

I leaned in close and said, "Oui M'sieu (yes sir)," and was lead back to the holding tank to wait for the bus back to Los Padrinos juvenile hall.

When I looked back, Mr. Crawford was stuffing papers into his worn out briefcase and looking at me with a grin on his face that said, '*I knew it.*'

I smiled back and said a little prayer thanking God that this part of the journey was over.

The ride back to the halls was unusually quiet. A lot of us had just signed away years of our lives and had donated rest of our youth to the California penal system. We arrived back at L.P. around 6 p.m. and were quickly directed back to our housing units.

When I walked into E/F (my unit), my boy Tiny Moon from Long Beach told me, "Rowdy you hit today," which meant that I had received mail, that it was being held in the staff's office.

After I was strip searched (for the 3rd time) I gave my homies the short version of what happened at court then made my way to the staff's office.

"Coop what's up?" I asked Mr. Cooper the senior staff member.

"C'mere son we need to talk" he said as I sat in the chair across the desk from him. "You got a pretty interesting letter today while you were out at court," he said, then threw the envelope across the desk to me and sat back in his chair and folded his arms across his huge belly. When the letter landed in front of me I saw it was from Kelis and instantly stood up to leave.

"Send it back." I said as I turned towards the door.

"Naw son, don't be hasty, least you can do is take a peek, then we got business."

"Business?" I asked curiously.

He made a shooing motion with his hand and said,"Come see me before lock up and tell me what you wanna do then."

As I made my way down the hall to my room my little homeboy, LK from O'Farrell Park fell in beside and walked with me.

"Su whoop, blood, wus brackin,'" he asked in his squeaky little voice, I immediately began to smile.

"Su whoop lil daddy, what's good?" I asked pointing to his freshly swollen black eye.

LK is 15 years old and already a legend in his neighborhood in San Diego. He was 5'7, 140lbs, but had the heart of a full grown lion.

"Aw blood, it ain't nuthin. That crab nigga Spanky got smart and I took off on'em."

I just shook my head and grabbed him around the neck. Spanky was 6'2, 240lbs and was the only nigga in juvenile hall with a full beard. Nobody believed he was 16 years old, including the staff.

"Who wrote you?" he asked looking at the envelope in my hand.

"My B.M.," I said sourly.

"Whoa, y'all talkin now?"

"Nope."

"Taco said you took 8 at court today, that true?"

"Yeah, I'm done with court dog," I said evenly. He sighed and looked away. We both knew this meant I'd be leaving soon, he was hurt.

"Blood you aiight? You ain't getting all Carl Thomas on me are you?" I asked releasing him out off the head lock.

He gave me his best fake smile and said, "Real niggas don't deal with emotions." Then he put his gangsta face back on.

I asked him, "You satisfied with that shit with Spanky or you wanna pop it off before I bounce?" He thought about it. Poppin it off meant a full scale riot with the Crips, one that we would probably lose because the Crips had us out numbered 3-1, but fuck it.

"Nahh I'm bool, plus I took off on him first." He said with a big grin that made him look more like a child and less like a dude that was on trial for double murder.

"Send Spanky down here, I still wanna holler at him." I said, then turned to go in my room. I put the letter on the bed, tied my shoes up tight and waited for Spanky to show up. He did five minutes later.

"Spank' what's up dog?"

"Whatchu mean? That shit with LK?"

"Yep."

"Shit, that lil nigga took off on *me*."

"Why though? You did something to provoke him."

"Man that shit is over." He said avoiding the question.

"You sure?"

"We had a head up fade. That's it."

"LK is hands off from now on blood." I said, then threw him 3 joints and 3 matches wrapped in cellophane. "Tell yo folks too, cause next time it gets ugly. For *everybody*."

Then I turned and picked up my letter signifying that the conversation was over. When I held the letter I noticed my hands were shaking. I don't know if it was from the prefight jitters or the bullshit I was about to read. The staff has to screen all incoming mail as a security precaution so when I pulled out the letter I noticed the red, white, and blue cashier's check. Pacific Bank: pay to the order of Mr. Kevon Dumas, $7,000. Seven thousand dollars and zero cents. I turned it over to make sure it was real then sat it down next to me and began to read the letter I had stopped expecting a long time ago.

***Date**: July 22, 1995*
***Time:** 5p.m*
***Feeling**: Missing you*
***Dedication**: Believe in me by; Mary J Blige*
***Reason:** I think we should talk*

Dear Kevon,
I know you probably hate me and don't want to hear a word I have to say but I'm hoping and praying that you at least hear me out. I know I fucked up and I'm sorry. I'm reminded of how bad I fucked up every time I look at our beautiful son. Yes we had a boy and yes he looks just like you. Mean! When that check came I gave my greedy ass moma her half which she lost in Vegas. Then I bought everything I thought the baby needed and got my car fixed. I sent the rest to you. I know it don't make up for what I did but I hope you can use it. I DON'T WANT IT! My family's not for sale! I have a lot more to say but I'll say it at visiting on Saturday. If you'll agree to see me. I guess I'm finished for now but I do love you and I'm very sorry. Call me, I mean us 213-901 7325

Love Always, Kelis.

P.S I saw Damion at the Compton Swapmeet but he wouldn't talk to me.

This bitch must've been smoking hard white if she thought she could rat me out to the Feds then, waltz back into my life like nothing ever happened. I picked the letter up then headed back to Coop's office, caught him at the water fountain.

"So what you gone do with all that loot?"

"Give it back."

"Why? Boy you been smoking some of that grass they got floating around here?" he asked with an,*I know everything* look.

"Nahh, it's dirty money, I'm cool."

"From the bank robbery?" he asked trying to catch me off guard.

"What bank robbery?" I said with a get the fuck outta here expression.

He laughed and said, "Just send it outta here with yo Grandmaw on Sunday when she comes to visit you." Then he let out a mean ass fart.

I winced and said, "Nasty bastard." As I walked back to my room. Before I got there I was stopped by a familiar voice calling me.

"Hey Rowdy, wait up!" I turned around to see my only Mexican homeboy joggin towards me.

Stryker was a character. He was 5'11, 185lbs and had tattoos all over his face and head. But, that's not what was funny about him. His neighborhood was in Watts, it was surrounded by Black gangs, and because of that, Stryker had a little soul. He had just come back to the unit from the BOX (solitary confinement) because he started a full blown race riot in church between the Blacks and the Mexicans. Why? He said *Nigga.* And he said it like he made the damn word up.

"Rowdy what's up Ese? What happened at court?" He asked as I gave him some dap.

"Shit, I took 8 and my crimee took 10."

"Daaaamn nigga, you outta here." He said a little too loud.

"Yep, I think I'm leaving on Monday or Tuesday."

"To Y.A., or the the Peenta?"

"Hopefully the Penn, cause I got tried as an adult."

"Oh, yeah. Fuck it homes 'least you outta' this kiddie ass shit," he said as I stared at the big ass 13 tatooed on his forehead.

"Man I hope I get a deal one day." He said in a far away voice.

"Stop carjacking old ladies." I said with a laugh.

"Fuck you nigga, she was 25." He said with a shove.

I said, "Keep that shit up and imma' go tell your people you saying nigga again."

He turned back towards the dayroom where everybody was watching Lethal Weapon II and screamed NIGGA! NIGGA! NIGGA! NIGGA! Then crossed his arms in a defiant gesture. A few people turned around, the Southsider Otto from Lennox just shook his head. LK laughed out loud and through up the "P." Stryker threw up a bunch of signs with his hands in response then turned back to me.

"Mann, yo ass is craaazy." I said laughing.Then Stryker turned and went back to the movie, strollin and sagging his LP jumpsuit, just like a nigga.

Saturday came faster than I expected and as it's customary, after breakfast there was a tackle football game against unit C/D. Those who were expecting visitors had the option of going to the game or staying behind on the unit to wait for their visitor. I stayed behind and watched as the visitors began to arrive. At around 10:00 a.m. I saw her.

Kelis was 5'2, 120lbs, maybe 150lbs with the new baby fat she'd gained. She was wearing a blue jean Guess skirt and matching jacket and her mocha colored skin was shining softly against the sunlight. As she struggled up the stairs with the diaper bag on her shoulder and the car seat in her hands, I noticed that she had changed over the last year. She looked, *older*. She was no longer the 16 year old girl I'd gotten pregnant. Now, because of our decisions she was a woman. And a Mother.

I jumped down from the window and rushed to the mirror to check my face and my breath, then I sat on the edge of the bottom bunk and waited for the staff to call my name over the P.A. system. When they did, I walked casually down the hallway with one leg of my orange jumpsuit pulled up LL.COOL. J style and made my way to the sitting area where my Ex and my newborn son were seated. When she stood to hug me I waved a finger at her and slid into the yellow plastic chair nearest to my son. His blue plaid Eddie Bauer car-seat was covered with a blue blanket decorated with white bears.

"Is he sleep?" I asked stupidly not knowing what else to say.

"No he should be up. I covered him because the sun was too bright outside," she said in a casual voice.

I dug in my pocket for the letter with the cashier's check, handed it to her and pulled the car seat closer to me. I reached down to remove the blanket with shaking hands, a racing heart and instantly fell in love. He was pale, with a nest of curly black hair and eyes the same brown as mine but with more of a slant. He looked just like me. As he blinked his way into adjusting to the lights he focused on me and we had the first of many wordless conversations. This was mine! My son! My baby! With those thoughts in my heart, my heart beat evened out and I began to let a smile out on my face.

"What's his name?" I asked hoping she didn't give him some fucked up name like Kevontae or Jaquarious.

"Pascal, like that village your family is from in Haiti. But my momma and them call him Cali cause they say Pascal is too hard to pronounce." She said with a wide smile that I still found attractive.

"I don't want that money Kelis," I said looking for my anger again and changing the subject.

"Why?" She asked, tears brimming in her eyes.

"Because it's dirty money, SNITCH money, and it cost'd me 8 years of my life!" I said looking through her.

"8 years….?" She asked in a little voice.

"Yep, 8 fucking years! Because of *you*! I don't get to see my son's first steps or hear his first words. I hope you're happy." I barked.

"I'm sorry." she tried to say but I just put my hand up as to say, 'save it.' My son could sense the negative energy and began to cry. Not the frantic all out wail of most new borns but a whimpering low cry. When I picked him up he stopped, then gave me a toothless smile that melted my anger.

"You're stupid." I told her as I put my son on my chest and patted his back lightly.

"I know" she said and looked down at the floor for something that wasn't there.

"You sold your family out for ten grand. I stopped hanging out, went to college, and got a job for YOU! Because I wanted to do right by YOU! And it still wasn't enough!" I continued, "Just make sure you tell him the truth. Or I will."

The visit continued like this until its conclusion and when it ended, I couldn't have been happier. I kissed my son's slobbery lips, inhaled the scent of his hair as I put his sleeping little body back into his car seat.

"I brought you some shoes and personals." She said pointing to a bag that Mrs. Bender was searching thoroughly.

I said "Thank you" and waited for the 5 minute warning.

When she bent to pick up my son's pacifier I noticed that her breasts had swelled by 2 or 3 sizes and she had a fresh tattoo on the left one. "***KEVON***" it said. I smiled to myself, then we both got up as the staff announced, "VISITING IS NOW OVER!"

I hugged her, not out of love or warmth, but because I noticed that she was really sorry and was trying hard to fix something that could never be repaired. I watched her make her way to the stairway then stop to wave once. I waved back, and she left.

The shoes she brought me were the grey,white and red Huaraches'. My favorite shoes at the time. The small bag of "personals" contained 2 tubes of toothpaste, 2 toothbrushes, a jar of Murray's hair grease and 2 sticks of Mitchum deodorant. All my favorites. I picked up the small bag and the shoe box and went back down the long hallway to my room.

Dinner came and went as usual, and for the first time since my capture I had a peaceful night's sleep. No more haunted dreams of Simone getting shot or Kelis betraying me. Instead, I had a dream of me pushing my son on the swings in some beautiful but distant future. The dream was vivid, maybe because it could be a sign. The fact that I could still smell my son's baby smell on my T-shirt helped a lot. I slept with it balled up, next to my face.

Sunday was my favorite day. Not because it was the day that Jesus rested or anything like that. It was the day that I got to see my Grandmother and my Aunt Janet. After hugs and kisses were exchanged I filled my family in on what transpired at court, about my upcoming departure.

"Huit ans? (eight years?)" My Aunt asked.

"Yep, I took it so they wouldn't give Simone life"

"Goot," my Grandmother broke in, "A goot Creole is loyal and keeps his word!" she said as she patted my knee.

"The good news is I don't have to do the whole 8 years, only half of it. Give or take a few months." This made my grandmother smile. I didn't mention my visit with Kelis because my family didn't like her. Especially the women. Towards the end of the visit, Coop came over and spoke to my Grandmother and flirted with my Aunt.

"Yep, the boy's leaving tomarah," he said in a huff.

"Where?" I asked hoping he'd say Chino Reception Center.

"C.Y.A. boy! Seems the judge didn't think you was ready for the big house." He laughed as my family and I began to fire words rapidly in French due to these new developments.

As Coop' just stood there amazed, I'd basically explained to my family that I wasn't going to the big Prison, that I'd probably be placed somewhere close to home. They were pleased and gave me words of encouragement. This all blew Coop away.I hugged my Grandmother tight as she began to cry like she always did at the end of our visits.

Then she stepped back and held my face in her strong hands and said, "Tell me the 5 virtues." She did this every time, every time to make sure I never forgot my Grandfather's favorite words.

In a strong French accent I said, "*Honor, Respect, Understanding, Patience, and,* ***LOYALTY***."

She smiled, kissed my forehead, and headed for the stairs with her head held high and her back straight. I truly believed that if she could, she would've done this time for me.

"What was all that voolay voo shit boy?" Coop asked with a confused look.

I smiled and said, "Spanish," with raised eyebrows.

"Boy if that was Spanish, I'm dumber than a Chinese hooker." I burst into laughter holding my stomach. Coop had a way of saying the most hilarious shit at the wrong time.

"French," I confessed. He covered his mouth and wagged his finger like I had just told him that I killed JFK.

"I knew it!" he said scratching his chin. "How much y'all get?" he asked in a hushed voice.

"The media said all the money was recovered." I said in a mocking tone.

"Screw the media!" he boomed. "They always say that shit to try to deter folks from robbing banks, how much y'all get?" He pressed as he danced from one foot to the other like a kid doing the pee-pee dance.

"Twenty?"

"Higher," I said.

"Thirty?" I pointed up.

"Fifty?" I shook my head.

"A hundred?" I looked insulted.

"Sonofabitch!" he said in an out of breath voice.

"Quarter mill", I said ending his misery.

He looked up and started doing math in his head. "You got four years to do, let's see, that's sixty thousand plus a year…"

"That's *if* I was involved." I said jokingly.

Coop laughed and said "If? If a hawk had a radio in his ass there'd be music in the air."

And I walked down the hall laughing my ass off. I was definitely going to miss Mr. Cooper.

Chapter Six

Downey California 1995

On the morning of September 12, 1995 a bus filled with 22 teenage boys left Los Padrinos Juvenile Hall destined for the Southern Reception Center of California, or SRCC as it's called.

SRCC worked as an orientation center for those inmates headed to the California Youth Authority. It housed teens from all over Southern California. From Los Angeles to as far as Vista California near the US/Mexico border. This promised a mix of different cultures, races, and definitely gangs. Some say the 'Y' is the breeding ground for building the perfect gangbanger and, if you can make it through the "Y" you can make it through anything.

SRCC wasn't a real Y.A. because it was only temporary housing. The maximum stay at SRCC was 90 days. Then you were shipped out to your permanent Y.A. to finish out your time. There were Y.A.'s all over California. Most were located up North. The ones you did and didn't want to go to were located conveniently right in Southern California.

The absolute best Y.A. to go to according to rumor was Ventura. Located not 60 minutes away from L.A., the reason Ventura was the best was simple; it was Co-Ed. This meant girls and girls equaled sex. Ventura also had a work program with T.W.A airlines called Free Venture. This program allowed the teens to build and assemble parts at minimum wage. Pussy *and* Money? Sheeiit, Sign me up. The only requirement they had was you had to have a high school diploma or G.E.D. I had both and was almost guaranteed a spot at Ventura.

The *other* Y.A. was an absolute no-no and was considered the most dangerous Y.A. in the state. At the Youth Training School

(Y.T.S.) more people died, got raped, and stabbed there than any and all of the other Y.A.'s put together. It was there that they sent societies worst. It was located on the Chino/Ontario border not 40 minutes from Los Angeles, but that still didn't make it attractive. To be honest, after the stories I'd heard, I much rather prefered adult prison.

Out of the 22 inmates on the bus with me I only recognized four. My boy Tiny Moon from Long Beach Insane, Droopy from Fo' Tray Gangsta's in L.A, and Black Flag from V.N.G. The 4th guy was this weird dude that didn't talk or interact, he just looked out the window and laughed at jokes that only he heard.

"You scared?" Tiny Moon asked as he leaned forward on my seat.

"Not *scared,* but nervous."

"Fuck it cuzz, I mean Rowdy, when we get there just don't change up on me." He said with a weak smile.

I smiled back and said "Never nigga, I'm the same everywhere I go."

"Yep, a asshole," he said and we both started laughing nervously.

"You dirty?" I asked

"Yeah, I got some pot and some matches. You?

"Just my key, I gave everything to LK when I left."

Black Flag ever the jokester started beating on the window and rapping …

On the way to Y.A. doing my duty
this nigga T-Moon got weed in his booty
Rowdy is a cutie he all light skinned
a big black nigga gone be his boyfriend….

The whole bus erupted into laughter as we pulled up to the security gate and waited to get buzzed in. I took a deep breath, said a little prayer, and put my mean mug on… let's do it!

After we got strip searched, we were divided into groups according to age, then given uniforms and gray sweatshirts.

Because of their ages 15-16, Droopy and Black Flag went to PICO unit. Tiny Moon and I went to GIBBS unit. We lied and told the staff that we didn't bang so they wouldn't split us up and we ended up getting a room together. The next 87 days passed relatively quickly and with minimal action.

SRCC was peaceful, probably because everybody was scared because they didn't know where they were going. Sure, there was the occasional fist fight over a foul on the basketball court or somebody crossing somebody's hood out, but for the most part, it was cool. Kelis and my family came to visit me often so my time passed fast.

On Thursday, the 88th day, the packing boxes were passed out. Splatt-pssst was the sounds they made as they were dropped in front of your door, then kicked under. Tiny Moon and I were in room 34 so when we heard the first boxes hit the floor that morning, we got up and waited tensely. As the staff got closer we could hear the screams of joy from those who received boxes that had Ventura written on them. And the death like quiet of those whose boxes read Y.T.S. Tiny Moon and I had already decided that we weren't tripping off of going to Y.T.S., but I still harbored secret hopes of going to Ventura and doing *easy* time.

"Brown, Dumas!" The staffer yelled as he dropped and kicked our boxes. "Gladiator school!" he said with a snicker.

There was no need to even look at the boxes. As I picked up my 2 boxes and handed Tiny Moon his 2 we both began to smile.

"Fuck it," he said.

"Fuck it," I said back, then held the boxes high above my head and did my horrible impersonation of the Crip Walk. He fell back on his bed, laughing, gripping his boxes to his chest.

Y.T.S? Gladiator School? Fuuuck it! I didn't know exactly what time it was when they got us up for transfer, but the sun wasn't out and it was cold as hell. When we got to the front of the unit to be handcuffed we didn't see any of the Y.A. staff doing the shackles or waist chains. Instead there were actual L.A County Sheriffs' deputies doing the work. They stripped us out, then chained our waists to the *front* which had never happened before in juvenile hall. I looked at Moon who was being attended to by a pretty dark skinned sheriff and stuck my tongue out to show him the handcuff key I had hidden in my mouth. He made a slight giggle and the lady looked at him crazy then pulled his chains so tight his face turned red.

After all the "Wards" (which was what we were now) were secured, we were loaded onto a Grey-Goose styled bus with tinted windows and bars. There were about 30 of us in all, 5 or 6 of which I recognized from juvenile hall. When the bus started moving I was seated 5 rows back from Tiny Moon. He was seated next to some fat nigga with a 52 tat'd under his eye.

I asked, "Hey folks, you wanna trade seats?"

He looked at me like I had shit on my face and said, "Hey Cuzz where you from?"

Here we go I thought. He called me *cuzz* which automatically made us enemies but because he was from L.A and a hood I technically didn't have beef with I said,"I'm from Compton homie" and waited on his response.

"Compton what?" he asked a little too aggressively.

"Man you gone trade seats or not?" I asked getting pissed off.

Tiny Moon said, "Fuck it, Rowdy I'll come back there." And tried to get passed ol boy.

He stood to block Moon's way and said, "Nigga, where *you* from?"

Why'd he do that? Tiny Moon rammed his head into the front of dude's face, his nose crunched and began to gush blood. By the time Tiny Moon started to kick him I was already out of my handcuffs and socking him repeatedly in the face and head. When the sheriffs had finally pulled the bus over on the freeway we had beaten Mr. 52 out of his clothes.

The female officer knocked me down on top of the unconscious guy and cuffed my hands behind my back. When she knee'd me in the side I swallowed my handcuff key with a gag. Tiny Moon was bleeding profusely from the forehead. After they secured us in the isolation cages at the front of the bus they sprayed us with pepper spray. It felt like my face was on fire, but Moon was screaming because he had an open cut on his fore head. Shortly after they tended to the tough guy in the back they started the bus like none of it had ever happened.

The trip from SRCC to Y.T.S. took less than 1 ½ hours thankfully.As we came onto the grounds the female deputy asked, "How the fuck you get out of your cuffs?"

I did what I always did when the situation was right, I spoke French. "Je ne compren pas (I don't understand)."

"What was that?" she asked a little amused.

Tiny Moon said, "He don't speak English, he's one of those French bank robbers." I just sat there looking purposely confused.

"He better not have a fuckin' cuff key," she said with a disgusted face.

I smiled through a face full of tears and a nose full of snot and said, "No."

Then the bus came to a stop. When the passengers began to unload they had to walk by the cages we were in and I just knew Mr. 52 was gone spit through the bars on one of us. It seemed he didn't remember me being involved because he hawked and then spit right in Moon's face and said, "Fuck yo dead homies bitch!"

He must've not seen me standing across from him. I said, "Hey Loc," and when he turned around I spit right in his eye before the cop pulled him down the 3 steps and out door. We sat on the bus for almost 20 minutes before the cops and two Y.A. staff dressed like cops came to get us.

"This them, the trouble makers?" the fat bald Y.A. staff asked.

"Yeah," the lady cop said, "The little French boy got out of his handcuffs, y'all better search him again."

I didn't say anything as they snatched me off the bus. They took Tiny Moon in a different direction, I assumed the infirmary. Then gave me a towel and took my handcuffs off. "Walk like this," the fat guy said stupidly as he demonstrated a guy walking with his hands behind his back.

"Oui (yes)," I said and mimicked his impression. They escorted me through the dock doors and onto the main campus. And that's exactly what it looked like, a campus. It had a football field complete with goal posts and bleachers. The living units looked more like apartment buildings and less like cell blocks.

I noticed the cell blockswere broken into units. Unit 1 housed A/B, C/D, E/F, G/H; unit 2 housed K/L, M/N, O/R; unit 3 housed S/T, U/V, W/X, Y/Z. The campus at Y.T.S. didn't look like jail, but as I looked into the faces of the residents, I knew where I was. They all had two things in common, they all had big ass muscles and they all looked mad!

Chapter Seven

Chino California 1995

I had just beat the shit out of somebodyand was being escorted by three cops so I looked mad too and made eye contact with some of the people I was passing. I wasn't really mad though. I was scared shitless and had been holding my pee since we left S.R.C.C. and, my face still burned.

We stopped at unit #1and I was herded up a ramp and into the unit. Amazing … as I walked through the dayroom I noticed the T.V was on MTV and the chairs were like fake leather love-seats, rows of them. And, they had a Solo flex weight lifting machine, ping pong table. This definitely wasn't jail.

The cops passed me off to the plain clothes staff that worked on the unit and left. The staff, a little red faced man named Bickard asked me to follow him and I did, still with my hands behind my back. I ignored the stares as he explained to me that I was only being housed here until they found me a compatible roommate.

He asked where I was from and I told him, then I was lead down the hall to my room. He opened it with a key, I stepped in, and he closed it back. The room was completely empty which didn't bother me as I set to the task of making my bed. As I was putting my pillow in its pillow case I felt eyes on me. And when I looked up, I noticed I wasn't trippin'. There were 2 faces crammed against the vertical rectangular window in the door.

"What's up?" I asked evenly.

“West Boulevard Crip,” the acne faced light skinned nigga said.

“Wrong room.” I said again evenly.

“Where you from cuzz?” the dark monkey looking dude asked, pushing the other dude out of the way.

“Compton.”

“Where at in Compton?” he probed.

“You a Crip?” I asked.

“Yep, West Side Gear Gang Crip!” he said proudly.

“Never heard of’em.” I said sounding uninterested.

This must have been funny because captain acne started laughing and said, “Aww cuzz, you let that nigga dis’ yo hood? Aww cuzz…”

Gear Gang asked, “Cuzz, you got jokes?” like I hurt his feelings.

By now I was pissed off and said, “Blood, get the fuck away from my door!” and walked up to the door.

“Where you from nigga!” he asked almost screaming.

“Whoever you don’t get along with!” I said with a snarl.

He looked stunned and was about to say something smart when another face appeared in the window and told them to go somewhere and stop acting hard in front of me. They left reluctantly, then the big dude said, “Don’t trip off them niggas, they busters.”

I said, “Good lookin out.”

And he asked, “Are you a Kiwe or Damu?”

“Huh?” I asked not understanding.

“You a Crip or a Blood?” he asked plainly.

“Oh, I’m from Fruit Town Piru.”

“I’m Baby Dave from Long Beach Insane.”

I smiled and said, “Tiny Moon just drove up with me today. He was my celly in SRCC.”

He smiled and said, "Yeah? That's my lil cousin, where he at?"

I told him about what happened on the bus and that Moon was probably on his way to the infirmary.

He left quickly, probably in search of his newly arrived cousin. Then turned and assured me that he'd send some of my homeboys to check on me. He was true to his word because about an hour later there were 2 more big ass niggas at my door. The tall one had to be about 6'6 or taller and the shorter guy had the chest and shoulders of a gorilla.

"Su whoop!!" They greeted me with the universal greeting for all Bloods.

"Su whoop!" I returned as I approached the door.

"Blood, wus hatnin?" The tall guy asked revealing dangerously crooked teeth.

"Bickin it." I said as we looked at each other, he looked familiar.

"I'm Stretch from Crenshaw Mafia and this the homie 5 fingers from BPS."

"The Jungles!" Five corrected in a voice too high to fit his muscled body.

"I'm Rowdy from Bompton Fruit Town Piru." I said in my big boy voice.

After the introductions were completed Five asked me for my paperwork. This interrogation is done to all fish (new guys) upon arrival at any new institution. It's a security measure and the ghetto version of a passport. I went to the small desk by the window and retrieved my court papers. What Five and Stretch looked for when I slid my paperwork under the door was: *why* I was in jail, if I'd snitched on anybody, and how much time I had. If I had a rape case, child abuse, or crime against old people; it would say so on my paperwork, and I'd probably never get out of Y.A. alive.

Five finished scanning my paperwork then passed it to Stretch and said, “Bank robber huh?” with a smile.

I smiled back and said, “Yep,” with pride.

We passed the next thirty minutes getting familiar and chatting excitedly as I gave them updates on their homies and their neighborhoods. Stretch had 6 years in on an 11 year sentence and Five had life for a double hot one (murder), I told them what happened on the bus, and about the guys harassing me on the door and they assured me that if I wanted a head-up with one or both of those dudes, they could set it up.

“Hell yeah blood,” I said excitedly. “Ol boy came at me sideways, I need that.” I said.

Five asked, “Which one you want?”

“Both.” I said, “line ‘em up!”They looked at each other then laughed. I asked, “What’s so funny?” in a serious tone.

As the welcoming committee’s laughter died Five said, “Blood, you gone fit right in around here.”

Before they left they assured me that they’d be back with a care package for me and something to read. I thanked them and went back to sweeping under my bed. I spent the next couple of hours pacing, staring out the window at the passing throngs of human traffic on the trade line and jacking off. It’s amazing the amount of erections and semen the young body can produce. My current record was seven times in a three to four hour span.

In the late afternoon the hallways and dayroom came alive with the sounds of the residents of unit A/B finally returning from school and work. I pushed to my door to see all the new faces and to observe how life was conducted in Y.A. A few of the guys mad dogged me as they passed my room, but for the most part I was ignored. These dudes had lives and set agendas. They could care less about the new guy in room A29. About two hours later, Five and Stretch came back and began to slide a bunch of items under my door; Top Ramen noodles, kool aid, candy bars, and stationary.Then, Stretch looked around and slid a "Hustler" porn magazine under the door with a snicker.

Five said, "We gone get you moved off of A/B and over there wit' us on G/H. Gimme a few days - til then Y.G., stay outta' trouble."

I asked, "Why Y'all being so nice to me?" skeptically. I'd heard a lot of stories about Y.A. and prison and the one I heard the most was, "If somebody tries to give you something, *don't* take it." These dudes were my Blood family but I still had to ask.

Five looked offended then said,"Huh," and took a long metal shank out of his waistline and kicked it under the door with a clank. Then he smiled and said, "When you trust me, give it back."And they turned to leave.

I sat on the edge of the bottom bunk and flipped the knife over and over in my hands. I learned years later that stabbing a person was much harder than shooting one. Using a knife or razor was more personal. Anybody could pull a trigger from a distance, but it took courage to get up on a person and feel the skin rip.

I walked back to the door to listen to the music videos through the crack on the side and when a commercial came on I noticed the dude from Gear Gang pushing a broom down the long hallway. Naturally, he stops at my room with his nose flared and his top lip curled up and says, "Cuzz, I'm finna knock you out, soon as the doors rack open."

I said, "Nigga, if *you* knock *me* out, I'll give my life to the Lord." And blew him a kiss. He went back the way he came and I sat on my bunk and thumbed through the magazine.

Some time later the staff announced dinner and all the wards filed out in a line and headed to the cafeteria to eat. Seconds later the staff, a cute light skinned girl with freckles brought me a Styrofoam tray with the night's dinner in it. Spaghetti. Hell no!

When I looked at the girl more closely I noticed two things. She wasn't that much older than me maybe 23-24. The other thing I knew for sure. She was Creole.

"Je ne veux pas," I said making sure I wasn't tripping."

She looked at me with wide eyes then looked down the hallway, in both directions and asked, "Who are you?" in English.

"Je suis un vrai Creole, et vous? (I'm a real Creole, and you?)." I answered and looked down to notice we were both still holding the tray.

She quickly let go and said, "I'm a woman trying to keep her job."

I smiled. One thing was for sure, she at least understood French. A curl of light brown hair fell free and she tucked it behind her ear and said, "Je vais paler lui demain (I'll talk to you tomorrow)," in the most beautiful French I'd ever heard.

"Quand? (when?)," I asked as she pushed me softly in the chest and closed the door. She looked back twice on her way down the hall. When she was gone I grabbed the Hustler magazine, time to break the record….

After my marathon masturbation session I washed up in the metal sink, then ate two of the top ramen noodles and two of the candy bars. After that I did five hundred pushups and went to sleep. That night, sleep came easily and I had a wonderful dream about the Creole girl. My Grandmother would be sooo pissed off.

I was awakened the next morning by the sounds of the wards being herded off to breakfast. When I heard the sound of keys approaching my door I rushed to the door expecting to see the Creole girl from the night before. Not the case… When the door opened, a huge black lady wearing a tight green uniform handed me my food then looked me up and down and snorted, "You must thank you special."

I just blinked and stepped back, "Huh?" I asked.

"You movin' after breakfast. Seems your homiesgot some just juice on G/H."

I said thank you, not knowing what else to say as the door was slammed in my face. Bitch! The breakfast was one I'd seen before a thousand times since I'd been incarcerated. Two boiled eggs, two hash browns and oatmeal, one milk and one frozen carton of juice. After breakfast I packed the few items I had remaining from the care package and waited tensely. There was a chance I'd run into ol boy from Gear Gang. If I did, it'd be too bad for him.

When "Bertha" came back she said, "Come on," in an irritated voice and told me to put my hands behind my back as was customary of an inmate walking with or being escorted by a staff member. Good. That's where the knife was tucked into my waistline. If ol boy tried something stupid I could get to it easily. At the same time, I was having nagging thoughts. Did I really have the nerve to bust on somebody with a knife? We'd find out soon enough because when we went through the doorway that separated the hall and the dayroom he was standing up with his back to me, changing the channel on the T.V.

"Fish walking!" Bertha screamed announcing my presence and destroying the element of surprise.

When he spun around I dropped one of my hands that was holding the brown paper bag behind my back. Outside of us three, there were only four other people in the large dayroom, a pair of Samoans talking harshly in the green backed chairs, hands flailing and afros shakin' as they argued in their rough language. And two wards in painter's uniforms and goggles. When Gear Gang made his attempt to come towards me Bertha, a lot faster than I expected, removed a large can of pepper spray from the utility belt on her giant hips.

"Move Dixon, before I spray your black ass." She told him.

He stopped between the rows of chairs and we glared at each other with hate filled eyes. Bertha obviously sensing some type of tension began to shake the supersized canister and said, "Fuck around if y'all want to." Then she called for someone named Rodriguez. A tall Hispanic man in civilian clothes came out of the front office with half a bagel in his hand, wiping his mouth with a napkin.

"Watch that bastard!" she said as she nodded at Gear Gang.

Rodriguez, obviously pissed off about having his breakfast disturbed said, "Dixon sit down or lock it up!"

This obviously got Gear Gangs' attention because he took one more look and said, "Rod, I'm cool" And turned back to the T.V. I was lead out the door and into the sunlight where I was passed to a pretty older black lady whose ID tag said, "Baker"

Ms. Baker was built like a stallion and her green uniform fit nicely. "Hey Wanda, where's this cutie pie going?" she asked

Bertha/Wanda as we approached. "His yellow ass going to G/H" She spit back. I looked at her like she was crazy and mumbled "Garce (bitch)," under my breath.

"What?" she asked reaching for her pepper spray. Then Ms. Baker grabbed my arm and spun me towards the ramp that lead to G/H.

"She is a bitch ain't she?" She asked with a girlish giggle. I nodded and asked

"Parlez-Vous Francais? (do you speak French?)"

"A little bit." She continued in English, "I just remember all the bad words and the food." She said, with another giggle. When we got to the door on unit G/H there was an older black man with a clipboard in his left hand and a hand held metal detector in the other. SHIT!

"Dumas?" He asked as he began to raise the metal detector in my direction.

Ms. Baker said, "I searched him already." And winked at me in an, I got your back type of way. The man in the street clothes said, "Good," and clipped the metal detector to his belt.

"Thank you Ms. Baker," I said as she made her way back down the ramp.

"You welcome," she called over her shoulder with a wave, as we entered the unit. The staff, Mr. Thomas explained to me in a very feminine voice that unit G/H was considered the honor unit of YTS. Everybody wanted to live on unit G/H because it was exclusive. All the older wards lived on G/H, and there was hardly any racial or gang tension. You had to actually apply and be interviewed to be housed there. The requirements were three fold; have a high school diploma or G.E.D, have a clean behavior record,(which was almost impossible), and be athletic. G/H had all of the best athletes in YTS, and as I entered the hallway I noticed the caliber of dudes was totally different. Yes, a few had their masks on, but in Y.A. that was part of the uniform.

I sat in the office which was buzzing with activity, and was asked a series of questions by two of the three men present. Rex was the football coach and Scott was the basketball coach. After determining that I *fit,* I signed a contract stating that if I got two level B's or 3 level A's (incident reports) I would be removed from unit G/H immediately. Scott told me that he needed a point guard and that tryouts were on Saturday.

"I'll be there" I said and was escorted to my room, the place that I would be living for the next four years.

When we got to the door Mr. Thomas said, "You know you're an M number and that you're supposed to be in prison. If you fuck up here, fights, riots, weapons or that gang shit; I'll personally make sure you end up in Pelican Bay. Go on." He said and nodded at the room door.

To my surprise, it was unlocked. I looked at Thomas and as if reading my thoughts he said, "We don't lock doors around here."Then reached across the hall and pulled open another room door to illustrate his point. "If something comes up missing, they have ways of finding out who did it." And with that he walked soundlessly back down the hall.

When I entered the room I was blown away. The floors were painted with a black/white checkerboard design and were polished to a brilliant shine. The walls were accented in a similar fashion. There was a T.V. on the desk and a radio on the floor. The bottom bunk was made up military style and had a Muslim prayer rug draped over the pillow. Shoes were lined up neatly under the bed and on a make shift shelf, books ran from end to end. Che'Guevara A Revolutionary Life , Blood in my eye, Karl Marx Quotes, the Qu Ran. This was a weird ass dude. I sat my bag on the top bunk and pushed the power button on the T.V. nothing. Again, nothing. When I looked behind the T.V. I noticed there was no cord or electrical outlet. Strange. As I put the few items I owned on my shelf the door opened and two dudes stepped in leaving the door ajar and making me nervous. I immediately drew the knife.

"Hold on Blood, Hol' up!" The short fat guy said in a rush. "We homies, dog" he assured me with his hands up. "I'm Bang from Avenue Piru, this Snake from NHB."

I noticed the big C.K. (Crip Killa) on Snakes forearms and put the knife down. "Rowdy, Bompton Fruit Town Piru." I said in a shakey voice.

"Five said you was comin' tomorrow, but when I saw you, I knew you was homie." Bang assured me.

"What's with this nigga?" I asked waving my hand at the prayer rug and the books.

"Blood is one of them Muslims" Snake said, in a slow deep voice.

"Like ol boy Farakhan?" I asked. They both nodded their consent.

After I put my stuff away they told me the rest of the homies that weren't at work or school were waiting to meet me on the rec-yard outside and we proceeded there. The rec-yard was full of activity. There were guys playing basketball, guys lifting weights, and an impromptu rap session going on at one of the tables. At the table in the far corner there was a crowd of guys sitting and playing dominoes. This is where we stopped.

"Hey, blood," Bang said to the table, "This the homie Rowdy from FTP."

The handshakes, daps, and hugs were passed out. Names and neighborhoods were said as I made my way around the table. Shady Grady from East Side Pain, Kre-Kre from Athens Park, Inch from Tree Top, G-Sex from Denver Lane….the list went on and on. I produced my paperwork then turned to watch the basketball game. I hadn't touched a basketball in over a month and was starving to play.

"You wanna play blood?" Kre-Kre asked noticing my desire.

"Yeah, dog," I answered. And he started to call for somebody named Baby Slim.

A tall lanky dark skinned dude trotted over, glanced at me then said, "What blood? I got next."

"This the homie Rowdy from Fruit Town. Let blood run with you." Kre-Kre instructed.

"Can he play?" he asked as if I wasn't standing right there.

I said, "Blood, I'll be starting point guard next season."

The homies at the table gave a collective ooh, and Slim said, "Aiight,let's go."

We won the next three games in a row then lost the fourth because our center sprained his ankle and had to sub-out. As we walked back to the Bloods bench I noticed Five and Stretch had shown up.

"You aiight?" Five said assessing my game with a smile.

Baby Slim said, "Don't listen to that nigga dog, you got game."

We all hung out until they recalled the rec-yard for dinner. When I got to my room I could hear music coming from the inside. Reggae music. Secretly, I loved reggae music because it was all my Grandfather used to listen to. When I opened the door my roommate turned the music down and I noticed the T.V. was on…

"What's up folks, I'm Rasan" My roommate said as he stuck his hand out.

"Rowdy." I said as we shook. He was about my size; dark complected and had noble African features.

"Where you from I asked?"

"San Diego."

"Where at in San Diego?"

"I use to be from SkyLine, but I don't bang no more. I serve a higher cause."

"I bang, I'm from the Fruits …."

"That's cool, that's yo' business. Just don't bring no drama to the room and we straight."

"I'm not, I'm on some other shit," I said.

Then I went to the sink to take a quick bird-bath before dinner. As we talked and looked at each other's paperwork I noticed I felt comfortable with Rasan. He had everything I wanted, intelligence, pride, and something else that I knew was out of my reach. He was an *individual*.He went out at the five minute warning to go assist in the chow hall with serving the food. As I sat flipping through the channels, I heard keys approaching and wheels of some kind. Then she appeared.

"Here's your property," she said in her soft musical voice. And began to unload my two boxes from the dolly she was pulling.

"Where you been?" I asked sounding a little too much like Ike Turner.

She laughed and said, "J'ai beaucoup de travail (I have a lot of work)." She began to inventory the boxes and hand me things.

I asked, "How old are you?"

She laughed again and said, "Older than you. Why?"

Now I laughed. She was rude. I liked that. "Cause I'm tryna' decide if you gone be my next ex-wife." I said in a playful voice.

She laughed out loud then looked around to see who was watching and said, "You think you're sooo cute, don't you?"

"Nope that's what *you* think." I said.

She cocked her head to the side and looked at me then said, "Yeah, you're cute but you got a big head." We both began to laugh again. When the boxes were empty I asked, "Where do you work ma?"

"Everywhere," she said. "I'm the property officer."

"So how will I see you?" I asked in a panicked voice, sensing our time was over.

"I work in the library on Mondays and Tuesdays. If you really want to see me you'll find a way over there."

As she finished her statement I grabbed her hand. She looked scared but didn't snatch it back. I looked directly into her eyes then bugged out my eyes and stuck my tongue out. She burst into laughter then covered her mouth to stifle the sounds. When she turned to leave I asked, "When you first saw me what did you think?"

Pulling the dolly quietly behind her she took a few steps, then stopped and said, "I thought you looked like Christmas morning," then continued down the hallway.

Wow, that was a good one I thought. Then grabbed my cup and spoon and headed to the chow hall. The meal was actually good, chicken fried steak & baked potatoes. But I was too busy thinking about Ms…? Damn I don't even know her name.

"Blood you alright?" Five asked in a voice that sounded far away.

"Oui (yeah)," I answered.

"We what?" he asked confused.

"Never mind," I said. Then changing the subject I asked, "What's Kiwe and Damu?"

"Swahili." Then sensing my confusionhe said, "It's an African language. Kiwe means Crip, and Damu means Blood. We started speaking Swahili so the Mexicans couldn't understand us. Kinda like how they speak Spanish around us and we can't understand."

I nodded my understanding.

After dinner, and the chow hall was safely secured, the day room, phones, and showers were opened. I took a quick shower then stood in line to wait to use the phone. When my turn came I dialed my Grandmother's number and my cousin Damion picked up on the third ring.

"Allo (hello)."

"What's up fool? It's me," I said smiling at the sound of my cousins' voice.

"Oh, hey," he said dryly.

"What's wrong?" I asked sensing something was amiss.

"Nothing. Wanna talk to Memom?" He asked in the same dry tone.

"No. I wanna talk to *you*! What's wrong?"

I was fifteen days older than Damion, but I had always played the role of "Big" cousin. Probably due to the difference in our natures. I was more outgoing and mischievous as a child. He was quiet and more of a house mouse. Finally he said "I need my money."

"What money? I asked knowing he wasn't talking about *the* money. "What money?" I asked again dismissing the fact that my call was being recorded.

"You know," he said weakly

"Are you high?" I asked becoming irritated.

"No, I'm not high," he said in a voice I didn't appreciate. "Tonya pregnant with twins and I need some fucking money!" he yelled. Now, I was pissed off.

"First of all, lower yo mothafuckin' voice, second, don't be cursin in my Grandmother's house, –'she's my Grandmother too' – third, there is no money!" I continued.

"So what am I supposed to do" he asked weakly

"Do what I did, get a fuckin job! Be a man and hold up your end of the contract!"

The agreement was nobody would touch any of the money until all three of us were present. Now he was getting weak and greedy. Damion was never really smart, but for the first time in my life I saw how stupid he was. If he went near the money he could blow everything. For everybody. And I knew the Feds were still watching my Grandmother's house. He wasn't thinking.

"Put Memom on the phone. And if you take 1 dime of that money, buy yo'self a gun."

"Hold on." He said softly and put the phone down.

"Bonjour mon petit. Comment allez-vous?" My Grandmother sang as she picked up the phone.

My anger immediately disappeared. She knew single handedly how to lift my spirits. She'd done this when my mother died. Then three years later when my father, her son put a bullet through his mouth.

"Hi Memom," I said feeling like a child.

We talked happily until a Mexican dude told me it was his turn to use the phone. We ended and she told me that she'd be up to see me on Sunday and she was bringing a special gift. I wiped the mouth piece with the front of my shirt and passed it to the guy behind me.

"Gracias," he said with an agitated look, then turned to dial.

I felt good every time I talked to my Grandmother, but I had a nagging feeling that Damion was gonna try something stupid. I passed by the noisy dayroom and headed back to my room to write Kelis a letter. It'd been 2 ½ weeks so I figured it was time. I put in the' My Life' tape that I had borrowed from one of the homies, then sat at the metal desk to compose my thoughts.

Date: *October 15 1995*
Time: *8p.m*
Feeling*: irritated*
Dedication: *I'm going down by; Mary J Blige*

Hey Ma, what's up? Not much on my end. I know it's been a while since you heard from me but I just been taking the time to get settled. I'm in YTS as you noticed. It ain't too bad and since I ain't too far I should see you and the baby kinda often. How is he? Kiss him for me and tell him I love him. In regards to what you asked me in your last letter.... I don't know. I think we should try to be parents then friends.Then if a new relationship develops. I won't fight it. I don't trust you! Anyway, I'd like to see you at least twice a month. But if you can come more, I'd appreciate it. I don't want to be a ghost to my son. I'm done for now. Write back if you want.
Sincerely, K.Dumas.

"Aww blood, you stressin?" Shady Grady asked as he entered my room and took a seat on the toilet.

"Nahh I'm good, dog. Just lettin' my folks know where I'm at."

He nodded then asked if I wanted some work done.

"What kind of work?" I asked confused. He showed me his chest and arms indicating that he was talking about tattoo work.

"Yep, I want my whole back done."

"Blood that shit hurts!" he notified me.

"How you know?" I asked and he stood up and took his shirt off. In the middle of his back was a huge red 'P' it went from the base of his neck to the bottom of his boxers. The rest of his back was lined with neat rows of seemingly all the Crip neighborhoods I'd ever heard of. And, some I hadn't. They all had a neat 'X' slashed across them.

"Daaaamn blood, that's active!!" I said in an excited voice. He beamed with pride and put his shirt back on.

"The back, the stomach, and, the ass hurt the worse," he told me.

"Blood you got a tat' on yo ass?" I asked amazed. He stood again and began to pull down his pants, but I screamed, "Whoa! Hold up!"

And he stopped with a wild cackling laugh."I just got some lips on there blood!" He said through his laughter.'

"Shit, I believe you nigga," I said laughing hard.

"What you gone get?" he asked seriously.

I thought about it for a moment then said, "A map of Haiti."

"Of what?"

" Haiti. The island my family is from."

"Oh, that's gone be active, blood." He agreed. Then stood, gave me the Piru hand shake, and left as quietly as he came.

Chapter Eight

Westchester California 2002.

Argh! Argh! Argh ... Argh!I was snapped back into reality. Not because I wanted to be but because Fiona had her head poked into the shower curtain and was barking like she'd lost her damn mind.

"What Fifi? What?" I asked, as I stepped out of the now cold water. Damn. My little Sports Illustrated clock read 2:10 p.m. a seventy minute shower. Damn!

"Gimme a towel Fifi," I said to the dog as I stepped out of the shower. "Yeah, yo ass ain't that damn smart," I said as she cocked her head to the side confused and followed me to my room dragging my underwear. "Gimme that nasty ass!" I said reaching for my drawls. She bounced back out of my reach and shook her head vigorously. "I'm not finna chase you!" I assured her then walked into my closet.

The weatherman said it would be 67 degrees and sunny so I decided on a pair of dark blue True-Religion jean shorts, white Pro-Club and my blue and gray Matsumoto tennis shoes. I put on some Mitchum and three sprays of Gucci cologne and headed out the door. Then I doubled back and grabbed my UCLA hoodie, cursed Fiona out and left. As I walked towards the elevator I decided to stop at apartment 260 and ask her out. Before I could push the doorbell the door cracked and then came open.

"Hey you," she said with a smile and I noticed immediately that she'd just gotten out of the shower. All she was wearing was a yellow silk rob that stopped just above the knee. Yep, I was definitely gonna hump her, I decided.

"You should let me take you somewhere, and put something in your mouth," I said tucking my helmet under my arm and grinning like an idiot.

"Wow, you're forward aren't you?" she responded returning my grin.

I looked at her with my fake shocked expression and said, "I was talking about dinner"

"Oh" she said with a giggle and began to twirl a lock of red hair around her finger.

"Too bad," she purred.

"You like Asian food?"

"Yeah, it's ok."

"P.F Changs, sound alright?"

"Oohh, I love it there," she said happily.

"You cold ma?" I asked pointing to the nipple that was now fully awake.

"Oh these?" she said pulling the other nipple. "They have a mind of their own."

"Yeah I have the same problem. A little lower though," I said in a serious tone.

"Mmm Hmm." she said biting her lower lip as we stared at each other.

"Friday?" I asked killing the quiet.

"Friday's cool. You drive and I'll pay."

"Okay, but you have to promise to swallow everything you put in there." I said gently touching her lips.

She laughed and said, "Promise."

I walked back in the direction of the elevator, when I got on, she was still standing in the doorway. As the elevator doors began to close she pulled both sides of her robe open flashing me and exposing some juicy looking pale titties with large pink nipples and a short patch of red hair that looked neatly trimmed. I pushed #5 repeatedly trying to go back up and could've sworn I heard her laughing.

When I got off in the garage I tried to call KD, but couldn't get any service. So I texted, "2:45- Be early, I'm on the bike," and hopped back on the bike feeling free. I turned into the Food 4 Less parking lot on Central Ave and Rosecrans Blvd at 2:56 p.m. and rolled through the parking lot looking for Chico's car and KD'S 2 door Tahoe.

I noticed KD was parked in front of the beauty supply store. When I passed by he gave me the usual irritated look and went back to the game he was playing on his cell phone. At 2:59 I saw Chico sitting in a purple '88 S.S Monte Carlo on 22" Irocs. Not *his* car. What a stupid nigga! I pulled up next to the S.S and put the bike in neutral.

"Sup' dumbass?" I asked as he opened the passenger's side door.

"I know I know," he said throwing up his hands in mock surrender, then the buyer got out and instantly started to laugh.

"Peaches?"

"Kevon?" she asked surprised. Then came around the car and gave me a big *manly* hug.

I met Peaches a long time ago, '90 I think. We were fucking with the same girl, then ended up being cool. She was not the average female. She was a Dude in every aspect except genitalia. In her neighborhood, Carver Park; she was known and *feared.* A LOT! Shit, I used to be a little spooked of her.

"Cuzz, you the one with all the heats?"

'Stall me out wit' all the cuzzes, Peaches."

"Alright. Alright blood," she said sarcastically. Then she got back to business, and askedin a no nonsense voice, "You bring'em?"

"Of course, where's the loot?"

She threw me a stack of money wrapped in rubber bands and said, “It’s all there, you know how I get down.”

“I know,” I said and put the money in my hoodie pocket, pressed send on my phone. KD instantly pulled up in front of Peaches, almost close enough to run her foot over.

She jumped back with a, “Watch out nigga!” as KD jumped out of the truck.

They stared at each other and I started thinking “Oh shit” both of them had guns I knew but only KD had a vest on. And he’d test it, and her…

“Can’t we all just get along?” Chico said with perfect timing.

KD ignored the joke and went to the back of his truck and started passing Peaches a bunch of small grey boxes with German writing on the front of them. She opened each box and put it in the trunk of her car.

When he handed her the 2 black and gold boxes I asked her, “Who y’all finna go to war with?”

She opened one of the boxes, pulled the gun out, smelled it, and then calmly said, “Each other.”

I didn’t ask anything else.“Those jam if you don’t clean’em” I told her. “And they fire three round bursts, Read the instructions.”

Chico got in the truck with KD and we left, headed back to the shop.“That was stupid,” I told Chico as he exited the Tahoe. “You know the rules Larry. *Never* get in the car with a buyer. Never!”

“I know,” he said weakly as KD walked passed us and into the shop. I continued to yell at Chico in the parking lot for another five minutes then we went inside the shop. As I passed my Camaro, I noticed the right front rim had fresh scratches.

The shop was full of activity.

Dannie had came to work finally so all the chairs were full. The waiting room was also full to capacity with men and kids watching Sports Center.

"Simone! Office! Now!" I said as I passed the carpeted area where the couches were.

She sucked her teeth and mumbled something under her breath then got up and followed me down the short hallway to my office. When she plopped down in her seat like a kid in the principal's office I noticed she had the nerve to have an attitude.

"Something on yo' mind?" I asked irritated

"No why?"

"Cause yo' attitude is stinkin' up my office."

"I don't have no attitude." She said giving me a fake smile.

"What happened?" I demanded.

"To who?" She asked in her, you're not my man or my daddy, voice.

"To who? To Wu Tang Clan… You know damn well what I'm talkin' about!"

"It's a scratch on the wheel, Kevon! It's not like I dented the car." She said pleadingly. "Imma get it fixed today, I already called 310 Motors"

"Fix my rim, Simone." I said dryly.

"I am, dang!"

"Oh, am I bothering you?" I asked getting mad.

"No, it's just busy today, and I'm bleeding."

Ughh! She knew I hated talking about periods and tampons and shit. But that did explain her attitude."Bye Simone. Don't bleed on the couch." I said sarcastically.

"I won't" she said, "But you should get your interior cleaned," and walked out of the office smiling.

Disgusting… When I walked back to the front of the shop I noticed more people had shown up. My Aunt had decided to come to work and was already getting started in the small kitchen. And one of my favorite homies in the world was there, Ase from Cedar Block.

Ase was a street legend in Compton. Like MoMo, China Dog, Rooster and the host of other niggas that held down their neighborhoods in good times and bad. I grew up with the Cedars. There were never more than 30 of them in their neighborhood at one time and when they went to war, they lost important members. Motor being one of the most memorable.

"Who is this?" I asked pointing to the tall cute nigga with the fresh CBP tattoo on his neck. I knew almost all the Cedars and he wasn't familiar.

"This my lil brother, he just signed his record deal" Ase said proudly.

"What's yo name, blood?" I asked feeling defensive all of a sudden.

"They call me Flame, homie," he said as he stuck out his hand. I took it and when I tried to give him the Piru handshake his fingers fumbled. *Yep, I was right.*

"So, you Flame huh?" I said sarcastically.He looked at Ase for help, but Ase knew this guy. His *brother* wasn't from around here.

"Aw blood, it ain't like that. I'm official like a referee's whistle." Flame assured me. Then Ase asked, "Is my dog ready?"

I said, "Yeah, come on," and lead the way to the patio. I opened the kennel and the puppies burst free. I immediately picked up Simone and watched Ase pick his puppy.

"You smoke?" Flame asked lighting up a purple blunt without asking.

"I don't smoke pot homie, I smoke enemies" I told him with exaggerated toughness.

"Ahhh that's active blood. Imma use that in one of my rhymes" He said through gags and coughs. Asechose his dog and gave me $500, then we went back inside.

"Rowdy, you still got some of those fully 9's,"Ase asked.

"Yep, $1,500. A rack to you though since you my boy."

"Told you nigga!" he told his brother "This nigga don't believe there's a such thang as fully hand guns," he said pointing at his little brother accusingly.

"Yeah, but don't nobody got'em, but us and the Asians." I said neglecting to mention that I had just sold two to a known enemy.

"When I get my royalty check imma buy like ten of them mothafuckas," Flame assured me.

"$15,000," I said doing the math for him. I hugged Ase as he began to leave and whispered, "That's yo' real brother?" in his ear.

"Pop's side," was his answer as he went over to the couches to flirt with Simone and her customers. He came back rubbing his arms where Simone had beat him with her combs and said, "Imma marry her," in a happy voice.

We all laughed as I walked them out into the parking lot. When I turned to go back in I noticed the cable repair man still working on the power lines outside. What struck me as odd was nobody had cable in this area. We all had direct T.V. The Feds were either getting sloppy or they wanted me to see them. "Hey!" I called to the cable guy, "Make sure they take good pictures," I said pointing at the van he came in.

When I walked inside I decided I felt like cutting so I opened chair #4 and called my first customer, Big Nubb, from Nutty Block. Nubb, like most of the original Compton Crips and Bloods had a loveable old school style. He was in his late 40's but still had youthful energy pouring out of his movements.

"Sup junior?" he said as he sat in the chair and craned his neck towards the T.V.

"Shit. What's good, Hub City?"

"Aw ain't nothin'. How many Pits you got left?" he asked knowing damn well they'd sold out.

"Three, but they're all sold and I'm keeping the female." I told him as I began to clean up his taper.

"You got a girl? Whatchu' want for her?" He asked diggin in his pockets.

"Nothin'. She ain't for sale" I said laughing at this bluff.

"Everything's fa sale," he assured me, then leaned back in the chair and closed his eyes.

Two years ago, this would not be happening. Our hoods were worse enemies and I'd had multiple incidents with the Nutty's. But when the race wars started, we decided to put our old colored beefs to the side and focus on the real enemies. In essence, the Crip/Blood war was over in Compton. Black was the only important color.

"Wake up!" I told him as I turned to trim his beard. "This ain't no old folks home, pops," I teased. He opened one eye then gave me a crooked smile and raised his chin.

In the chair next to me Dannie and Rodney were having the same tired argument they always had when nothing was on T. V. 'Who was the best rapper ever? Biggie or Tupac?' As I tuned in, Dannie was saying, "Pac was a gangsta! He kept it real!"

"Gangsta? That nigga claimed like five different hoods," Rodney shot back. "N.Y., Oakland, Compton"…."

"He bust' on the police, went to the Penn, and all that! Big ain't do shit! He's just a rapper!"

"Both of them niggas had flaws," I said butting in. "And, they both was liars." They looked at me, clippers in mid-air and said, "What?"

"Look," I said, "They're probably in everybody's top five favorite rappers and deserve to be, but don't confuse rap with the streets."

Dannie nodded his agreement but Rodney just wouldn't let go.

"Big wasn't no rapper, he was a M.C. there's a difference!" he said proudly as he went back to cutting his customer's hair.

"You a B.I.G. Fan?" I asked rhetorically

"Yep!"

"So you bought all of his albums right?"

"Yep, Ready To Die and Life After Death." He assured me.

Good I thought, he took the bait, "That's not all of 'em," I said, and as Rodney realized my trap I sealed the deal. "Big put out three albums, two was done while he was alive, the third, when he died. And that shit didn't sell 100,000 copies. It sucked!"

"That was Puffy!" he cried.

"Puff these nuts" I said and humped my crotch at his chair. The kid sitting in Dannie's chair burst into laughter.

I finished with Nubb and when he handed me the $10 bill I pushed it back towards him and said, "Keep it, just lace me up with some old school knowledge."

He paused to think. Nubb had some of the best quotes. I don't know if he made them up or just read a lot. *"Men do what they want, boys do what they can,"* he said as he stood and dusted off his blue khaki suit.

"I like that," I said, as I tumbled the words across my mind. I cut three more heads, then closed my chair and walked to the counter that separated the kitchen and the sitting area. My Aunt was stuffing money into her apron and handing a customer a Styrofoam tray filled with food.

"How's business?" I asked jumping onto a barstool.

"No' bat" My Aunt said with her heavy accent.

"What's on the menu?" I asked knowin' my aunt only made three dishes. Fish, Chicken, and, Shrimp.

"Chicken and' Rice Pilaf" she answered.

She was the darkest of my grandmother's children but was more like my grandfather than any of her siblings. She'd been on and off drugs since the 90's but she always handled her business. High or not, we were close, because she looked after me when my mom died.

"So, you want to be organ donor eh?" she asked pointing at the motorcycle through the window.

"No, I'm a safe rider." I lied as she put a plate of chicken and rice on the counter. I took it and got up before the lecture started and headed to my office.

"Come here, Simone," I said as I passed her area and went to the office. When I turned on the light, I saw KD sprawled out on the couch near the desk. Drooling on the leather and clutching his gun.

"Oww, him so cute," I said in my baby voice as he sat up and adjusted his clothes.

"I've shot people for less," he reminded me as I handed him the plate of food. When Simone came in the office and closed the door I started the meeting.

"I'm going away for awhile." I said shocking everybody including myself.

"*Away* away?" Simone asked. "Like Top Ramen, sharing showers away?"

"Nahh. Vacation." I said unsure of myself.

"Where?" KD asked, "I hear Baghdad is nice this time of year." He said through a mouthful of chicken.

"Haiti" I said as I watched Simone sit on the arm of the couch and take a chicken wing right out of KD's mouth. He growled in protest but she just rolled her eyes and asked, "When are we leaving?"

I put my palms to my eyes then dragged them down my face as I said, "You can't go." Then turned to KD and said, "You either." They burst into protest for a full thirty seconds and when they finished I said, "That's it! I'll leave in two weeks and stay a month. I trust y'all. And because of that trust we've been successful. Simone you have to take care of the shop and KD you got the other shit. I love y'all but I gotta do this for my Memom. She's getting older, and it's the only thing she's ever asked me to do." KD nodded and seemed to understand, but Simone kept complaining.

KD said, "Call me," and got up to leave. When he did, the fireworks started.

"Do you love me?" She asked me in a hurt voice.

"Don't do this Simone …"

"Answer the question!"

"Of course, more than I love myself. You know that."

"Then what're we waiting for?"

Uh-oh. I thought, 'her period's fuckin' with her brain. "Do we have to do this now?"

"If you're going to the island without me, then yes."

"You make it seem like I'm going to get married or die," I joked.

"Don't say stuff like that, its stupid."

"Simone what would you like for me to do, huh? I have to do this ma"

"And what about me eh? How long Kevon? How long am I supposed to wait? For you to make me feel whole." She asked as the tears began to fall.

"Simone I-…..

"You know what? Never mind, you're stupid. You can't see the forest because the trees are in your way."

I sat in my chair feeling *stupid*, and watching the woman I was in love with pour her heart out.

"You know, I'll be here. I'll wait. Until I'm old and dried up. I'll wait for you." She said then palmed her tears and went across the hall to the bathroom.

I sat back in my chair and closed my eyes. What *was* I waiting for? I loved her, wanted her, needed her and she was physically perfect. Yeah, I thought, I am stupid.

I needed to leave. I couldn't face her again so I grabbed my helmet and left to go to the bank. The weather had changed appreciably I'd noticed as I started the bike. The wind had a nasty bite to it so I decided to put the bike up and go get my truck. Simone got on my damn nerves. She was the only woman that had that type of mind control over me. Not even my baby-moma had the power to control my moods. When it suited her, she used my son like a weapon or a shield. And it still didn't have the effect that Simone could conjure with just a few words. I'd make it right I told myself as I circled my Grandmother's block then turned up the driveway.

When I got to the garage and parked behind Simone's Jeep I noticed my Grandmother's car was gone. That meant she was out visiting relatives or doing her favorite thing, grocery shopping. I looked to make sure the kitchen light was off then opened the door to the Range Rover. When I turned the key the T.V.'s and sound system came on and the sounds and images of a gang of people fucking came into view. 'Brazillian Orgy, part IV.' I forgot I had been watching this the last time I drove the truck. I jumped out of the truck and closed the door with a laugh, then pushed #1 on my phone. My Grandmother's speed dial code.

Chapter Nine

Compton California 2002

"Allo," she answered on the first ring.

"Ou etes tu? (Where are you?)," I asked in a playfully demanding voice.

She laughed and decided to be pert. "Je suis avec un homme (I'm with a man)," she told me. I could just see her sitting in the passenger's seat of the Benz I'd bought her, loving our fake argument.

No doubt the man was my Uncle Chris or one of my other relatives. "Quel homme? (what man?)" I asked.

She laughed some more and then said, "J'ai beaucoup jeunes hommes! (I have a lot of young men!)"

I laughed out loud and said, "Memom you're a pimp." When I opened the door to see how much gas I had the sounds of the video invaded the conversation.

"C'etait quoi? (what was that?)," My Grandmother asked, alarmed.

"Les voisins (the neighbors)," I lied.

She told me she was at the Farmers Market in Torrance with my cousin Billy, and that she would be home at around eight.

I told her that I had some good news and that I'd see her when she got home, then we hung up. After I changed the video to Carlito's Way I jumped in the driver's seat and pulled out of the driveway. As I sat at the stoplight on Alondra Ave and Avalon Blvd the conversation with Simone started to replay in my mind. Thankfully, my Sidekick began to ring.

"Hello?"

"Daddy, it's me."

"Duhhh," I said. "What's up?"

"Nothing, my Moma said you was coming over here tonight." He said expectantly

"She's confused, not tonight, tomorrow night."

"Oh," he said, accepting my lie.

"You do your homework?" I asked quickly changing the subject.

"Yes."

"All of it, Pascal?"

"Yes."

"Good, cause pretty girls like smart guys." I told him.

"Cute guys too," he chimed in.

"Who says *you're* cute?" I asked jokingly.

"Are *you* cute?" He asked, trying to trap me…a bit.

"Of course I'm cute! Are you crazy?" I said through my laughter.

"Then I'm cute too cause I look just like you," he said in his 'take that' voice.

"I guess so huh," I agreed. "But you don't got no hairs down stairs suckaaaa," I said in my Day-Day voice.

He burst into laughter then answered, "Gimme a minute sucka mannnn," in the same voice.

When the laughter stopped I said, "Tell me about this girlfriend of yours," in a fatherly tone.

"Aww mann…" he said, and I could hear him get up, go to his bedroom, and close the door.

"She's pretty and she's the smartest girl in the whole school."

"Uh huh," I listened.

"Her mom's a nurse too. Oh, and she's Mexican."

"Really?" I asked not knowing what else to say. My son and I were only seventeen years apart so we had a lot in common. But as he got older and I tried to hold on to my youth, the gap would close quickly.

"You kiss her?" I asked being nosey.

"Aww mann," again.

"Boy, answer the question!"

"No not yet. I touched her booty though," he assured me. Even through the phone I could see him smiling like a jackal.

"Booty?" I asked, "Mexicans ain't got no booty," I joked.

"Uh huh, she got a big ol badonka donk," he said with a giggle

"A badonka what?" I asked feeling old.

"It means *butt,* Dad," he explained in a bored voice. I smiled again feeling old.

"Tell me about niggas," I told him as I pulled into Bank of America behind the Carson Mall.

"Niggas ain't nothing," he began. "They do drugs and gang bang because they're followers."

"And what about you?" I asked, knowing his response because we'd been having this conversation since he was about six years old.

"Me … I'm a Dumas, and a Man. I don't follow anybody. *I live with Honor, Understanding, Respect, Loyalty, and* ***Patience****!*"

"Good boy!" I said proudly.

"Dad, can I order a pizza?" he asked.

"Your Mom must be cooking something new," I said knowingly.

"Yeah, it smells funny. And it's green..."

"Yeah, order some Dominoes'. And don't put jalapenos on everything. You have to share with your sister. I'll pay for it when I leave the bank."

"Oooh you putting money in my account?" he asked excitedly.

"Maybe," I said drawing him in.

"Pascal, who you talking to?" His Mom blurted as she picked up the other line.

"My Daddy."

"Tell yo lyin' ass Daddy imma' slap his ass when I see him!" She said ignoring my presence on the phone.

"Bite me!"

"I already did," she said sarcastically.

"Bye Pascal, I love you." Click.

I got a chill as I walked in the bank and made my way over to the merchant teller's line. Maybe it was a warning, or maybe it was all in my mind. As I filled out the deposit slip I noticed a cute chubby girl staring at me. Not chubby, just round in all the right places. I did my business then went to deposit $2,000 in my son's already bulging account. The cute girl made her way over to my roped off divider and said, "Hi," in a sprite like little voice.

"Hi, you," I said trying to sound cool.

"What's your name?" she asked sounding too sexy.

"Rowdy."

"Hi Rowdy, I'm Misty."

"Hi Misty." I said as I let an old Chinese couple cut in front of me.

"Where're you from?" she asked, probably catching a bit of my accent.

"Compton. You?"

"Inglewood!" she said proudly. "So Mr. Rowdy, tell me something about yourself." She said as she put a hand on one of her soft hips.

"I'm ignorant and negative. Oh, and I think I know everything." This made her laugh so loud she covered her mouth with the stack of bills she was holding.

"You're funny. I like that." She said with a cute smile.

"So, tell me something about you."

"I'm twenty five, a nurse, recently divorced, and I have a son."She said, looking for some sign of disappointment on my face.

"Me too," I said. "How old is your son?"

"He's five. His name's Jermaine."

"My son's eight, his name's Pascal."

"You should call me some time." She said as she handed me her card, then took it back and wrote another number on the back. I agreed to call her then she turned to leave. I watched as her Badonka donk bounced and she looked back laughing and tried to cover it.

"Sorry," I said to the two construction workers that were covered in dirt and glaring at me for holding up the line. After I made my deposit, I walked over to my truck and called the number on the back of the card.

"Hello," she answered softly.

"Hey ma, it's Rowdy," I said as I got in the truck.

"Oh hey. I was kinda hoping you'd call."

"Where you headed?" I asked hearing traffic in the background.

"To the day-care, then home," she said sounding tired.

"Where's home?"

"Hawthorne, what about you?"

"Watts," I lied

"You don't look like an Eastside guy."

"What's that supposed to mean?"

"Nothing," she giggled. "You just look too neat"

"You shouldn't judge people. It says so in the Bible," I teased.

"Can I call you later?" I asked.

"Of course. If you don't call me, can I call you?"

"Yeah, did my number show up in your phone?"

"Yes."

"Okay then, call me if I forget."

"Okay drive safely."

"You too, Ma," I said then pulled the Range Rover onto DelAmo Blvd. I left Dominoes' feeling played again. How could an eight year old and a five year old eat $40 worth of pizza? His ass was spoiled, and I meant to call him and tell him so before the night was over.

When I got back to the shop I noticed all the cars were gone except the Camaro and that only the light from the T.V. glared through the front window. When I let myself in with my key I saw Simone standing at the Mrs. Pac Man game focused intently. The only time she got like this was when she was really happy or really sad. The pile of Kleenex balled up on the floor next to her indicated the latter. I walked in and she gave me a weak smile as I made my way over to her. Her body tensed as I stood behind her and wrapped my arms around her waist. She didn't pull away which was a good sign. "Ow!" She said as I pushed the hair back from her face and bit her cheek. Her skin and hair smelled freshly washed, like peaches.

"What's the score?" I asked as I rested my chin on her shoulder. She pointed at the screen then sniffled and reached for another tissue. I took it then turned her to face me, put it to her little nose, and said, "Blow" like she was a little kid. She did, and we just looked at each other for a while. It was now dark outside but even in the dim light I could tell her eyes had taken on a goldish color, with a hint of green.

"That's disgusting," she said pointing at the Kleenex I was still holding.

"Imma try to sell it on EBay," I said as I continued to get lost in her eyes. She smiled then allowed me to take her hand and lead her to the couches. When I layed on my back, I pulled her on top of me and made small circles on her back as she listened to my heart beat.

"I want you to do me a favor while I'm gone," I said softly into her hair.

"What?" She breathed into my shirt, "Fix your rim?"

"No smart ass, I want you to find us a house."

She sat up, put her chin against mines and said, "What do you mean *us*?" with confused eyes.

"I know your English isn't that good, but us usually means you and me, puppy."

"Don't play with me Kevon," she said as she bit down on my goatee.

"I'm not Simone. I've been avoiding us for a long time. It's time I did the right thing. We've always had love. That's never been the problem. But love is an action, not just a word," I said as I palmed her ass through her skirt.

"Find a house and then what?" she asked avoiding the real question.

"Then we move in and if we can stand living together, we make other plans," I said carefully avoiding the "M" word.

"Would you really marry me?" she asked as she sat up and straddled my lap.

"Yeah. I think I'm supposed to," I said in a smiling voice.

"Says who?" she asked placing her forehead against mine.

"Says me," I said as I sucked her bottom lip into my mouth.

She closed her eyes and began to caress my face then I thought, *Her Period*!

"Are you still wounded?" I asked pointing below her waist.

"Yeah, it's a light day though," she said as she jumped from my lap and headed towards the hallway.

"Let's go out," I called to her long swinging ponytail as she turned the corner.

"Okay, where?" she yelled sounding happy.

"The casino, then dinner"

"Which casino? Crystal Park or Hustler?"

"Not Hustler. Gardena Police be too hot at night. Let's go to Crystal Park, then to the Red Lobster in Lakewood."

"I don't want fish," she whined.

"They don't just serve fish," I said as I stood in the doorway and watched her wash her hands.

"I'm not dressed for dinner, let me go shower and change then I'll meet you at the casino."

"Okay," I agreed. Then kissed her deeply and let her suck my tongue. When she opened her eyes she gave my ass a two handed squeeze, then bounced to the front door and left. When I heard the Camaro pull off I sat down at my office computer and logged on to CheapTix.com. After I'd made all the necessary arrangements for my trip I went to the floor safe and took out $5,000 for us to gamble with.

With that done I let my dogs loose in the patio, locked up the shop, and went to get gas. I paid for the gas, bought a "Mango Madness" Snapple and a pack of Altoids, jumped on the 91 Freeway headed to the only Casino in the ghetto. I usually valet my cars but since Simone and I drove separately, I parked in the front of the casino so she could find me easily. The casino was jerkin'. It was packed with Baller's, Broke Niggas, and, Working Class folks. All trying to beat the house. I went to the cashier, turned $3,000 into chips and headed for the emptiest Blackjack table. Just my luck, I found a dealer alone at the $25 table.

"Welcome to Crystal Park," the Samoan looking lady said as I placed a $100 bet. I got a jack of hearts and an 8. She had a 6 showing so I had her, unless some miracle shit happened. It did of course. She got a 10 and hit a fucking 3. Cheating Bitch! We went back and forth like this until my phone rang. "Yo?"

"Where are you?"

"At the $25 table, getting swindled."

"Oh, I see you."

When I turned on my stool I saw her coming. And everybody was staring at her. She had on a black one piece body suit by Dior. What wasn't jiggling in the front was bouncing in the back. "Come here," I said as I grabbed her and zipped up her top just a little. She let me as she dug in my pocket for some chips. "You look nice," I said as I kissed her cleavage, pissing off the male onlookers.

"Behave," she said as she pulled her stool next to mine.

"For now," I said then gagged on my Ginger-ale as she put $700 down in front of her. I decided to sit this one out and watch.

She got an Ace, the dealer got a paint card, then Simone got her second card, a Queen. The dealer got a 7. I sat there with my mouth open. Simone smiled and said, "Go hard, or go home," and kissed me on the neck. I stood and gave her a squeeze then went to the Cashier to cash in my chips and use the bathroom. When I returned Simone was arguing with some dusty looking dude at the table.

"What's wrong?" I asked irritated.

"Nothing. He was just leaving."

"Oh this yo man?" The drunk, Swap Meet, nigga said. "My bad folks," he said lifting his empty glass and stumbling away.

"You okay?"

"Yes," she said as she raked another pile of chips toward herself.

"Nothing can ruin this night," she said smiling beautifully.

I pulled her close then slid my hand between us and tweaked her nipple through the soft material. Her face flushed, I let go, and watched her win for the next hour. At 9:30 I said, "Cash out ma," and she knew I wasn't asking.

When we got to the Cashier's window the Cashier counted out $4,300, to my surprise and Simone's amusement. She pushed the money across to me then took my hand and said, "Let's go."

When we got outside I noticed Simone had parked directly across from me. I released her hand as we walked to our separate cars. When I got in the truck I took out my phone and began to text message Misty.

"Su Whoop," some voices said in front of me.

"Su Whoop," I answered before I looked up. When I did, what I saw was the front of a dark Blue Chevy Caprice, two Hispanic males, and two handguns. BOOM-BOOM-BOOM-BOOM! PAKA- PAKA- PAKA –BOOM-PAKA! The guns exploded as bullets tore through the windows and the body of my truck. My waist felt hot and wet, like I had spilled coffee on my sweater. And my face was burning. They say you never hear the bullets that hit you. That's some bullshit! I heard all four that entered my torso and face. All I could do was grab the seat lever and lay all the way back in the seat. The last thing I remember hearing was screeching tires and a collision. Then I passed out. When I came to I remember being cold and Simone screaming my name. We were flying on the 91 freeway headed to Kaiser Hospital. When I opened my eyes Simone was driving the Range Rover with the front windshield and driver's side window shot out, mumbling in French.

"Cold," I said in a weak voice. Then coughed up blood on my sweater and gold cross.

"No baby, I'm taking you to the hospital," she said as the wind blew her hair all over her face.

"No, take me to Memom," I said then passed out again. If I died, I'd die with my family.

When I became conscious again I was staring into my Grandmother's beautiful face, she was holding prayer beads tightly. She wasn't crying or panicky. But calm and composed. The pain in her eyes she couldn't hide though.

"He is awake," she said in a commanding voice. Then took my hand and squeezed. "You are a Dumas," she said proudly." We can not die so easily, no?"

Then I saw Simone and the neighbor Cynthia Nunn who worked at St. Francis hospital in Lynwood.

"You lost a lot of blood," she said in a relieved voice. "You're lucky, but two of the bullets are still in there, I couldn't get them."

I whispered, "Thank you," then went back to sleep lying on my Grandmother's kitchen table and holding her hand. They said I was out for two days, when I woke up I had pain and stiffness everywhere. Simone was asleep when I opened my eyes. When I touched her hair she jumped sending a fresh jolt of pain through my body. "AGHHH!"

"I'm sorry, I'm sorry," she said. She stood and called my Grandmother from the living room.

"Simone hit me!" I told my Grandmother as she entered the kitchen wearing a weak smile.

"You are alive, no?"

"Yes."

"Then no talk English in my kitchen," she said as she squeezed my toes and left Simone and I to be alone.

"The Camaro's totaled," she said rubbing my head.

"Huh?" I asked not understanding.

"I rammed them… when they started shooting. I just crashed right into them," she said as a tear made its way down her cheek.

"It's ok puppy. You did good," I told her and put my good arm around her waist. She was still wearing the same black pantsuit from the night of the shooting which meant she'd never left my side. Not even to change clothes.

"How many times was I hit?"

"Four. Two in the arm, one in the chest, and a bullet grazed your face," she said touching the cracked scab under my eye.

"I think I killed one," she said smiling.

"Good girl." I said patting her on the butt. "What did the police say?"

"They're looking for us and the truck."

"Burn it." I closed my eyes and went back to sleep.

Chapter Ten

Compton, California 2002

On Wednesday morning, I got up on weak legs and went to the bathroom, clutching a sheet around my naked, patched-up body. When I got in the shower, Simone came in the bathroom and began to undress.

"Move," she said as she stepped in the shower behind me.

"Hey you gotta be nice to me, I'm injured." I joked as I began to soap a towel.

"No, I don't," she said as she took the towel and began to wash my body in soft circles.

"Turn around," she said as she began to wash my chest and noticed the hardon I had.

"You're terrible," she said, as she began to massage my erection with a soapy hand.

"Ow-oww!" I said, as I stopped her movements. "That hurts too!"

She laughed and began to soap her own washcloth, "Wash my back," she said as she began to take her hair down.

"I love you," I said as I began to wash her tummy from behind.

"I love you, too," she said, and pushed my hand down to the stubble that had grown over her pussy.

"We both need to shave," I said giggling. Then the water went cold.

"Memom!" we screamed at the same time.

"Sorry!" my uncle said through the door laughing.

I got dressed, then ate and asked Simone to take me home. I had a zillion things to do and a million phone calls to make. My turn…"Didn't you wear that last week?" I asked Simone playfully as we made the left on Compton Blvd.

"Ha ha," she said rolling her eyes."

"This doesn't change anything," I assured her as I adjusted my arm in the sling. "This only pushes the plans back a little," I said squeezing her thighs reassuringly.

"I know," she said looking in the rearview mirror.

When we got on the freeway I decided to make the first of the hard phone calls.

She picked up on the first ring. "Hello?"

"Yeah, it's me."

"Where the fuck you been? I've been calling you for two days!"

"I had an accident"

"What? What kind of accident?"

"A minor accident. I'm straight"

"What kind of accident?" she asked in a low scared voice.

"I got shot," I said and waited for the tornado.

"Whatchu' mean shot? Like with a gun? Who shot you? Oh my God, I'm coming up there, what hospital you at?"

"I'm not at the hospital. I told you, it was minor."

"Ain't no such thing as minor bullets," she said sounding out of breath. "How many times they shoot you?"

"Four. All flesh wounds," she got quiet and I knew she was having a panic attack. "I'm cool ma, Simone's taking me home. I'll lay low for a few days, then be good as new."

"Should I tell Pascal?"

"No, it'll scare him."

"You said Simone's with you, huh? I knew you was fucking that Bitch."

"Man, don't start."

"You gotta be fuckin her, she knows where you live and I don't!"

"Bye, Kelis."

"Don't hang up, Kevon."

"Then watch your mouth!"

"Why? Cause I called that Bitch, a Bitch?"

Click… When I sat back in my seat, I could see the angry vein throbbing in Simone's forehead. I sat and waited for tornado number two.

"I still don't believe you gave my baby to that easty-ass ghetto Bitch!" She said it in a quiet voice that gave me a chill.

"Simone, don't start."

"I'll start if I fucking feel like it!"

"Fine. Argue with yourself."

"No, imma argue with your selfish ass!"

I turned up the Anthony Hamilton CD, Simone ejected it and threw it out the window, almost hitting a beige van full of church people.

"That's enough Simone. I'm serious."

"You're a selfish bastard!" she said, having to steal the last word.

We parked and rode the elevator to my floor without speaking. When we entered I checked the automatic feeder for Fifi.

Simone went to my room to get a t-shirt. She stopped in the bathroom doorway and said, "Losing me would be your biggest mistake." She slammed the door and got in the shower again.

I went on the patio to change Fifi's litter box and water, then sat on the couch and made more phone calls.

After I hassled with the insurance company I made sure my Uncle took the truck to Victorville and burned it. Simone came out wearing my t-shirt and didn't speak to me. Instead, she called Fifi who jumped off the couch with me and went with her.

“Fiona!” I yelled. She looked back, yawned, then followed Simone into my bedroom where she closed the door. Damn, she even had control over my dog.

When my Uncle called me back to confirm the deed was done I called KD to fill him in.

“What? Why are you just now calling me!” He yelled.

“I was laying half dead on a table, Dog, I couldn’t get to a phone.”

“That ain’t no excuse, cuzz!” He said *cuzz* which meant he was pissed off. I let him get his big brother on for a while, then I explained what had happened.

“You said it happened outside?”

“Yeah.”

“I can get the tape.”

“How?”

“Dana still works there, in the security booth.”

“Dana? You sure you wanna go there?”

“Do we need the tape or not?”

“Yeah.”

“Alright, then let me deal with Dana. You need to call Boomer too, cause all we got is pistols and that A.R.”

“Yeah, I’ll set up a meet.”

“Tell Simone I said she did good. Again!”

“I’ll tell her.”

“I’ll bring you those pain bills later, when I come out that way.”

“Tell Dana I said, Hi,” I joked

“Fuck yo’self!”

Click. Dana was KD’s version of Simone, except she was bigger… Much bigger. When I crept to the bedroom to check on Simone, she was in my bed asleep, under the blankets. Fifi who knew she wasn’t allowed in my bed was next to her sleeping as well. Simone was beautiful. But she looked even more beautiful when she was asleep. Fifi lifted her head as I approached the bed. "I'll deal with your ass later" I told her. If a dog could smile, I think she did. I ran my fingertips across Simone's sleeping cheek, then found the business card I was looking for and went back to the living room.

"Thank you for calling Ernie's Autobody, can I help you?" The perky receptionist said when she answered.

"Damn Maria, you sound just like a White girl," I said as Ernie's wife started to laugh.

"Travieso?"

"Yeah Mommy it's me. Is fat boy around?"

"Yeah, hees fat ass is in da back, I'll go get heem," she said losing the fake American accent and letting the Chicana back in. When they came back into the office, I knew because they were arguing loudly, and in Spanish. When Ernie came on the line he sounded winded. "Wassup?"

"Nada," I said to the only Mexican friend I had.

"What's up? I'm trying to run an honest business here," he said with a laugh. I laughed too because Ernie was the most crooked dude I know. He did it all, from computer crimes to running his auto body/chop shop. But his specialty was cars.

"I need a car, and a truck," I said waiting for his tirade.

"What! I just sold you a brand new car and a new truck, what happened?" I told him, then he asked if I needed his help. I told him, "no." He asked me how much I wanted to spend.

"Depends…" Was all I said because Ernie had all the connections and could get almost any car I asked for. And by the end of the week, I would own it. Legally.

"What you got in the shop now," I asked.

"A Jag, two Benzes and a Viper."

"What year is the Viper?" I asked getting excited.

"2000 but it has the 2002 kit on it and 22" Niche's."

"What color?"

"Yellow, with black guts..."

"I'll give you ten for it."

"Fifteen, and you can have my fucking bitch wife too."

"Good! At least he can fuck for more than five minutes!" Maria screamed through the office door.

I laughed then said, "I'll give you fifteen if you can get the truck I want."

"What kind? Tahoe, G5?"

"Nope, Cayenne."

"The Porsche SUV? That's easy fool. Gettin' those is like stealing a Honda!"

"Good, what's the ticket?"

"Imma' have to pay my DMV connect double, plus tax, about a dub."

"Nigga, that's rape!"

"Yep, but you love me so pay me"

"Alright, I'll give you thirty grand for both, but I want'em hooked up clean."

"Puto, for thirty grand, you can have that bitch for real." He said laughing.

"When can I pick'em up?"

"Gimme three weeks, 'cause I gotta order some parts and shit."

"All right fool. I'll holla' at you in a couple weeks," I said getting ready to hang up.

"You *sure* you don't want that bitch?" he asked laughing. Then she burst in the door and started slapping and hitting him,"Gotta go!" he said.

I hung up laughing so hard I almost popped my stitches. I stood up to stretch and noticed I had spots of blood on my bandages which meant I need them changed. My stomach was also growling which meant I had to wake up Simone. This wasn't easy. Waking up Simone was like pulling the pin on an old grenade. It could go off and blow your ass to pieces, or it could be a dud. There was only one way to find out. When I walked in the room Simone was laying on her side with her back to me sleeping soundlessly. I almost didn't want to wake her up.

"Simone," I said softly with a light shake.

"Samooan," I whined again shaking her harder. She began to stir then Fifi raised her head. "Out Fifi!" I yelled a little too loud.

"Leave her alone," Simone said sleepily.

"Wake up ma, I need you."

"Oh, *now* you need me?"

"Look," I said pointing to the spots of blood.

"Gimme that bag and come here," she said through a yawn. When I came back with the medical bag she kneeled in my bed and began to change the bandages. I gritted my teeth as she removed the old tape and gauze, and decide to occupy my time and hands with Simone's body. I heard her breath catch as I pulled the T-shirt up and caressed the swell of her hips. She pretended to ignore me as she moved on to the second bandage but as her nipples began to rise under the T-shirt, I knew I had her.

"Su-stop," she purred, as I began to drag my fingertips across her lower back. She shuddered and I could feel the goose bumps rise on the areas I'd touched.

"You want me to stop?" I asked softly putting my cheek against hers.

"Yes," she said unconvincingly.

"No." I said and traced my finger down the crack of her ass, down to her damp pussy.

"Sil vous plait, Kevon" (Please, Kevon), she breathed as she dropped the roll of tape between us.

"Please what, mommy? Please stop, or please don't stop?" I asked as I found her swelling clit.

"Nooo…" she whimpered and grabbed the back of my neck to steady herself.

"Don't tell me no," I said as I began to lick and suck on the spot behind her ears.

"Lay back Simone." I said as I eased her onto her back and put a pillow under her ass.

"What're you doing?' she asked in a whisper.

"Shhhh..."

I grabbed her ankles then raised them high in the air and pushed her legs back. Her pussy was a golden color with a touch of pink from the inner lips that were parting like a flower. There was a pearl of a pussy juice right below her clit and as my tongue made contact with it she arched her back and partially lifted off the bed.

"No, please," she said as she began to shake her head.

"I want you to watch me," I said as I planted soft kisses up and down her inner thighs.

"I, I can't."

"Watch." I said louder as I gave her whole pussy a long lick.

"Unhhh…" she moaned through clenched teeth.

"Watch." I said again, pushing down on her flat stomach. When she propped herself up on her elbows and put herself in a position where she could see, I looked at her then pointed my tongue and eased it slowly into her tight pussy.

"Oooh, don't do that," she said as she lifted the t-shirt and began to pinch her nipple. I slid my tongue out of her pussy and let her see that it was coated with her juices. Then I slid it back in and began to tongue fuck her slowly. When I looked up she had her eyes closed, so I softly bit down on her clit.

"Unhhh…." She moaned loudly and opened her eyes. I let her see the mess I was making as I pulled my big lips off her mound. I raised my head and let the mix of drool and pussy juice run down my chin. Then I asked her,

"You want me to eat it?"

"Un huh…"

"Tell me."

"Eat it."

"Eat what?"

"Eat my pussy."

"Say please."

"Please Kevon, please eat my pussy …"

I pulled the hood of skin covering her clit up and then let saliva ooze out of my mouth onto it. "Ooh yeah," she cried.

Then I slid my middle finger into her fat pussy until I found her G-spot. When I did, she jumped off my fingers and pulled her pussy away from my lips with a loud,wet, smacking sound.

"Bring your ass here," I said as I chased her on the bed.

"Oooh, please don't, please don't," she begged as I put her back in her former postion. I locked my lips on her clit then eased my finger back into her pussy and quickly found the nub of her G-spot. I sucked hard on her clit as I made the "come here" motion with my finger to stroke her electric place.

"Motherfucker…" she said, as she put the corner of the silk sheet in her mouth and began to hump against my face. I stopped sucking her clit and began to lick her pussy with the same motion as her humps.

"Ooh fuck, ooh fuck yeah," she screamed so loud Fifi started to bark.

"Motherfuckerrrrr …" she screamed as she came on my tongue. She grabbed my head with both hands and humped hard against my face and as her orgasm slowly faded she fell back on the bed breathing harshly and murmuring, "Oh my God, oh my God," with her hands covering her eyes. I slowly withdrew my finger then gave her pussy one last peck and drew myself up so we were face to face. I took her hands from in front of her face and noticed she was crying.

"Puppy, you okay?" I asked bracing myself with my good arm.

"No, I'll never be okay again," she said smiling. "Where did you learn how to do that?"

"Why, you like it?" I asked stupidly.

"Like it? I almost passed out," she asked pulling me close for a kiss.

"You're nasty," I joked.

"Marry me," she giggled.

"Oh, *now* you wanna get married….?"

"Hell to the yes," she said and kissed me deeply.

"Taste good huh?" I joked.

"Wow…."

"Wow?" I asked confused.

"Yes, wow. I came so hard I cried. Wow."

"You're such a perv'."

"Can you …?" She asked pointing at my bulge.

"Nahh, not yet. Wanna lick it though?"

"Yeah," she said with a sly giggle.

"Nope!" I said then gave her big breasts a squeeze.

"I'm hungry."

"If I can stand up, I'll make you something."

"Want me to do it again?" I joked puttin' my head near her pussy.

"Please. No. I can't take it." She said as she locked her legs closed.

"C'mon then, I'm hungry," I said getting off the bed.

"Okay, okay. Can I have time to recuperate at least?"

"Five minutes." I said and went to the bathroom to brush my teeth. When I walked to the kitchen Simone was on the phone.

"KD's on his way, he sounds mad."

"That nigga always sounds mad." I said.

"I know." She went to the bathroom to take a quick shower. When she came back she was wearing my blue and gray flannel pajamas and a Notre Dame t-shirt. KD and I were locked in a fierce game of Tekken 4 and discussing how to proceed.

"Hey Kenneth," Simone said as she began to prepare the food.

I paused the game and watched KD as he stared at Simone's bouncing double D's as she scrambled eggs in a pan. I waved my hands in front of his face in a "earth to KD" motion.

He snapped out of his trance and said, "Hey Simone." I un-paused the game and took a bunch of cheap shots on his man. "Hey fuckin' cheater!" He grumbled and tried to snatch the controller out of my hand. "Anyway," he continued. "If we can get the tape, we can get the license plate number then just run it through the DMV to get an address."

"I got a DMV connect," I interjected.

"Good. Then we can run it, get the address, and kill everybody that lives there."

"What's if it's all old people?" I joked.

"Then we won't have to chase'em," he said seriously.

"I wanna help," Simone said as she brought three plates of cheesy scrambled eggs, turkey bacon, bagels and handed them out. "They won't expect me," she said tucking' her legs under her in the Lazy Boy.

"We'll see" I said noncommittally.

"She's right," KD said. I just looked at him like he was retarded. He looked back at me like *what?* Then we ate in silence.

"Those look like 9's or .380's," he said pointing his fork at the three bandages on my arms and chest.

"Probably both, they had two heats." When Simone took the empty plates, KD stood to leave and gave me a bottle of pills.

"Those is Oxycontin," he warned. "Take one if you can bear the pain. Take two if you wanna go Night-Night." He smacked me on the elbow and laughed as I screamed in pain.

"Get out!" I said, as he laughed some more, then walked towards the elevator. When he left, I pulled Simone into my lap and snuggled with her while we watched old reruns of the Golden Girls. When she fell asleep in my arms I called my P.O. and told him to come by the house instead of the shop. I was feeling sick, was the message. I was smart to play hooky, and even smarter not to go to the hospital. Getting shot was an automatic parole violation and would've sent me back to prison for 12 months flat. I couldn't afford that. I had places to go and people to kill. Jail didn't fit into my schedule. I looked at Simone cradled in my good arm, then took two of the Oxycontin and joined her in a deep drug induced sleep.

Chapter Eleven

Y.T.S 1996

I hadn't seen my Grandmother in almost two months. When they announced I had a visit, I reacted like a little kid. After rushing to get dressed and trimming my freshly grown goatee, I grabbed my visiting pass and headed down the ramp to the visiting area. I tried to hide the big ass Kool-Aid smile I was wearing and was failing miserably.

The visiting area was set up just like every other visiting area I'd seen: A large hall-type room packed wall-to-wall with chairs, tables, and people. I saw my Grandmother as soon as I walked in but what didn't seem right was she was holding a baby… *My* baby I noticed as I got closer.

"Sava Grandmere (hey Grandmother)," I said cheesing despite myself, giving my Grandmother a noisy kiss on the cheek.

"Dis child is a special child," she told me as she rocked my son adoringly.

"He does not cry, he watches," she said in a serious tone.

"Who drove you up here?" I asked scanning the room and failing to find my Aunt or Uncle. Then Kelis came walking towards us, carrying two trays and two bottles of juice.

"Hey," I said as I stood to hug her, then looked at my Grandmother confused. She patted my leg knowingly then passed me the baby.

"That child has been 'ere before" she told us as I covered his face and slobbery lips with kisses.

Most Creoles belong to one of two religions: Voodoo, or Roman Catholicism. My family believed in a mixture of both. By saying that my son had possibly been on earth in another life time meant he was reincarnated spiritually as one of my deceased relatives.

"Who?" I asked my Grandmother, curious as to who she'd say.

"I dun' know, Christiane perhaps" she said in a faint voice.

"Grandfather?"

"Perhaps. We'll see as he grows," she said grabbing his chubby cheeks. After a pause she reached down, grabbed her Crochet supplies, and said, "Go!" Sending Kelis and I outside to the patio area.

The patio was nice. It was large and shaped like a small park, complete with benches and a slide for the bigger kids.

"Hold the baby!" I said hurriedly as he approached.

"This Holy ground cuzz." Dixon stopped carefully, out of swinging distance. "We don't bring that bullshit out here," he continued.

"So, when?" I asked feeling my heart race with the pre fight jitters.

"You'll get a pass," was all he said as he walked back over to the slide where he picked up a pretty little girl and swung her around in a wide circle while she screamed with delight.

"Who was that?"

"A dead nigga."

"Kevon, please don't get in trouble."

"I'm not, *that* nigga is the one in trouble," I said, again reaching for my baby.

After an hour of being alone we went back to the visiting room and enjoyed the rest of our visit. They brought me a care package and my Grandmother put $200 on my books. Then the five minute warning was announced. To my surprise, my

Grandmother didn't cry. She just held my hand and played with the baby while I held him.

I gave Kelis a kiss and fondled her breasts clumsily, when my Grandmother left to dump the trash. She told me she'd be back every other weekend, then slipped me two $100 bills, and caught up with my Grandmother in the exit line.

Immediately I went on alert and spotted Gear Gang. He was in the front of the search line, getting undressed. I made sure he saw me, and then I threw up a big "B" with my fingers. He answered by throwing up a "C" as he sat to take his pants off. I spit on the ground and turned my back to him disrespectfully.

"Sup fool?" Tiny Moon said as he made his way over.

"Nothing nigga, what unit they got you on?"

"K/L, it's cool"

"Who's yo roommate? Is he cool?"

"Squirt from 20's. He straight."

"Where you at?"

"G/H, it's live over there."

"Lucky ass nigga. We just got off lockdown."

"Sucks to be you," I joked as we got closer to the front of the line and began to undress.

"Ol boy must think you cute the way he keep staring at you," Moon joked.

"He's a poodle," I said as I handed the staff my clothes so he could search them.

When we got dressed and got on the Trade line, I gave Moon one of the hundred dollar bills, and a hard hug, then we headed in different directions. When I got back to my room Rasan was reading a novel and listening to the Mary J Blige tape I had borrowed.

"You have a good one?"

"Yeah, my G-moms and my baby moma came."

"I used to get visits," he said in a sad voice.

"What happened?"

"Life moved on without me."

"Yeah," I said feeling sorry for him. That situation was common. When you came to jail, people abandoned you. You become a ghost, a memory.

"You got a pass," he said handing me a small square piece of paper. It said I was supposed to report to the library at 8a.m. on Monday. The pass was signed C. Malveaux. Malveaux was one of the most common Creole names there was. It was the French version of Jones or Williams.

I grinned and put the pass to my nose to smell it.

"You trippin,'" Rasan said staring at me suspiciously.

I laughed feeling stupid and promised to explain later. After that I grabbed my knife and went to the dayroom.

"Wassup bloods?" I said as I plopped down between Five and Grady on the green backed chairs.

"Su Whoop."

"What's brackin?"

"What y'all doin?"

"Watching the Raiders get smashed!"

"Watch yo' mouth!" Five warned.

"Fuck the Raiders. This Piiiiru!"

"This nigga's stupid. You have a good visit?"

"Yeah I saw my son," I said smiling.

"That's decent. That's decent."

"I got a pass to the library," I said pulling it out of my pocket.

"Eight a.m.? The library don't open 'til nine."

"I know," I said smiling.

"Oh shit!" Grady said finally catching on. "Don't that new lady work in the library on Mondays and Tuesdays? The fine one."

"Yep."

"Damn blood you just got here and you already knocked a bitch?"

"Stop Hatin'," Five joked.

"Hating? Blood all I hate is crabs and them doo-doo ass Raiders!" Grady said then jumped off the chair before Five could grab him.

I laughed and then pulled the knife out and passed it to Five.

"I'm good blood. Thank you."

"Ain't nothing Ru Ryda, but in the future, just look a nigga in his eyes and you can tell what his intentions are. And remember, all Bloods ain't yo homie. Aiight?"

"Aiight."

"Come on blood it's almost chow time."

After chow I went to call my Grandmother to make sure she made it home safely, then called it a night. I had big plans tomorrow....

At 7:45 a.m. I head down the ramp where I was stopped to be searched, and wanded with the metal detector. When I raised my right foot to be wanded I saw Unit A/B coming out for early Trade/School release.

As they were passing by us I saw Gear Gang in the back of the line, walking with a staff member. When I looked down to raise my left foot I heard the staff scream, "Dixon get your ass back over here!" Then I heard footsteps running towards me and felt the first two punches on the back of my head and jaw. My vision went black as I went down on one knee. He continued to rain punches on my head and face. Now numbed by adrenaline, I grabbed his legs and pulled him down. Bleeding from my eye and nose I pulled his sweatshirt over his head and began to ram my knee into the top of his head. That's when I heard the alarms and felt the pepper spray as the staff struggled to pull us apart.

Ms. Baker was screaming, “He didn’t do nothing!” as a crowd began to form. I got one last kick off as they pulled me off of him. When they had us layed on our stomachs, cuffed behind our backs I saw through blood soaked eyes that that motherfucker was smiling. He blew me a kiss and said, “Fuck Slobs!” then coughed hard as Bertha put a sharp knee into his back and told him to shut the fuck up.

He got me. I got caught slipping, point blank. But, losing the fight ain’t what hurt. What hurt was the fact that I knew I’d blown my chance with the Creole girl. That fact was further confirmed when she rolled up in a Golf cart and shook her head in disgust.

Two hours and seven stitches later I was escorted back to Unit G/H and CTQ’d (confined to quarters). I was staring at my newly damaged face in the mirror when Mr. Thomas opened the door.

“Ms. Baker says that you weren’t the aggressor in that little incident a few hours ago so you won’t receive a write-up for it. But, you are on CTQ for seventy two hours, and will receive your meals in your room.”

“Okay,” I said feeling relieved. He left, and I continued to survey the damage.

“Blood what happened?” Grady and Five asked as they barged into my room.

“Ol boy dope fiend’ me when I was getting searched.”

“Sheeiit, when I walked up they was pulling *you* off of him,” Grady said through his cackling laughter.

“Nahh, blood got me. He did that.”

“He’s gone now though, they put blood on the Rock.”

“The Rock?”

“Unit O/R. that’s lock-up. That’s like his third time too, so blood finna get shipped out.’

"Shipped out? Where?" I asked, seeing my revenge slip away.

"Probly' El Paso or Chad. Somewhere up North."

"Blood I need my run back."

"You'll get it. He got two homies on E/F."

"Good!" Five lifted my chin, looked at the damage and said, "You'll be aiight. It's just a few scratches."

"No it ain't," Grady said still laughing. "Yo face is fuuuccked up."

"Get yo Mexican ass outta here!" I said pushing Grady out the door.

"Nigga, I'm Puerto Rican!" he protested.

"Same shit!" I said laughing through my pain.

"We gone get'em blood." Five assured me in a calm voice.

"On Jungle Stones blood," Five said looking at my face again before he left.

I took off my damaged clothes, then took a nap before Rasan and chow came. I didn't feel like explaining my ass whuppin again, and I was dead tired. When P.M. chow release was announced, I got up and tenderly brushed my teeth, and waited for my dinner to arrive. Ten minutes later I got dinner and a surprise.

"So, you're a gangbanger huh?" She asked in a disappointed voice.

"I am what I am," I said as she passed me the Styrofoam tray.

"I hate gangbangers." She said looking me right in the eyes.

"Then maybe you should leave."

"Or maybe *you* should stop being childish."

"Maybe, I was on my way to library when it happened so it's partly your fault." I said trying to break the tension.

"My fault? You were the one rolling around on the ground like a jerk while I was in there freezing and half naked!"

I coughed up most of the juice I was sipping on the floor then said, “What!?”

“You heard me. Stupid bank robber, gangster. I might have caught a cold because of you.”

“Sorry,” I said feeling my dick swell.

“I have your package also. I’ll bring it to you in the morning at Trade release.”

“You gone be naked again?” I asked hopefully.

“Nope you blew that. Just like you blew the scene at Washington Mutual.”

“Did I?”

“Did you what?”

“Did I blow the scene at Washington Mutual?”

“The media said you did.”

“The media is controlled by the Jews, the Jews killed Jesus. You sure you wanna listen to the folks that killed Jesus?” I said, quoting some of the stuff Rasan had taught me.

“So you got the money then huh?”

“I never said that.”

“You think you’re smart don’t you?” she asked in her cutesy voice.

“Nahh, I’m just a dumb nigga from Compton.” I said eyeing her. Not sexually… suspiciously.

“I’ll see you tomorrow”

“Don’t wear no panties,” I said smiling as I closed the door. Then I sat on the cold metal toilet shaking. When I steadied myself, I riffled through my paperwork and read it carefully...twice. Nowhere in my shit did it mention the name of the bank I was accused of robbing, money, or if we’d blown the robbery. She knew way too much. She had to be a Fed’. Or maybe I was tripping off the pain pills I had taken. Either way, I’d check her out tomorrow.

“Wassup Tyson?” Rasan joked returning from dinner.

"Shit, more like Buster Douglas." I said pointing at my face.

"You alright?" he asked genuinely concerned.

"Yeah, it looks worse than it is," I assured him. "Hey, when did Ms. Malveaux start working here?" I asked knowing he'd know.

"About the same time you got here."

"Yeah?"

"Yeah, why you like her?"

"She's cute but too thin. I like'em wit so much ass you can see it from the front."

"You're crazy," he said through his laughter.

I laughed too, climbed on the top bunk to eat my dinner. When the dayrooms were opened, Rasan went to make his phone calls and I layed in bed nursing my ego, and my thoughts. How far would she go to bust me? What did she want, an arrest? Or the money. Fuck it. If she wanted to play I'd change the game and put the ball back in my court.

That night I slept with my back to the cold wall and with a huge smile on my face. Breakfast was at seven a.m., Trade release was an hour later. When the hallways reached the eerie silence of emptiness, I carefully washed my face, dick, and balls. Then I stripped down to my boxers and waited. I was sitting on Rasan's bed flipping through the Hustler magazine, with my dick sticking up like a Japanese flag pole when the door opened.

"Uh, excuse me, you want me to come back?" she asked embarrassed.

"Why?" I asked cool as a fan.

"You're umm… showing."

"Oh that?" I said nodding at my hard on, "I don't got shit to hide." I said as I got up and walked to the door, dick bouncing to the beat.

"What if somebody comes?"

"That's the plan," I said smiling. When she went down to pick up my package I inched closer to her, when she raised her head my dick grazed against her cheek.

"AGHH!" She screamed jumping backwards and wiping her cheek frantically.

"You need to put that away!"

"Touch it," I said arching my crotch in her direction.

"No."

"Yesterday you said you were waiting for me half naked right?"

"That, that was yesterday," she stammered.She slid the rest of the contents of the box to me with her foot.

"So I guess I've blown it again huh?"

"Yes," she said staring at my deflated penis.

"No bitch!" I said bitterly, "What's blown is your fuckin' cover!"

"What are you talkin about?"

"You're a fuckin Fed', do you think I'm stupid?"

"You're trippin'."

"Oh am I? Suck my dick then." I said massaging my dick back to its full size.

"I, I don't do that."

"Oohh, but you wait naked in libraries for teenagers?"

"I… That…"

"Bitch tell your boss *you* blew it, and that in three years and eleven months I'll be wiping my ass with free money. Now get the fuck outta here, Pig!"

Then I slammed the door in her shocked face. I watched her walking briskly down the hallway pulling the dolly and looking back repeatedly. I laughed nervously as I got dressed then sat down to write Simone and warn her about the hardball tactics the Feds were using.

Chapter Twelve

YTS 1996

By the end of Spring, beginning of Summer I had settled in to life in California Youth Authority (C.Y.A.). My hunch was right. Ms. Malveaux disappeared as fast as she had appeared, never to be seen again.I received a job working on the unit under the watchful eye of Mr. Thomas. I played basketball, baseball, and football, and even began to take college classes via the satellite program set-up with the University of Laverne.

On Saturday July 17, as the football team tracked wearily up the ramp after a gruesome "hell week" practice, Mr. Thomas approached me with cautious steps. I had an emergency phone call in the Chaplain's office. These phone calls were always bad. Somebody was either sick or dead. I dropped my helmet and pads and followed him to the Chaplain's office. When we walked inan open Bible sat limply next to the phone on the desk. I snatched it, and without thinking said my Grandmother's name, praying she'd answer.

"Allo mon petit (hello little one)," she answered in a small choked voice. But to me it sounded like music. She was alive.

"Qu'est-ce que le problemme? (What's the problem?)"

"Votre cousin (your cousin)."

"Quel cousin? (which cousin?)" I asked nervously remembering the last conversation I had with my cousin Damion.

"Damion…."

"Qu'est-ce qui ne va pas (what's wrong?)," I asked nervously, fearing the answer.

"Il ya un accident (there was an accident). Damion est mort…. (Damion is dead)."

I dropped the receiver and just stared at the bible passage. Not really reading it. Just staring at it as tears burned their way down my face.

The story was: Damion got drunk and crashed into a tree. The only problem I had with that was Damion didn't drink. Neither one of us did, but I'd been gone almost two years so maybe he'd developed a habit. I told my Grandmother I loved her and ended the call then walked back to unit G/H alone. When I entered the unit I was in a daze, and my vision was blurred by tears that refused to fall. I picked up my helmet and pads and walked to the hallway where I was stopped by a voice.

"Hey Dumas," coach asked, "You okay?"

"Yeah," I lied. "Any word on Ms. Baker?" She'd been missing for four days and nobody knew where she was.

Before I got back down the hallway I was stopped again by a voice and a face that was vaguely familiar.

"Wus' hatnin, Cuzz?"

"Not now homie." I said, and then I recognized the 52 tattoo under his eye and felt the spit land on my face with a nasty splash.

"Member me now nigga?" he asked in an amused voice.

I just stood there, feeling the spit run down over the spot where my stitches were taken out. Some of it even got in the corner of my mouth. First, I just smiled. I stood there and smiled letting the rage build from the bottoms of my feet up through the rest of my body. Then the tears started to fall and I watched his feet shuffle backwards. Then for some strange reason, I started to laugh. Low at first, then louder and louder. Then it stopped.

"You should hit me," I whispered.

"Huh…?"

"Hit me, nigga! Hit me!" I screamed…then I hit him. Square in the face with my football helmet. Blood splattered on the window and walls like ketchup. He made a watery "Arrgh" sound in the back of his throat then stumbled backwards grasping at nothing. By that time, I knew it didn't even matter anymore. So I hit him again and again. For Simone, for Damion, for the Fed bitch, and of course, some of the blows that destroyed his face and skull were for me, and all the pains I kept buried under my heart. I don't remember much else, but voices yelling and being tackled to the ground. But not much else...

I woke up in a padded room. Not like on T.V., but close to it. The lights were blinding.

"You almost killed him." A soft voice said.

"My cousin died…"

"He was taken off life support Monday."

"What's today?"

"Wednesday."

"He spit on me," I said weakly remembering the incident.

"I know, I saw that in the report, but you're still being charged with assault and mayhem."

"It doesn't matter…"

"What doesn't matter?"

"I shoulda gave'em the money"

"Gave who the money, Mr. Dumas?"

"It doesn't matter..."

After my psych evaluation I was moved to O/R (The Rock), and given 365 extra days for my assault on Mr. 52. While I was on the rock Mr. Thomas came to visit me and told me that they'd found Ms. Bakers body at the Pomona trash dump. She'd been stabbed and strangled. Because the inmate accused of the crime was a ward on unit E/F, had confessed Governor Pete Wilson had ordered all wards with M numbers to be immediately shipped to adult prisons. All the Y.A.'s were on nationwide lockdown until the transfers were completed.

1996 was the year of death I'd realized later on. Me and 500 other wards were awaiting another life change. On my birthday weekend I sat eating a jailhouse pie made of candybars, peanut butter, and graham crackers. I received three birthday cards: one from my Aunt Janet, one from my Grandmother, and one from Kelis. The card from Kelis had a letter and a newspaper article from the L.A. Times. What it said shocked me, and the world forever.

"Notorious gangster rapper Tupac Shakur gunned down in Las Vegas..."

'Pac was dead...like I said, the year of death. By December 1996 all M-numbers were cleared out of all of the various California Youth Authority campuses throughout the state. The Juvenile/Ward system was happy to be rid of us. The California Department of Corrections (CDC) had an entirely different outlook. It appeared to the forty of us stepping off the bus at the Kern County Reception Center, that the cops in the CDC system were actually afraid of us. We were all kept together and separated from G.P. (General Population), probably because they expected us to start riots or other various forms of trouble that were commonplace in Y.A. The funny thing was we all pretty much stayed together anyway. We were just as scared as they were. The bus I was on didn't have that many Blacks on it. And even fewer Bloods. I counted three of my homeboys and fourteen Crips. Everybody else on the bus was Hispanic.

"Look blood," Evil said pointing to a sign on the wall that gave me a chill...

That sign alone let me know I was in an entirely different world. There were no guns in Y.A., but here, they brandished high powered rifles and used them with little or no provocation.

"Y'all see that?" I asked Kre-Kre and D-Dog from Athens Park.

"Dog that's just a scare tactic they use to keep niggas from poppin' it off." Kre-Kre said in a not so sure voice.

"No it ain't." A squeaky voice said, we all turned to the back of the line and saw one of the few Crips we all liked, C-looney from Venice Sho'Line. "They killed my cousin in Corcoran."

"Why?" I asked now even more scared.

"He was choking out a Whiteboy that called him a nigger."

"For real?"

"On the set, shot cuzz twice with a mini-fourteen."

"Daaaamn…."

"If you choke a nigga or if they see a weapon, they can shoot you," he said in a warning voice.

I said "Good lookin out." And we continued to our new housing units.

When I walked in, it was nothing like I had expected. It was dead quiet and there weren't any bars on the doors. In a way, it resembled a Y.A. unit except there were two tiers and a bunch of metal tables. I assumed were the eating areas.

Evil screamed, "Su-whoop!!" at the top of his lungs and before he could take another breath, there were four big ass white cops on top of him. I took a step forward to go help him and Kre-Kre grabbed the back of my paper jumpsuit and pointed up at the tower. Standing on the catwalk was a 6'6 Whiteman pointing his Mini Fourteen at the crowd and smiling in an, "I dare you," type of way.

All you could hear was Evil yelling in pain, and the cops saying, "Stop resisting! Stop resisting!" as they beat him with their billy clubs. By now the unit had came alive as the lights in the cells began to turn on one after the other.

"He didn't even do nothing.'"

I said to nobody in particular and was grabbed by the back of my neck and tripped to my knees.

"Shut the fuck up boy!" The cop spat into my ear. His breath smelled like baked ass and cigarettes.

"Man, fuck that," I began defiantly then he put his knee in my back and his club under my chin.

"Are *you* resisting?" he asked in an angry but expectant voice. "Huh?" he asked pulling my head back so far I could feel the neck muscles stretch.

"No." I managed to say.Then he let me go and screamed, "Prone out!"

Everybody laid on their stomachs with their arms stretched out in front of them and listened to a speech that had obviously been given a hundred times before.

"You are now the property of the California Department of Corrections. You are no longer a name, but a number.

"If you speak, I will club you, If you move too quickly I will club you, If you try to incite a riot (he said giving Evil a kick), I will club you. That gunner up there has one instruction. Shoot one or all of you motherfuckers dead." Then he stopped in front of one of the Mexicans and stood on his fingers. Five minutes later a cute little blonde officer with yellow sergeant's stripes on her shoulders entered the unit and asked what happened. What I heard was the biggest lie I'd ever heard in my life.

"That one over there, he tried to incite a riot." He said pointing at Evil who was cuffed behind his back and groaning in pain."Jackson took him down but he kept resisting, so we all loaned him our assistance." He said completing his lie.

The Sergeant eyed the C.O. suspiciously then went over to Evil and asked what happened. Evil told his version and was taken to the infirmary to be checked out. When the Sergeant left we were told to get up, given a bedroll and escorted to our assigned cells. I was placed with Evil, and Kre-Kre and D-Dog were celled together. After I took a piss and washed my hands I started to make my bed. Before I could unfold the thin mattress a voice appeared in the vent that connected my cell to the cell next door.

"Hey cell 220!"

"What's up," I said as I stood on the toilet to hear him better.

"Hey, where y'all come from?"

"T.S."

"Cause that Lady got killed huh?"

"Yeah!"

"Hey, where you from folks?"

"I'm a Damu from Compton."

"Right, Right. I'm Scrooge from Grape Street Watts. My celly is V-Dog from Park Village."

"Which V-Dog?" I asked excited. "Big V-Dog or Lil V-Dog?"

"Lil V-Dog," a new voice said.

"Vili-Vili?" I said using his real name.

"Who is that? Cuzz, you know me?"

"It's Rowdy fool, Kevon."

"Ahhhh, what's up nigga? He asked in a happy voice. V-Dog was from Park Village Compton Crips, a mostly Samoan gang close to my neighborhood but more importantly, I used to date his sister a long time ago.

"How much time you got left fool?"

"Four years. I caught a year in Y.A."

"Yo' ass still crazy."

"How much time you got?"

"I got eight years."

"For that shit at Miracle Market?" I asked, remembering the shoot-out he'd had with the Compton police.

"Yep. I beat life 'cause the cops lied on the stand."

"That's good nigga. I thought yo'ass was washed up."

"Nahh, I'm aiight."

"What's up with Lelani?"

"Oh you fucked up. She just got married."

"Daaamn."

"You had her, but you did her dirty."

"Yeah. I fucked that right up."

We continued to reminisce for the next hour then he told me which Bloods were on the unit, and that he'd let'em know I was here. Two hours later, Evil came back looking defeated and walking softly.

"Blood, you aiight?" I teased, hoping to lift his spirits.

"Hell naw blood, that fat ass Cracker fucked my back up," he said smiling.

"What the Sergeant say?"

"She love me."

"Nigga stop playing, for real?"

"On Lanes, blood."

"Not Pasadena Denver Lanes! Maybe bowling lanes," I said joking.

"Nahh, she said I aint' gone get no write-up but to chill be-smuzz we only gone be here ninety days."

Then he jumped in the air and landed on the metal desk screaming like a girl.

"Blood what was that?" he asked smiling nervously, and a little embarrassed.

"A rat?" I said not knowing, then looked on the floor and saw a bar of soap with a piece of string looped through it. I picked it up and went to the door.

A voice on the tier said “Pull!” so I did. A note was attached to the middle of the string.
“Don’t open that” Evil warned looking at me cautiously.
“Why not? It’s addressed to you!”
“Let me see, It just says “Su-Whoop,’ That’s *both* of us” he said opening the kite.

> “Greetings Damus, this Memphis from BPS and Tweet from Swans we just wanted to let y’all know we was here in 217, in cell 232 is LB from Bebop watts & Screwy Louie from LA Lanes, in 169 is B-Krazy from 2P’s and Tom Slick form 456, in 140 is Slug from TreeTop & Chuckstone from Bity Stones. I’d appreciate it if y’all shot y’all paper work and names back at us. Just tie it on the line. ”
>
> With Respects,
> Damus.

Evil read the kite then passed it to me. After I read it I looked at him unsure.

“Well?”

“Fuck it blood,” he said and started digging for his paperwork.

I did the same. Plus, I knew Slug from the streets. So I knew wouldn’t no funny shit happen. I wrote a quick kite back to them then secured everything on the line and screamed, “Pull!” As I watched our information being dragged back down the tier.

An hour later one of the officers came and asked, “Which one of y’all got fucked up earlier?”

I laughed and pointed at Evil.

“Welcome to CDC,” he said then opened the food slot in the door and handed us two orange jumpsuits and two pairs of sandals. After we got dressed we bullshitted and told stories about our young lives as gangsters and waited for our paperwork to come back. When the soap came flying under the door I picked it up and read the new kite. It said, Slug sent his regards to me and that he'd get at me when they did showers on Wednesday. I gave the kite along with his paperwork to Evil and did my push-ups before I went to bed.

My sleep was haunted as it had been since the night I found out Damion was dead. I tossed and turned as visions of Damion's car crashed into a tree invaded my mind. I could see him laying bloodied and broken in his car. I still refused to believe my cousin died a drunk driver. It didn't make sense. When sleep finally did come I wasn't even tired, my body and mind just kinda' shut down, an act of duty and necessity. The morning came with a bunch of fucking noise. It seemed like everybody that came out of their cells for breakfast slammed their doors on purpose. When Evil finished his morning routine I got up pissed and brushed my teeth, reluctantly accepting the fact that another miserable day had started.

"Morning, ugly blood."

"Fuck dinga lings," I said through a foamy mouth of toothpaste.

Evil laughed, and said, "Ol die'ru ass nigga!"

I laughed spraying toothpaste on the small mirror. When I looked out the window I saw Slug immediately. He smiled and threw up a "P." I smiled and did the same. Then he leaned across the table to an older lookin' guy who in turn threw up a"B".

"The homies are at that table," I told Evil, then moved so he could get a look.

"Damn they look old," he said almost sounding disappointed.

"Nigga they *are* old. Everybody can't stay a Y.G. forever."

"I am."

"So what, you gone be a 48 year old Y.G.?"

"Yep, Y.G. active blood til I *B.I.P.*"

"Yo' ass is stupid, move fool." I said trying to jockey a spot in the window so I could watch the goings on. When chow was over, the inmates that lived upstairs made little stops at cells to visit their friends, comrades and homies.

When Slug made his way to my door we talked briefly then he passed me a note and a small bag of coffee. The cops hurried him along. Not long after another guy not much older than us came to our door and asked, "Who from Lanes?"

"Me, I'm Evil from PDL"

"Wus Brackin', Blood. I'm Screwy Louie from L.A Lanes."

"Lane-tainin."

"Right right. I'll get at you later, Blood. What's hatnin' Rowdy?"

"Bickin it," I said from the back of the cell.

Then he too was hurried along by the cops. When chow was concluded I watched as the cops rolled a metal cart into the unit and started putting on kitchen hats and plastic gloves. The food was exactly the same as in Y.A., except in prison, you got a lot less.

"This shit's cold blood," Evil complained as he took in a mouthful of Grits.

I laughed and began to wolf down my food like I was in a race. Before I was done the cop appeared and opened the tray-slot on the door and asked for the plastic trays back. I noticed Evil hadn't even started on the little sandwhich he'd made out of the toast and scrambled eggs. "Trays!" the lady said in an irritated voice, stuck her hand through the slot. When she left, Evil had a handful of Grits in one hand and half a sandwhich in the other.

"Fuckin White Bitch!" he mumbled and licked the remainder of the grits off his palm.

I laughed and sat down on the toilet to read the kite I'd gotten from Slug.

"Blood don't open no kites from Tweet or Screwy! They Kutt!
And they're recrutin'. Don't take no open food either!"
Big Slug W.S TTP'S

I didn't know what the hell he meant by "they kutt" but the message was loud and clear. I flushed the kite and decided not to tell Evil about it.

"What was that?" he asked pointing to the torn up pieces of paper floating in the toilet bowl.

"Nothing. The homie sent us some coffee."

"Boffee."

"Whatever nigga." I said feeling bad about lying to him but not knowing why.

We did our time like this for the next eighty-nine days. Spending most of the time playing chess by numbers through the vent with V-Dogg and Scrooge, and listening to the T.V since we couldn't see it. Then, one by one we started leaving. Kre-Kre was the first out of the homies to leave and he got lucky. He got transferred to Lancaster State Prison which was one of the very few prisons located in Southern California. The large remaining majority were located either in Central or Northern California. D-Dog and Evil left two weeks later, both to Mule Creek State Prison. I stayed alone in my cell for almost another month before I received my transfer papers. Represa California was all I could understand out of all the initials and numbers. I asked my new neighbor Beto from Primera Flats which prison I was going to.

"That's New Folsom, Homes."

"Where's it located?"

"Sacramento Ese. Buster-Ville."

"Huh?"

"Busters, Homes. Nortenos!"

"What the fuck is that?" I asked confused.

Beto explained that all Mexicans didn't get along in Prison. In fact, the Southern Mexicans hated the Northern Mexicans more that they hated the Blacks. I stood on the toilet as he explained the war history and still didn't understand how they could hate some dudes that they've never seen before, and that had the same last name as them. "Just like you hate the Cripos"

"Yeah," I said. He had me. I sat down on the toilet confused and did what I'd been doing for the past two years. I waited…

Chapter Thirteen

Sacramento California 1997

I slept most of the eight hour bus ride to Folsom State Prison. We were hooked up to three man chains. I had the pleasure of being chained to a big ass White dude with a Nazi tattoo in the middle of his forehead, and a little Asian dude that looked like he didn't belong on the bus. There were thirty two of us in all. Mostly Hispanics ofcourse but this time there was a nice sprinkle of Blacks here and there. I listened to all the bullshit stories and lies that the various passengers told, while the cops blasted Country music and talked about how Pete Wilson was the savior of California.

I awoke several hours later and noticed that we had arrived. As we went thru the first of many checkpoints I noticed there was a passenger in one of the separation cages on the front of the bus. And, it was a female. I figured they would drop her off at a female prison close to here after the bus was cleared of all the male inmates. She was looking quietly out the window with her arms folded across her small breasts.

"Hey up there!" I screamed over the noise. No response…"Hey Ma," I said again, this time the girl looked at me and smiled.

"What's up? What's your name?"

She pointed to herself in a *who me*? gesture, then scooted closer to the front of the cage and said, "My name is Delishis," in a voice that was deeper than all of my uncles. I must've jumped because the big White dude gave me a nasty look. The old Asian man burst into wild laughter, exposing a mouthful of broken yellow teeth.

"You go boom-boom wit' cissy boy!" he said through his laughter. I laughed a little bit too, then looked at the fag again in amazement. It looked just like a girl except now that I looked closer, I saw the shadow of a beard. I shook my head in disgust. Then, shook it again to try and clear my thoughts. After that, I purposely avoided the fag's attention.

"Hey… don't be like that youngster," the fag said as I continued to ignore him/her/ it. "You know you want some of all of this!" It said now sensing how uncomfortable I was, and enjoying it.

After a while the fag left me alone and began a conversation with a guy it knew from another prison. After we cleared the last gate, the bus made its final stop and we began to unload as our row was called. After we were unchained, we were placed into 'holding' cells that held 10-15 inmates. Once situated we were given a cold sack lunch. My tank held four Blacks, six Mexicans, and the crazy Asian guy.

Once everyone was uncuffed, we immediately segregated ourselves. All the Mexicans and one of the Blacks went to one side of the cell, all the rest of the Blacks and the Asian guy went to the other side.Everyone began to eat their lunches, and use the bathroom.

"Hey?" I asked an older Black man that was eating the core of his apple, "Why's he over there with the Mexicans?"

"He's a Blaxican" he said sounding irritated.

"A what?"

"A Blaxican. He runs with the Ese's"

"Oh" I said feeling a little naïve.

After we formally introduced ourselves the third Black guy came over and joined our group. "How y'all Africans doin'?" He asked in an unusually smooth voice.

"Fine." The other O.G. said as they shook hands.

"Nigga, you from Africa?" I asked in a surprised voice. I immediately noticed a change in the man's face. It instantly became hard and it looked like he gritted his teeth. Then the angry shadow passed and was replaced with the same previous look.

"Where you from youngsta?"

"Compton, why?"

"You're a looong way from Compton," he said masking his anger. Then he continued, "We don't use that 'N' word up here young soldier."

"What word? Nigga?"

"Yeah. A lot of people killed and died for that word so we respect each other and don't use it.

"You been here before?"

"Yeah, I been living here for the passed fourteen years. I just went back to court on a child custody case for my grandson."

"Fourteen years?" I asked amazed.

"Yeah, I'm Mousey by the way," he said sticking his hand out. I shook his big brown hand and noticed the tattoo on his forearm. It was of an African warrior, or maybe a Pharoh standing in the middle of the African continent, with his arms out stretched. Under it neatly written was the word Kumi. I assumed that was his name or something.

One by one we were called to the Nurse's Station and given medical evaluations and tuberculosis shots. I noticed that everywhere the Mousey guy went the police deferred to him. Calling him Mr. Brown and asking him how his custody case went. I found out later on exactly why he was treated that way. After the medical exams, cops from the various housing units began to show up to pick up their new arrivals. At around 6:00 p.m a tall, balding, blond cop and his partner came to pick up me, three of the Mexicans, and to my surprise, Delishis.

When we arrived on C-yard the recreation yard was totally vacant, I imagined what it would be like with three to four hundred people cramped into the small spaces of the two basketball courts, the boxing ring, and the various tables.

"Dumas, Jackson, Rivera, You're going to the gym!" the tall cop announced as we stopped on top of the hill, in front of the Gymnasium. When the three of us stepped out of line I looked back and the fag gave me a little wave. I wanted to vomit. Then we entered the Gym. The smell was the first thing that hit me. It smelled like, a giant dirty clothes hamper soaked in piss. I held my stomach as we walked to the office. There were people and triple decker bunk beds everywhere.

It seemed like everybody came to the office to stare at the new arrivals. I heard a voice in the crowd say, "Oooh Wee, sweet man pussy!" and the fag started to laugh. Ughh. After we received our assigned bunks and combination locks we were turned loose in the gym. I was assigned to bunk number 160-middle and as I made my way over there I could feel niggas staring when I passed. When I reached bunk 160, it was occupied. Two guys were there slamming Dominoes and laughing.

"This a Blood rack," the one with the long braided goatee said in a blunt voice.

"I know." I said and waited for them to move out of the way.

"Where you from?" the slightly chubby guy asked in a quiet voice, then slammed a Dominoe so hard I jumped.

"I'm from Bompton" I said starting to feel irritated, but playing along since I was the new guy. Eventually they moved and watched quietly as I made my bed.

"You got yo paper work?"

"Yep."

After they both read my paper-work the guy with the goatee left, and the other guy introduced himself as Silent from

Crenshaw Mafia. We sat and talked for a while then the other guy returned with a bunch of other dudes that introduced themselves; Nella and Moose from Campanella Park, Hang Out from Denver Lanes, Lil M-Rock and Lil Killa Jess from BPS, Project Mike and Godd Father from PDL, and a little guy no more than 18 named Solo from OutLaw 20's. After I met everybody and answered all of their questions, Silent walked me around the Gym and explained the rules to me. Don't use that shower, Don't use those phones. Don't walk down those aisles… It was crazy. There were invisible lines set up all over the gym, and if you crossed them it was a sign of disrespect and an automatic riot. Or a D.P (disciplinary) which meant your own people beat the shit out of you.

"What's up with the Crips?" I asked silent cautiously.

"The ones that's in here are bool. But on the yard, everything is different." As we approached the T.V area I saw something that I hadn't seen since juvenile hall. Blacks and Mexicans playing cards together. "They Nortenos," Silent said, obviously reading my expression. "Yeah, I heard of them" I said trying not to sound too shocked. Then the argument started. "Sports is mandatory!" the big black dude said as he changed the channel.

"Cuzz golf ain't no mothafuckin sport!"

"I ain't yo mothafuckin Cuzz, folks!" the dark dude said, taking his shirt off. My eyes instantly went to the tattoo that covered the entire left side of his chest. It was the exact same tattoo Mousey had. The Kumi tattoo.

"Don't get too close," Silent warned as the entire T.V/Game area parted like the Red Sea. Little Solo came and stood next to me as the argument continued.

"Nigga on Gangsta Crip you better turn!"

"Fuck Gangsta Crip, this East Oakland!" the big dude said, then hit the guy standing to his left so hard I thought he broke his whole face, not just his nose. In the same motion, he hit the guy he was arguing with. He too went down, quietly still holding the remote. Then the big dude left and came back with a cup of water and was about to pour it into the T.V.

"Hold up Kabooby!" Silent said in a stern but pleading voice. Kabooby stopped and smiled, then poured the water on the guy laying asleep with the remote in his hand. I stood with my mouth open as he casually picked up a cup that has "415" written on it, and drank his coffee while he watched Tiger win the Master's Tournament. I guess Golf *was* a sport

"Why'd he hit ol boy?" I asked Silent pointing at the guy who was holding his face and mumbling threats that Kabooby obviously didn't believe. Silent pointed at the floor and I saw the knife for the first time.

"Pay attention"

"How'd he know?"

"Everybody knows everybody," was all Silent said, and we walked back to our bed area. Our other Bunkie, Casper, from CPF was reading one of those freaky Zane books when we walked up.

"Booby again?" he asked Silent knowingly.

"Yep."

"The T.V?"

"Yep."

"Them niggas betta leave that dude alone," Casper said, then went back to his book.

"Where's ol boy from, Kabooby?"

"The Bay. East Oakland I think."

"Why the Crips let him do that?"

"It wasn't all the Crips, it was the Gangsta' car."

"So the Crips are all separated?"

"Yeah, but not always."

"When are they together then?"

"Against us." Silent said in an amused voice, then Kabooby came over."

"You seen that shit, family? I'm putting niggas to bed," he said laughing.

"It was aiight," Silent said.

"Oh this a new Damu? What's good family?"

"Sup homie?"

"I'm Booby from 69 Village."

"Rowdy, Compton Piru's."

"Right, right."

"You know they gone try to take that shit to the yard," Silent said, warning him.

"Nahh, the Homies agreed that what happens in the gym, stays in the gym."

"But you know how the 'rips get down."

"If they do, me and my folks will be ready," he said between sips of coffee.

Chapter Fourteen

SacramentoCalifornia 1997

I was placed on orientation for three days which meant I couldn't go outside to the yard. I spent my days on the phone with my family and Kelis. She had been acting kinda odd lately but I didn't pay much attention to it because my focus wasn't a relationship with her, but one with my son.

I'd formed a bond with Moose and Nella since they were both from Compton, but I'd also taken a liking to Solo. He was like a bad ass little kid. The difference was he knew a lot of people in the Blood world, more than I did.

Nothing happened between Kumi and the Crip's because when the facts came out, it was determined that Kabooby was right about all sports being mandatory. And for initiating the violence since one of the Crip's had a knife. The atmosphere in the Gym remained tense until two guys came in and settled the issue permanently.

The cops announced yard release over the Gym intercom. "Rowdy, c'mon!" Solo said,I followed him to the Gym door where we showed the cops our I.D's, got patted down for weapons. When we finally made it outside the sun was blinding. I didn't know Sacramento got this hot. "C'mon blood, the homies is ova' here." Solo said as I followed him down the asphalt hill to an area containing three tables. When we approached I felt at ease immediately. There were red cups, red flags, and a bunch of familiar tattoos I recognized right away.

"Hey y'all, this the homie from Bompton," Solo said as we stopped. After hugs and intros were handed out, I sat on the corner of a bench and watched the action of a level IV prison yard. The Asian's and Norteno's were having a softball game and seemingly having a good time. The Blacks were scattered in various sections of the yard and holding down the basketball courts. At the top of the hill there was a large group of Blacks, about forty, engaged in a military styled exercise routine. The old guy calling the cadence had to be at least sixty years old, but his body looked twenty five.

"Who's that?" I asked Solo.

"Who them? They Jama."

"Is that Kumi, too?"

"Nahh, blood they on some Black Power shit."

"Like the Panthers?"

"Yeah. Some of them used to be Black Panthers."

I sat and watched in awe as the old guy went up and down the rows of soldiers, counting in Swahili.

"You like that shit, huh blood?"

"Yeah, it's organized, but why they call they'selves monkeys?"

"Not *that* kind of gorilla fool!" Solo said laughing.

"Oh…" Row by row they began to hit the jogging track looking like a well oiled machine. In a way, I was kinda jealous as I looked around at my homies drinking homemade wine, playing table games.

"Get Down!" The cop in the gun tower screamed through the intercom.

I jumped and started to get down until China Dog grabbed me and said, "Never get down until they get down," and when I looked in the direction he was looking, I saw the Southern Mexicans still all standing. Then, one by one they began to get down on their stomachs in the prone position.

Three Crips were jumping the guy that got knocked out in the gym the other day. He fought back valiantly for a while, and then turned to run towards the Program Office. I assumed that was his punishment for getting knocked out with a knife in his hand.

"Damn, blood is fast," China Dog joked. Then the cops handcuffed the assailants and we were allowed to get up and resume normal program.

I was about to ask China Dog what part of Compton he was from when the tower cop screamed, "Get Down!" again. This time, I waited and watched as two of the Southern Mexicans stabbed and punched one of their own people. Then, for the first time I heard gun shots. It was deafening. And even though I was already down, I tried to get down some more.

"Damn, they killin' blood," I said to myself as I watched the victim's white t-shirt slowly fill with red blotches. A cop on one of the roof tops fired his rifle and the two assailants got down on their stomachs. The victim stumbled in a small dazed circle, and then touched his bloody shirt, looked at his hands, in a surprised way, and collapsed.

Two over weight nurses came flying out of the infirmary and immediately began to work on the victim, while the cops arrested the other two guys.

"Is blood dead?" I asked China Dog in the little voice I had left.

"Probly," was all he said. Then took a hand rolled cigarette out of his shirt pocket. He took a few puffs as they rolled ol boy off on a stretcher. "You see those mothafuckaz over there blood, that's who run prison. Not us. The Blacks. We stay too busy fightin' and killin' each other." Then he took a pull on his cigarette and coughed a little. "They move as one, all the time.And when one get outta' line..."

"Blood that's yo first time seeing a sticking?" Solo asked, obviously amused at my discomfort.

"Yeah."

"That's normal here, dog. Get used to it." As soon as he said that, the cop said, "Resume normal program." We all stood up and dusted our clothes off.

"That was crazy. We ain't even going on lock down or nothing?"

"Nope"

"Damn." When the yard was finally recalled, I went back to the gym haunted by the visions the day's events.

"Blood, you bool?" Silent asked me as I laid on my bunk staring at nothing.

"Yeah, I'm bool." I said giving him a fake smile I hoped seemed convincing.

"C'mon blood, they just brought some new people," he said as he made his way towards the C/O's office. When we got there I saw four dudes. Three Mexicans and a short Black dude that had ears that stuck out so far his head looked like one of those baby cups. Then I looked closer at the Mexican with the long hair and smiled.

"Blood, that's a homie right there," I said pointing in the general direction of the office.

"Who? The lil nigga with the ears"

"Nahh, the Mexican wit' the long hair, that's Art from the Tree's"

"Ahh man…" Silent said dryly.

"Ahh man, what? Blood is official," I said defending Arturo.

"It ain't that blood, it's the politics involved."

"Huh?"

"The SouthSiders ain't gone let blood stay on the yard."

"Why?"

"Cause he's a Mexican, and a Blood."

"They got Blaxicans, I saw one…"

"Niggas don't care. But they do."

"That's stupid."

"I know."

In about twenty seconds, I went from being super happy about seeing my homeboy to wishing he never showed up.

"Blood, wus' bracking?" He screamed as soon as he saw me. I returned his hug with less energy then said, "Blood, wus' up?"

"Shit, Bickin' it. Where da homies at?"

"Over here I said then lead him to my bunk area. As we passed by the SouthSiders I could feel the heat coming out of their eyes. After he passed me his paperwork, the homies began to show up.

Before I could warn him about the situation Solo blurted out. "Blood you stayin' here?"

Arturo looked at me and said, "What blood talkin' about?" I looked at Silent for help then thought fuck it, "The SouthSiders don't allow Mexican Crip's or Blood's on this line."

"And! Fuck what they allow, this Trees or nothing!"

"I know blood, but….."

"But nothing, Rowdy you already know how I do mine dog. P.I. til' I B.I. blood!"

"So you stayin'?" Solo asked again.

"Mothafuckin' right!"

Silent left and came back with two older crips and Kabooby. After the situation was explained and everybody understood what was at stake we went to talk to the Mexican shot caller, Sporty, from Florencia 13.

"He gotta go homes, rule are rules."

"And if he chooses to stay?"

"We go to war…." He said it in a simple tone. Like, if he was saying, I'm hungry or what's on T.V.? We all walked away from the meeting knowing what came next. The rule was; Arturo had 72 hours to get off the yard, or a war between the Southern Mexicans and the Bloods was definitely on the horizon. Arturo would be on orientation for the next 72 hours so we had to work fast. The Bay and the Crips said it would be a "Black" war. Not a Blood war so that would at least even out the head count.

"Well?" Arturo asked nervously, but with a proud tone.

"Right now," Silent said, "We wait until tomorrow to get input from outside and follow the chain of command. But you're a Blood and it don't matter if you're a damn Cambodian. A Blood is a Blood." He said then hugged Arturo tightly.

Solo screamed, "Su whooooop!!!" Then we all joined him and "Suwhoooop'd" together. Letting everybody in the gym know our homeboy wasn't going anywhere. The rest of the night was tense. Yes, the SouthSiders would follow the 72 hour rule, but we still had to watch them because they were known for sneak attacks with loose razors or locks in socks. We took turns keeping watch and Kabooby stayed up the entire night talking with Arturo since they were neighbors.

"Is blood official like that?" Silent asked me in a, "Is he worth it," type of tone.

"Yeah. Blood saved my ass on the bus one day when the Palmer's had me trapped."

"Alright. We'll see what the homies say tomorrow, but most likely, a war is coming."

I closed my eyes, but couldn't sleep. I would stand by Art'. And if so, die with him. But in all actuality, I wanted blood to just leave. When the morning came, it was tense. All the guys from the Bay Area were wide awake and in full gear, coats included. Arturo came and stood by my bed as we got ready for chow release.

"Huhn blood." He said passing me a folded up piece of paper. "If something happens to me, call my moms for me blood," he said in a sad voice.

"Ain't nothing gone happen." I said not believing the lie I had just told. Chow went as usual, and when we went out for a.m. yard release the tension was so thick you could cut it with a knife.

I noticed that the homies were all assembled when I got there and that the Compton homies were in a separate circle. China Dog was addressing the group when I pulled up;"Blood that's our homie in there! And if blood is down enough to stay on the line, then that's it! Period!"

We all nodded and listened closely. Bloods don't have "shot callers" in their cars like the other groups, but there is always a pecking order. China Dog was about 46 years old, and had been in prison since 1989 which automatically put him at the top of the pecking order, along with Smallwood from PDL. They both were legends in our world and good leaders.

"So do we wait on them to move first?" Jay-Ru asked. "Cause on Westside P's I'm ready to get it on." He said, smiling and cracking his big knuckles.

"We gotta holla at the other Africans first. So we don't' tip our hand" Smallwood said. "Right now, the SouthSiders thinkin' we finna make blood roll it up. Good, let'em think that…" The rest of the yard continued quietly. Too quietly. No radios blasting, no baseball or basketball games being played, just everybody standing in their areas in huge packs, waiting.

The cops obviously figured out something was going on because there was an extra cop on every roof top with a rifle doing the same thing. Waiting…..

"Yaaard Reeecall!!! The cop in the tower screamed nervously. I guess the cops weren't taking any chances on a full scale riot, so they recalled the yard thirty minutes after they opened it. "Yard recall!" He screamed again and still nobody moved. It was like waiting on a bomb to go off. Then Looney from Rollin' 60's, Mousey, and two other guys from the Guerrillas approached our area.

"We moving or we going in?" Looney asked Big June from Denver Lanes.

"We're going in for now 'cause the gunners is ready," he said pointing to the roofs.

"Alright," Mousey said then turned towards his table and nodded. Instantly the Bay Area began to clear out like Mousey had given a command that only they heard. The Crips instantly followed suit and the Guerilla soldiers brought up the rear. It was amazing to see. I guess we could come together if we had to.

The older homies and the visitors walked off a few feet and had a private conversation while we watched the rest of the yard empty out. When we finally made it back to the gym the fear and adrenaline passed and was replaced by the bubble guts.

"Blood I gotta shit." I told Silent as I headed towards the huge bathroom area.

"Hold up," he said grabbing his knife and walking with me. "Blood, when it's like this don't go nowhere by yourself," he warned then he stopped and looked at me. "Blood, I'm serious."

"Alright I hear you," I said irritated. After I used the bathroom I decided to go call Kelis and my son. It had been a while since I'd called and I knew she was worried. The phone, to my surprise was empty when I walked up so I hopped on and called. The first time I called, the phone just rang. So I hung up and dialed again to make sure I'd dialed the right number. On the third ring a voice came on the phone that I didn't recognize.

"Hello," the male voice said.

"Hello? Let me speak to Kelis."

"Who is this?" The voice asked, amused.

"Nigga who are you!" I asked instantly pissed off that some dude was answering my phone.

"Hold on, here she go," he said, then I heard him playing with my son in the background.

"Hello," she said in a small scared voice.

"I know you don'tgot no nigga ova' there!" No answer…"Girl don't play with me!"Still no answer…"Is that nigga touching my baby?" I said through tightly clenched teeth.

"I'm sorry…"

"So that's how you do a nigga huh?" I asked so mad I could feel my heart pumping through my grip on the phone.

"I'm sorry, Kevon. I…"

Click. I hung up. I had to. The thoughts of that dude holding my son were too much. I wanted to scream.

I was still holding the phone when Oak Park Mark asked, "Rowdy you still using that blood?"

"Nah," I said quietly, and got off the stool. I didn't need this. I held my hand in front of my face and noticed it was shaking badly. I just needed to be alone. When I approached my bed area it was vacant except for Solo who was flipping through Casper's photo albums.

"Blood you look sick." He said in his squeaky little voice.

"Yeah, I don't feel too good" I said climbing in the middle bunk.

"Go 'head. Lay down blood, I got you." And before he finished that statement I was already asleep. She did it again. I let that bitch in and she betrayed me again. I just felt hot all over. Hot. I slept until dinner then got up and ate not tasting any of the food. When we came back from the chow hall I climbed back in the bed and laid there until mail call. I got two letters. One from my Grandmother containing $50, and some pictures of a BBQ at one of my relative's house, and a letter from Kelis which I threw in the trash.

"Rowdy you straight blood?" Arturo asked in his usually calm voice.

"I'm good. Just tired."

"Blood's stressin," Solo said from the bottom bunk. I didn't respond.

"Hey, did y'all know dude that came with me is a blood?" Arturo said changing the subject.

"Who?" Solo asked smelling the drama in the air.

"Ears, he from Hawthorne Piru."

"Why blood didn't check in?" Solo asked, now fully aware that an ass whippin' was in order.

"He said he don't bang no more."

"Fuck that shit blood, I'm telling Silent."Solo said and disappeared around the corner.

"Go get that little bastard!" I said as I rolled out of the bed. When we got to the T.V. area it was too late. Silent had the same shocked look that the rest of the homies were wearing.

"What he mean he don't bang no more?" Silent asked Arturo.

"Blood put his flag down."

"Let's mash blood!" Solo said rubbing his little hands together. He didn't check in. That's an automatic D.P." He said, reminding everybody about the rules.

"Let's wait 'til tomorrow. We got other real problems to deal wit!" Silent said to everybody. Then looked at Solo and said, "Don't do or say shit!"

"Mann…" he protested, sat down and sulked.

I walked back to my bed area to write my Grandmother back and chill the rest of the night. It had to be early in the morning when I got up to take a piss 'cause the whole Gym was dead quiet. No sound, no movement. As I slept walked to the bathroom I heard noises coming from the bunks behind me. I pulled out my small ice pick and walked down the aisle that the noise was coming from, what I saw scarred me for the rest of my life.

The nigga Squeak from Compton Ave. was sitting on the faggot Delishis's bed naked. Delishis was riding Squeak while Squeak jacked him off. Standing in front of the faggot, getting his dick sucked was the nigga Ears from Hawthorne Piru. First I just stood there amazed. Then I quickly turned away and went to get the closest homie in the area, Cereal from Pacoima Piru.

"Blood wake up!" I whispered loudly

"Hunh, wha…"

"Blood wake up. Come look!"

"Is it chow time already?"

"Nahh nigga get up!"

"Blood, what's wrong?" M-Rock asked, in a sleepy voice from the top bunk.

"These nigga's runnin' a train on the faggot," I said in a disgusted, but excited voice.

"Ughh blood, who?" Cereal said, now up and putting his boots on.

"The Crip nigga Squeak and y'all homie Ears from Hawthorne," I joked.

"That nigga ain't my homie!" M-Rock said with a scrunched up face.

"C'mon," Cereal whispered, Lead the way to the Homo-Orgy.

"Unghhhh," Cereal said laughing, then M-Rock joined us.

"Blood that's nasty," I said turning my head.

'Let's go wake up Boxer from East Coast," Cereal said smiling.

"Nahh, this ain't Damu business, I told them, and then screamed "Booty Bandits!!!" and ran back to my bunk laughing like a maniac.

Chapter Fifteen

Sacramento California 1997

The next morning we told the rest of the homies what we saw and as I expected, they all were thoroughly grossed out. Except Solo. "Blood, why y'all ain't wake me up?" he asked, sounding disappointed. Then the Ears guy walked by and got in the shower.

"There he go," I said pointing.

"Ughh, imma fuck blood up when we D.P. his faggot ass," Solo barked.

"That's probably why blood put his flag down. He's a fag-hag, and he know the homies don't play that shit." Silent added in a thoughtful voice.

"Probly," I said in agreement. Today was the last day that Arturo had to get off the yard, so outside of the comedy with the fags, it was business as usual. Kabooby came over with a huge cup of coffee and asked about last night's events afterwards we all went to the yard.

The scene was identical to the day before. Quiet and tense. When I made it to the Blood's area Steel-Toe from Fruit Town Brims pointed quietly at the basketball court, what I saw confused me. Smallwood and China Dog were in the SouthSiders area. Alone. Talking to the SouthSiders shot caller, an old Mexican guy with a long black moustache. Directly to his right was a big Ese with the numbers 18 tattoo'd down the length of his face.

"Are they safe?" I asked.

"Yeah, we ain't at war yet. They probably tryin' to find a way to avoid the bloodshed."

"Is there a way?"

"You believe in Unicorns and Tooth fairies?"

"No."

"Then there's yo answer," he said putting his hand on my shoulder and squeezing sadly.

When the older homies came back from their meeting with the SouthSiders, they briefed everyone on the conversation.Afterwards they went to talk to the elders of the other groups. In a way, we were like a bunch of different African tribes. It was funny.

"Blood, what they asked for was brazy." Scheme from Oak Park said, "A ounce of go fast and one of our phones…Fuck No!"

"That's like twenty G's," Steel-Toe added.

"What's twenty G's?"

"A ounce of go fast. Crystal."

"Damn!"

"How much is the…"

"Get down!!" The cop screamed, and like they were conjured up by witches, a cop with Mini Fourteen riflesappeared on every roof. We all looked around and didn't see any action on the yard, then all the cops from all the housing units started running in the direction of the gym. I immediately thought 'Oh Shit'.

"Blood who's all in there?" Smallwood asked us as he crawled towards us on his stomach.

"Just the orientation."

"Yeah, but who?"

"Arturo, and three SouthSiders."

"What about blood from Hawthorne?"

"He went to medical," I said in a distant voice because I knew for sure Art' was sleep when we came out to the yard. The main gate opened on the yard and cops from all the other yards flooded through it dressed in riot gear and equipped with various weapons. Block Guns that fired non-lethal rounds, Concussion Grenades, and guns that fired huge bursts of Pepper Spray.

Inside the gym a gun went off and I prayed that it was just a block gun. Or that they missed with the Mini Fourteen. The riot cops spread out in a military styled fan and covered all the different areas that contained 3 or more people.

"You dirty?" Cereal asked as the cops made their way to our area.

"No. You?"

"Yeah, I got my heat cheeked," he whispered.

"Don't move!" an old Mexican cop screamed at Cereal then kneeled into his back.

"I'm just scratchin' my ass," Cereal said in a choked voice. Immediately there were cops covering our entire area.

"Get me a metal detector!" The cop screamed. The female officer left and came back with a hand held wand. They stood Cereal up and wanded him repeatedly focusing on his butt area looking for a weapon.

"He's clean." The old cop told Cereal, "the next time you wanna scratch your ass; raise your hand." Then he walked off holding his Block gun tightly.

Cereal layed back down next to me in the dirt, "plastic," he smiled.

I nodded then watched as the Gym doors opened and the first of the nurses came out. Her white latex gloves had blood on them. Not a lot, but we could see it clearly. Then they brought the stretcher out and we all held our breath. The passenger was laid on his back and strapped down so we couldn't clearly see who it was, then he turned his head. He was bald.

"That ain't Art'," I said feeling myself smile.

"How you know?" Steel-Toe asked

"Blood got hair down to his ass."

"Oh. So far so good then huh?"

"Yeah."

Five minutes later they brought the other two SouthSiders out. One had a lot of blood on his shirt. The other was bare chested and drenched with Pepper Spray. The cops escorted them both in the direction of the infirmary. Then they brought out the second roll away stretcher. Arturo was on it. His long black hair hung lifeless over the sides, and a nurse was holding a blood soaked towel to his face. I instantly thought about the phone call I would have to make. As the procession of cops and nurses made their way carefully down the hill with the stretcher Arturo screamed, "Suuuu Whooop" and sat up before the cops and nurses struggled to lay him back down. Instantly all the blacks; Bay, Crips, Bloods, and even some of the Northerners started screaming, "Su Whoop, Su Whoop!" It was crazy. The cops tried to control it but it was impossible.

"What now?" I asked Smallwood.

"We find out what happened in there."

"I thought you said blood was sleep," Steel-Toe asked.

"Shit, I thought he was."

"It looks like he did his thang in there." Smallwood said sounding surprised.

"Of course he did, he from Bompton," I said proudly. The cops began to stand all the homies up and strip search us. When I looked over at Cereal he was smiling and had his hand in his pants. "Blood, whatchu' doing?" He smiled, said, "Watch this." Two female cops told us to stand up and strip out. When Cereal handed the fat White lady his boxers his dick jumped out like Jackie Chan.

"Oh my," the cop said, then, "Brenda bring me that metal detector."

The Black female cop said, "Guurl," and pointed at his dick like she was scared. I burst into laughter. I tried to hold it in but I couldn't. This fool was standing asshole naked with a hard on and a straight face. The old White lady handed Cereal his boxers back. But instead of putting them in his hand, she draped them over his erection; this made me laugh even more.

When we got dressed and stood in line to go back to the gym Cereal said, "That's Mrs. Daniels. She's a freak."

I just shook my head and laughed as we walked back to the gym. When we approached the gym I noticed only Blacks, Whites, Asians, and Nortenos were allowed to go back to the gym. "Wassup' with them?" I asked nodding at the Soutsiders.

"They gone put them somewhere else 'til they figure out if it's cool or not to bring'em back."

"How long will that take?"

"Couple days."

The gym was a wreck when we entered, and the Pepper Spray that hung in the air had everybody gagging and coughing.

"Your friend's a crazy fucker," the cop near the office told Silent as we passed him. "He attacked those three guys all by himself. He got sliced up pretty good though." He said, then went back to writing his incident report.

"Arturo rushed *them*,"I said trying to not sound surprised.

"Guess so," Silent said smiling. After everybody cleaned up their bed area, Silent called a small meeting and explained what the cop had just told us.

"Where's the baybay kid?" I asked, looking around for Solo. When he showed up he was walking quickly.

"Blood, let's get some of that shit!" he chirped in an excited voice.

"Summa what shit?" Casper asked.

"The Norteno's is breakin' in the SouthSiders lockers and stealing all they stuff," he said happily.

"Bloods don't steal!" Silent said in his no nonsense voice

"I do." Solo said defiantly.

"Go ahead then," Silent said with an I dare you tone. Then Kabooby and two of the Crips came to join the meeting. "Tell yo folks not to get involved in that stealing shit." Black Cuzz from West Coast 30's said.

"We already know."

"So what we gone do when they bring the Ese's back in here?" Bandit from PlayBoy Gangsters asked.

"Well we know they ain't gone make a move on us cause it's sixty blacks in here and only thirty eight of them. Plus, when they find out the Norteno's stole all they shit, they gone get at them."

"Unless they think we did it," I said. Nobody said anything. We all just stood around bouncing that idea around in our heads.

"Let's go and talk to the Norteno's," Silent said, and got up. "Hey Spooky let me holler at you." Silent watched the Norteno shot caller prance around in his new, stolen Nike Cortez.

"What's up homie?"

"Look, we ain't trippin off what y'all doing cause that's y'all business. But, when they bring them dudes back in here, y'all need to take responsibility for y'all actions. Feel me?"

"Yeah I got you," he said, not even listening to Silent. Then he said, "Wanna' buy a Mack 10 C-D?"

"Nahh, I'm straight."

"What about a new bowl?"

"I'm cool," Silent said then walked away. The yard was put on lockdown for two weeks, pending review of the incident. In the middle of the second week they brought the Southsider's back into the gym. We watched as they walked to their bed areas, and noticed their personal belongings were gone.

"You guys have twenty four hours to give my Raza back their property or it's on!" The Gym shot caller told Silent and Kabooby as he crossed the invisible lines and came to the Black T.V area, alone.

"Who the fuck you think you talkin' to?" Kabooby asked as he stood up from his Chess game.

"Booby, hold up," I said.Turned to the intruder and asked, "What makes you think we have any of that shit?"

"Y'all don't?"

"Of course not!"

"Twenty four hours homes." Then he walked casually away, out of the lion's den.

"I shoulda' K'O'd his bitch ass for coming over here wit' no security."

"Fuck'em. He's in for a surprise."

"Yeah, Fuck'em! Rowdy you alright, you know that."

"I try to be," I said, then walked back to my bed area, shaking like hell. After I explained what had happened to the homies, I said what nobody wanted to hear. "The Norteno's didn't take responsibility for that stealing, to be honest; I think they lied on us."

Everybody looked at me, then Silent said, "We get off lockdown tomorrow. Let's see how it plays out." The gym was the last of the buildings to be released for yard. When we got outside the older homies were back in the SouthSiders area talking to their shot caller. It was decided that they knew the Norteno's had stolen all of their property and a cease fire was called between the Blacks and the SouthSiders. To everybody's amazement, the war we had been expecting between the North and the South never came. The Norteno's simply gave the SouthSiders their stuff back plus interest and a war was avoided. Peace it seemed had been restored.

"So that's it?" I asked China Dog in a disappointed voice. "No war, no beef, nothing?"

"Guess not" he said through a cloud of cigarette smoke.

I couldn't believe it. How could they just let an infraction like that go? True, I heard the Norteno's gave the SouthSiders their stuff back plus an ounce of speed but still…. Whatever happened, it played out peacefully so I let it go like everybody else.

It was May but it felt like summer had already arrived in full swing. There were baseball and basketball tournaments, rap contests, and track meets. Ears got wind that we were going to D.P. his ass, so on the morning of May fifth he packed all his stuff and told the cops that his life was in danger. He was placed in protective custody.

When the cop announced a.m. yard he also said Happy Cinco De Mayo to all the Mexican inmates. After that we were released into the burning Sacramento sun.

"Blood, you going out?" I asked Nella before he got on the phone.

"Nahh, Imma' call the pad and check in."

"Aiight, I'll see you in a minute Ru Ryda."

"Su Whoop."

"Su Whoop."

"Sup, Groove?" Straw-Dog from Hoover said as I approached the basketball court near the Crip's area.

"It's hella' Mexicans out here," he said looking up the hill and dribbling the basketball.

"I know" I said now realizing that there *was* a lot of Mexicans out on the yard. It seemed like every SouthSider was out.

"Do they have mandatory yard today?"

"It's Cinco De Mayo, so maybe." With that said I walked to my area and to my surprise, none of my homies noticed the number of Mexicans that were out. A lot of Blacks had stayed in to watch the Basketball game, and to use the phone or catch up on letter writing. There was only a few dozen of my homies in our area. The Bay Area and Kumi were out in full force as usual, the Crips were deep also. It still felt wrong for some reason.

"Blood how you feel?" I asked Silent, interrupting his Chess game.

"Fine why?" he said looking up, then moving his King out of check.

"Something's wrong."

"No it ain't, the Mexicans do this every Cinco de Mayo. Jus' like we deep on Juneteenth or the morning before the Super Bowl.

"You sure?"

"I'm positive. I been here for three years, stop being paranoid."

"Aiight, I'm finna' go holler at Sante and Matata then."

"The Guerillas?"

"Yeah, they got some books for me."

"Su Whoop!"

"Su Whoop!"

The rest of the time on the yard passed quietly and peacefully. On my way to the Bay Area tables I passed by Squeak and Delishis arguing over a Pinochle game. It was nasty, but they looked like two lovers in the park. I looked over the yard and noticed the SouthSiders were walking in packs of ten and twenty. I let the thought pass as more paranoia.

"You ready for this heat?" Sante asked as he handed me two books. Both written by a dude named George Jackson.

"This it?" I asked faking like I was disappointed.

"Just read'em" Matata said annoyed.

"Aiight. Have y'all noticed anything strange?" I asked them as I read the preface for the Soledad Brothers.

"There's one hundred and six of them out here," said Sante matter of factly.

"So, I'm not trippin' then?"

"Nope. A good soldier pays attention." I hung out with the Guerillas until five minutes before yard recall, then as I made my way across the baseball diamond I noticed that none of the packs of SouthSiders that were walking on the track were moving. They had all stopped. There were two packs of about thirty between our area and the basketball court where Solo was playing one on one with Straw-Dog.

At the top of the hill the old shot caller kneeled with his back against the hand ball wall. Standing directly in front of him was about fifty SouthSiders. The big dude with the 18 on his face pulled a long metal knife that looked like it came from Big 5 out of his boot and screamed, "RAZAAA!!" and started running full speed towards the basketball court where Solo was.

The rest of the Mexicans responded, "RAZAA!!" in a united voice that sounded like thunder.

Then the chaos started…

All 106 of the SouthSiders attacked the small groups of Blacks spread out across the yard. At first I froze. I just stood there, my feet wouldn't move. Where was I supposed to go? Everywhere I looked Blacks were being slaughtered. I saw Silent running up the hill towards the basketball court where Solo and Straw-Dog were fighting eight or nine Mexicans. Then Solo went down. I immediately broke into a run as the cops screamed, "Get Down!" and the emergency alarm blared. I started to sweat or cry or both as the big dude with the 18 on his face repeatedly jammed his knife into Solo's little body. The other SouthSiders had Straw-Dog's entire body covered and were stabbing and kicking him. Silent just dove into the crowd, landing on top of them in a fury of punches and kicks. I hit the guy on top of Solo with a football tackle and he hit his head on the basketball pole and layed lifelessly unconscious.

"He stabbed me blood," Solo said in a small voice choked with blood.

"I know blood, I know." I said as the Guerilla's and Crip's showed up to help Silent. I picked up Solo's damaged little body and ran towards the infirmary. By now guns were going off in rapid succession, but I just ran trying to save my homeboys life. There were fights and bodies everywhere as I made my way to the nurse's area and put Solo down on the ground. A cop tried to grab me but I spun out of my t-shirt and ran shirtless back across the grass. I stopped in the Crip's area where KD from 40's was dropping Mexicans every time he hit one. I kneeled down and picked up a knife then jammed it into the face of an already knocked out SouthSider. It went in easy at first, then banked off of something deep behind his nose. "Mothafucka!"

"C'mon," KD said as we ran to the top of the hill towards the SouthSider's area. Kabooby was up there alone, surrounded by a pack of ten SouthSiders, screaming, "Black Power Mothafucka!" He fought all of them. Ignoring the fact that he was covered in blood and had multiple stab wounds in his side and shoulders.

Then, the gun went off directly behind me and the top of a young SouthSiders face disappeared right in front of me. The blood and brain matter splashed on my neck and got in my eyes. I screamed, then got down as the riot police finally showed up. At least eighty to ninety cops arrived, and I was happy as hell to see them. I laid directly next to the dead SouthSider and watched as his warm blood soaked into the asphalt.

KD asked, "You alright?" I couldn't answer.

"Hey Rowdy… Don't go into shock nigga!" he screamed as he shook me, and the nurses came over to check us for injuries. "I'm okay" I said but nobody heard me. I just layed there and watched the dead guy's body shake and spray blood.

"Get off me Bitch!" Kabooby argued as the nurses tried to clean his wounds.

It took thirty four nurses and one hundred and twenty eight cops to clean up the carnage of the Cinco de Mayo massacre. The report said one hundred and nine Southern Mexicans attacked seventy nine blacks on that fateful afternoon. They found fifty four knives and countless razorblades. Three Blacks were killed. Straw-

Dog, old man Sam, and the homosexual Delishis. Solo was air lifted by helicopter to an outside hospital, where after two surgeries he pulled through. All the other injuries were minor. Only the Mexican that got shot died. But, many of them had serious injuries. One in particular lost vision in his right eye where a knife had been plunged. After the media circus was over New Folsom State Prison was placed on an indeterminate lock down. It was with these conditions that I left prison and went home. Worse than when I went in.

Chapter Sixteen

Compton California 2000

"The following people have rides so listen up," the burly corrections officer said as he read from a list on a clip board. "Garcia-J47691, Hunt-K11704, Johnson-H97181, and Dumas-J69260."

We all grabbed our brown paper bags full of personal belongings and followed the cop out of the Receiving/Release section of the prison, and out to the Visitor's parking lot where our loved ones would be waiting to take us home. The other six or seven inmates that were still in the R/R holding tank would be dropped off at local bus or train stations and set free that way. It was sad that nobody cared enough to come and pick them up.

As I passed officer Rooney he said, "You'll be back." He spit on the curb, splashing some of the chewing tobacco on his own boot.

I said, "Maybe for killin' some Crackers." I smiled and walked towards the direction of my Aunt's parked car.

"Hey Auntie," I said as she gave me a hug. My Grandmother had fallen asleep in the front passenger's seat. She looked old to me for the first time in my life.

"Long drive," my Aunt said as she walked over to the driver's side, and I got in the back seat. The drive back was uneventful. My Grandmother slept, while my Aunt and I talked lightly about the changes in the city, and the escalating violence between the Black and Hispanic gangs. I noticed she carefully avoided talking about what happened to my cousin, Damion.

"Where's he buried?" I asked finally.

"Who?" she asked in a quiet voice.

"Janet, tell heem da truth," my Grandmother said as she stirred from her nap.

My Aunt put both hands on the wheel, glanced over at my Grandmother with an irritated look and said. "It wasn't an accident. The damn Mexicans killed Damion. They ran him off the road on Greenleaf Blvd, he crashed into a tree."

I could feel the heat rising from my stomach all the way to the top of my head. I dug my finger nails into my palms and asked, "Whose idea was it to lie to me?"

"Mine," my Grandmother said. "If we told you da truth, what you do huh? Fight the Mexicons in dere, no? I weel not bury two of my Grandchildren! I weel not!" She began to cry.

Seeing my Grandmother cry was like somebody squeezing my soul. "It's okay Memom." I said as I reached forward to take her hand.

When her tears stopped, she rubbed my hand absently and said, "You should have babies with Simone!"

"Huh?" I asked as she turned to face me.

"Simone is a good Creole Garl. A good *Creole* garl, eh?"

"Where's this coming from?" I asked my Aunt.

With a crooked smile, she said,"Leave me out of it!"

My Grandmother continued, "We do not have enough babies in dis family. An' most of dem' are mixed. The Dumas blood must remain pure," she said matter of factly. Everybody knew that when Elizabeth Dumas talked about blood and Creole heritage, her passion was unmatched, and to let her have her say.

"Okay Memom. How many babies from me and Simone?" I asked holding my stomach.

With a brisk nod of her head, she said, "Seven!" I laughed out loud and my Aunt even joined in.

"Seven, Memom?" I asked still giggling, with watering eyes.

"Oui!" she said, now smiling herself. "You are strong, you can do it!" My Grandmother smiled even wider, but serious as hell.

We switched from the 5 freeway to the 91 interchange and I started to feel the pangs of familiarity pulling at my mind. After five years, I was home. When we got off on the Rosecrans exit my Aunt asked if I wanted to go and check in with my Parole Officer. I declined, and asked to be taken home. I had other things on my mind. Killing Christopher Daniels and the money.

We had buried the money in one of my Grandfather's old suitcases, in the vacant lot next door to my Grand Parents house. Damion put the combination lock to his bike on our chain link fence. If you took ten big steps over into the vacant lot, that's where the money was buried. A sort of ghetto treasure map. As we turned on Piru Street and turned into the driveway to my Grand Parents home, my heart fell to the floor. The vacant lot was no longer a vacant lot. It was now, Story Land Day Care. And I wanted to throw up.

When I got inside my Grandmother's house the scene was 100%, uncut fake. All of my Aunt's, Uncle's, and other various relatives were there to greet me and welcome me home. These were the same people that called me stupid and campaigned against me, to have my Grandmother throw me out of her home. Now, here they were, with their fake smiles and even faker hugs. The truth is, outside of my Grandmother, only Aunt Janet and Aunt Paulette wrote to me.

Yeah, different females popped in and out of my life, but nobody was consistent. I hugged and waved my way through the crowd until I found my Aunt Paulette. Damion's death was still very much present on her face, and in the slackness of her thin body. "Sava Tante Paulette. (Hey Auntie Paulette)" I said in French because we were indoors.

"Sava Neveu (hey Nephew)."

"J'ai besoin de parler avec vous (I need to talk to you)." I made her eyes meet mine. My Aunt was a devout Catholic, and had never, that I could remember, ever done or said anything negative.

"Quand voulez-vous parler? (When do you want to talk?)"

"Demain (tomorrow)," I said as I kissed her cold cheeks.

In the kitchen the table and counters were covered with all of my favorite foods. Jambalaya, Chicken Soleil, Etoufee, Dirty Rice, Gumbo, and my number one favorite, Chili cheese fries covered in pastrami meat from Louis Burgers on Rosecrans. My Grandmother knew me well. I piled a plate full of food, then went to my room and closed the door.

After doing half a decade in prison I learned to dislike crowds. I finished most of my food and was watching Sports Center when someone began to knock on my door. "Entrée Vous (come in),"I said, then sat up on the edge of my bed. My Grandmother came in smiling and holding the telephone.

"C'est Simone (It's Simone)," she said in a whisper, then picked up my plate and left as quiet as she came.

"Hello."

"Hello to you, Mr. Freedom."

"Hey Ma. What's up? How'd you know I was home?" It was Simone. I was surprised to hear her voice.

"I have my ways."

"Yeah, that Voo Doo yo Gram's be doing."

"How's it feel, you know, to be out?"

"Empty."

"Why?"

"Cause my better half ain't free yet,"

"Kevon don't make me start crying. I got a reputation to uphold," she whispered.

"I do feel empty Simone. I got holes in my life that only you can fill."

"So, what are you saying?" she asked between sniffles.

I took a deep breath, let the words form in my mind, then I warmed them in my heart, "I love you," I said. "I've loved you since we were kids. When you got shot I thought you were dead, and in wanted to die too. You Simone Belleu live in all the rooms in my heart."

"Je t'adore aussi" (I love you too), she said between soft sobs.

"Wipe your face," I said.

"Shut up! You don't know me like that," I could hear her blowing her nose.

"Un huh, and I got pictures of you naked," I said playfully.

"I was like four years old," she said with a giggle.

"So, a back shot is a back shot," I said.

She laughed, then said, "I've been waiting to hear those words from you since Jr. High."

"You didn't even speak English in Jr. High," I reminded her, then told her what my Grandmother said.

"Damn. Seven!" she gasped.

"Yep, want me to tell her you said no?" I teased.

"No, we can have *seventeen* if that's what you want."

"So, you wanna' do the grown up with me?"

"I've been saving myself for you, stupid ass."

"You're still a virgin?"

"Duhhh…"

"How much more time you got left?"

"Ten months."

"I'll be there to get you, oh and I'm diggin' up the money if that's okay with you."

"Go ahead."

"You sure?"

"Go ahead. I never cared about the money."

"Je t'adore."

"I love you, too."

Click.I sat holding the cordless phone for a while and thinking about Simone, pumping myself up to do what needed to be done. After I took a long hot shower I walked out on the porch and stared up and down the small street that I grew up on.

I paid particular attention to the new day care center next door. It said, "Coming Soon" which meant it wasn't officially open yet. That made me feel a little better.

"Uncle Chris!" I called as he made his way up the driveway.

"What's up nephew?"

"Nuttin', I need a favor, some info."

"I was in Florida when Damion died," he said quickly, assuming I didn't know the truth.

"I already know what happened," I said, instantly feeling sad again.

"What then?"

"I need to set a fire. But make it look like an accident," I confessed as his eyes got wide and then very small.

"What kind of fire?"

"A house fire."

"Why? Never mind. Here's what you do…" After I got the details on how to start a gas fire I went back to my room and called my son's mother.

"Hello?"

"Can I speak to Pascal?"

"Kelis's not here."

"I don't want Kelis, put my son on the phone!"

"Oh my God! Kevon?"

"Who's this?"

"It's me, Pinky."

"Pinky put Pascal on the phone Please."

"Hold on, Pascal!" she screamed. I walked back out to the front porch on nervous legs and waited to talk to my six year old son for the first time in three and a half years.

"Hello," he said in a happy little voice, and I almost melted.

"Hello, can I speak to Pascal Dumas?"

"I *am* Pascal Dumas, who are you?"

"I'm Kevon Dumas"

"My Daddy's name is Kevon Dumas. But he's in the bad place."

"No he's not!"

"Yeah, huh."

"I'm your Daddy and I'm not in jail anymore."

Silence… I guess he had to process all the information first, because he came back on the line and carefully said, "Daddy?" in a small, uncertain voice. My heart froze as my worst fears came to life. He doesn't know me.

"Hello?"

"If you're my Daddy, what's my birthday then?"

"Your birthday is June 25, 1994, you were born at Saint Francis Hospital, you have a birthmark on your tummy, and you hate the Ninja Turtles."

He laughed and said," Daddy!" His happy little voice was back again, this time he was sure.

We talked happily for the next hour and I told him that I'd be over there to get him later. When I got off the phone I felt good, warm in places that used to be ice cold.

When I opened my eyes, Mrs. Patterson was walking up the driveway. In an exaggerated voice, she said, "Oh my God! Little Kevon?"

"Hey Mrs. P," I said looking at how nicely her stretch pants and t-shirt clung to her hips and breasts.

"I see you finally home huh?" she said walking up the porch stairs and stopping in front of me.

"Yeah, I'm home," I said cooly, setting the cordless down on the porch rail.

"Damn, you look different," she said looking me up and down.

"Yeah, how so?"Not believing I was flirting with my old babysitter.

"Shit, you look good," she said licking her lips "Was you working out and stuff?" She squeezing my arms and patting my chest.

"Yeah, I hit the weights."

"I could tell."

"Where Danny at?" I asked, changing the subject and asking about her husband.

"He back in the County for drunk driving, can I have a hug?"

"Yeah," I said and opened my arms. When we embraced, my dick pushed right into her crotch area.

"Oh-oh, somebody just woke up," she said in a sexy, but playful voice.

"Yep," I said, then said fuck it and palmed her big ass.

"Ohh, Kevon, you bad …."

"I'm also grown," I said as she pressed her middle into my hard on.

"What yo Grandmother gone say?"

"I don't know, probably, 'use a condom'." Then I laughed at my own joke.

"I always wanted to give you some, every since you was little."

"For real?"

"Umm hmmm."

I slipped my hand between us and started to rub her pussy through her stretch pants. "Damn this mothafucka fat."

"You like that?"

"Hell yeah," I said continuing to rub softly.

"Come over my house tonight, or do you got a little girlfriend?"

"I don't do girlfriends."

"Good. Imma cook you dinner then eat your young ass for dessert."

"Promises, promises…."

"Hello Barbara." My Grandmother said coming around the side of the house.

"Oh hey, Mrs. Dumas." She said nervously pulling out of our embrace and straightening her clothes.

"Can I 'elp you?"

"Oh, no. I just came to see if Chris could change my tire; it has a nail in it."

"Christopher is no' here."

"Okay," she said making her way down the stairs. "See you later Kevon."

"Bye Mrs. P," I said avoiding my Grandmother's glare and trying hard not to laugh. When she passed me on her way into the house, she intentionally bumped into me. I burst into laughter. "What Memom?" I asked when she stopped in the doorway.

"Just like Charles," she said, smiling but trying to fight it. I raised my eyebrows and hunched my shoulders in mock confusion. She shook her little head and went into the house. I laughed some more.

When I turned around to look back after Mrs. Patterson, a burgundy '96 Impala was flying down my block. A 'P' sign was banged out the passenger's side window. I threw up a 'P' back to the car as it pulled to the corner of Matthisen. Like I expected, the car busted a U-turn, then came back. When it pulled in front of my Grandmother's house, I saw the occupants and immediately started smiling. It was Muscles from the Trees and my homie Lil Man.

"Blooood," Muscles said as he exited the passenger's side. Lil Man just smiled ear to ear as they came on the porch.

"Damn nigga whatchu been eating?" Lil Man asked, hugging me roughly.

"Hella State food."

"Damn blood, what you pull like six?"

"Five and a half."

"Where was you at? Didn't you go to Y.A.?"

"Yeah, but I got kicked out. I finished the rest of my time in Folsom."

"Ain't that where Art' got sliced up?" Muscles asked knowingly?

"Yep, I was there. Blood, took off first."

"He told us that, but we thought he was lying."

"Nahh, Blood is the real deal. Did he ever get out?" I asked curiously.

"Yep, Blood live in San Bernardino."

"Hey blood, can I ask you something?" Muscles asked in a safe voice.

"What nigga? Did I get hooked up?" I asked, enjoying the look on his face.

"Nahh, blood. P-fonk, no kutts."

"I was just wondering blood."

"Where y'all on y'all way to anyway?"

"We finna go fuck with some bitches in the New Jacks"

"In the Mobb?"

"Yep, wanna roll?"

"Nope, but y'all can drop me off at the swap meet though."

"C'mon dog."

"Aiight, let me change my clothes."

It seemed like we got to the Compton Fashion Center in two minutes because Lil Man drove like damn NASCAR driver. When they dropped me off Lil Man gave me $250.00 and a bag of rocks. I gave the rocks back and took the .32 pistol he had under his seat instead.

"If you need a ride call me, Rowdy, we'll be across the street."

"Aiight blood, su whoop!"

"Su, whoop!"

Chapter Seventeen

Compton California 2000

The swapmeet looked just like I remembered. Bright, loud, and full of people. It wasn't really in anybody's hood "officially", but the Santana's and the Luedars Parks both claimed it. First I just walked around all the booths that sold fake and refurbished merchandise. Then I made my way to one of the many hat vendors.

"Can I help you?" The cute Mexican girl said as she wrapped up a sale with a previous customer.

"Yeah let me see that blue 76ers hat."

"The one with the "P" on it?"

"Yeah!"

I looked at it and liked it instantly. It was a dark blue with the red "P".

"You got this in a 6 7/8?"

"Let me see," she said looking through her inventory. When she turned around, I noticed she had a nice ass.

"Nice butt," I said as she climbed up on the ladder.

"Gracias," she said with a smile then came down empty handed.

"Sorry I don't have your size," she said seeming genuinely disappointed.

"It's cool ma, let me get that Phillies hat with the "P"on it then."

She rung up my purchase then wrote her name and phone number on my receipt. I said I'd call her then headed out of the swapmeet to call Lil Man. On my way out I bumped into two of my big homies, Toochie and Chilly Dubb. Chilly Dubb was getting a gold chain repaired at a jewelry booth.

"Rowdy, wus brackin blood? I heard you was home" Toochie said with a heavy lisp.

"What's up wit y'all, old niggas?"

"I ain't old nigga, I turn 25 every year," Chilly Dubb said holding his big belly.

"Damn blood, you still fat," I joked as he grabbed me in a bear hug.

"Whatchu doing up here by yo'self?" Toochie asked in a serious voice.

"I'm heated dog, don't trip," I told him, raising my shirt and showing him the tucked .32.

"Nigga, ain't you on parole?"

"I'd rather be caught wit' it, than caught without it." I said ending the conversation.

"Yeah blood these messkins ain't playing fair,"Chilly Dubb said showing me his .38.

That's when they explained to me the who, what, and why, of our war with the Tortilla Flats. When they told me the body count so far, I felt weak.

"Damn blood, 30 niggas?"

"Yep, most of'em youngsters, 15-16."

"Damn…"

"What's up with the crabs though?"

"The Crips?" Toochie asked surprised.

"The Crip/Blood war is pretty much over in Compton. I mean, there's petty little shit going on, but the on-sight beefs are over blood. Some Crips live in the hood."

"What?" I said not believing the shit I was hearing.

"It's true blood,"Chilly Dubb added.

I stood there feeling dumb.

"$19.75," the Chinese man said handing Chilly Dubb the gold chain, then we headed for parking lot.

"Blood, you still got this car?" I asked as we approached Toochie's gold and green '63 Impala on 14" Dayton's.

"Nigga, this a classic," he said lighting a cigarette then hittin the switches. I laughed and asked them to drop me off at my Grandmother's house.

"Dat crazy girl call twinty times," my Grandmother told me as I walked up the porch stairs.

"Sorry, Memom," I told her as she worked in her rose garden on the side of the house.

"Jus' call her back," she said then I kissed her forehead and went to look for the phone. Pascal picked up on the first ring.

"Hello."

"It's me, daddy."

I was happy he knew my voice. "Me who? What's your name?"

"Pascal Cherron Dumas."

"Are you sure?"

"Dad…"

"Okay, was up kiddo?"

"Nothing, when are you coming over here?"

"In a few hours."

"How many is a few hours?"

"Hello?"Kelis said as her voice came on the line.

"Put my son back on the phone."

"Are you coming to see us?"

"Us?" I snorted, then laughed out loud. "No, I'm coming to pick my son up so pack him a bag."

"He has school tomorrow."

"Then I'll take him to school in the morning."

"You can take him on Friday."

"Whatever, where do you live?"

After I got off the phone I felt the old familiar hate that I had for her start to warm up again. When my uncle got off work I borrowed his car and made my way to 108th and Main, to my babymoma's house.

When I pulled on front of the raggedy duplex I heard loud music blasting out through the black screen door.There was a little boy of about 6 or 7 and a little girl about 3 or 4 playing in the small front yard. The Nerf football they were playing with rolled to the gate, the little boy chased it and when he looked up, I saw me. The way I looked on my baby pictures.

He dropped the ball and we just looked at each other. Then he rubbed a dirty hand across his forehead and said, "Daddy?" Before I could stop them, the tears had already started to run free. I didn't even bother opening the gate; I just reached over it and grabbed my son. He hugged me tightly around my neck and we just stood like that for what seemed like hours.

"You need a haircut"I said wiping my eyes and looking at him closely.

"I know," he said, then started to touch my face, as if to make sure I was real.

"Are you going back to jail?" he asked in a strong voice.

"No, never."

"Promise?"

"Promise," then we hugged some more and I noticed Kelis standing in the doorway. She looked, I stared, then the little girl called her "Mommy," and I jerked out of my trance.

"Are you coming in?"

"For what? I have the reason I came over here." I said, then told my son to go and get his backpack.

"You still hate me huh?" She said as she approached the gate.

"Hate you? Nahh, I don't even know you." I said hoping I hurt her feelings.

"What happened to your eye?"I asked with a giggle, pointing at the fresh black eye she had.

"He got drunk and ...."

Good! I thought, bitch you got what you deserved. Instead I said, "Bad shit happens to bad people."Then opened the gate so my son could get out.

"You can't hate me forever." She said as my son and I walked to my Uncle's Camry.

Feeling mad all over again, I said, "Imma try."Then got in the car and left.

I stayed up until about 9 p.m. playing with my son. When it was time for bed, I told him the story of our family history and my Grandparents horrible boat ride to the U.S. It was a story my Grandfather used to tell me and Damion as children, and one of my favorites. When my son was in a deep sleep Icrept out of the room and ran into my Grandmother in the hallway.

"Vous vous souvenez l'histoire? (You remember the story?)."

"Oui, toute ma vie (yes, all my life)."

"Bon garcon (good boy)," she said, then went to bed.

At 10:00 p.m. when I was sure everybody was asleep, I put my shoes on and walked down to the house on the corner. She opened the door on the second knock and smiled like a fairy.

"I thought you changed your mind."

"Nahh, I had business," I said as she took my hand and lead me to the beige sofa.

"You hungry?"

"What's on the menu?"

"Me."

"Hell yeah..." When she took her gown off she was wearing a pink thong and nothing else. I grabbed one of her big brown titties and stuffed the hard nipple in my mouth.

"Oooh," she said as I held her heavy breasts with both hands and pushed them together.

"Bite my nipples," she said as she tugged at my basketball shorts and massaged my hard on. "I knew you had a big dick." She said as she took my hand and led me to her bedroom,

Two hours later, she was snoring lightly.

I slid quietly from under her and went to wash up in her bathroom. When I came back I said, "Mrs. P." in a quiet voice but she was really asleep, so I went and got the comforter off of her bed and covered her up. I locked her door from the inside and stepped out into the cool summer air. Damn, Mrs. P. is a freak I thought to myself as I made the short walk back home.

When I let myself back in, everybody was still asleep. Good. I put on some of my old clothes, then headed to the garage to get some supplies. After I grabbed all my tools and gloves, I climbed the small wrought iron gate in front of StoryLand Daycare and went around the back. Yes, I felt bad as I broke the small window and realized what the hell I was doing. But, I just kept telling myself, it had to be done. Once I rigged a few of the electrical outlets like my Uncle instructed, I took out the spray bottle of gasoline and my lighter and started to light a series of little fires throughout the daycare center. When I got to the front window in the living-room, the place I assumed the money was buried, I poured the remainder of the gas on the floor and lit it.

The fire caught fast, too fast and I screamed as my Reebok classics caught on fire. I kicked them off and ran towards the rear exit bare footed. After I gathered all my supplies, I went out of the window again feeling bad about destroying the innocent building.

When I sneaked back into my room I checked on my son, dumped my clothes in a bucket ofbleach, and took a quick shower.

My Grandmother started beating on the door and screaming, "Il y a feu! Il y a feu!(There's a fire, there's a fire!)." When I came out of the bathroom she was holding my son. She quickly passed me his sleeping body, then headed out of the front door and into the yard.

When we made it out onto the lawn, it was like a scene out of the movies. All the neighbors on both sides of the street were on their lawns in their pajamas and watching the spectacular fire burn the new daycare center to the ground. I stood next to my Grandmother, holding my son and feeling horrible as the Compton Fire Dept arrived twenty minutes too late. My Uncle came out in his robe and looked at me in a disgusted way. I held his gaze and rubbed my son's back as the flames caused the roof to cave in. What I didn't see was the look my Grandmother was giving me.

"You fire dis school for da babies?" She asked in an accusing but calm tone.

'Oui Madame (yes ma'am)," I said, refusing to lie to the woman that raised me.

"Di money?" she asked knowingly.

"Oui," I confessed. She grabbed my chin and turned my face towards hers. Even at twenty three I still felt like a child under her gaze.

"Give back when you can," was all she said. She adjusted her flannel house coat and took my son inside, out of the cold. I stood on the lawn a little while longer, then turned to go inside, still telling myself that it had to be done.

The a.m. news said an electrical fire destroyed the daycare center and that the damage was so severe, it was immediately condemned. I sat and ate breakfast nervously with my son and Grandmother, feeling anxious about part two of my mission.

"Il a l'ecole au jour dui? (Does he have school today?)"

"Non, il a conge (no he has the day off)," I told my Grandmother as I decided to keep my son out of school.

"What are you saying dad?" My son asked me through a mouthful of cheesy scrambled eggs.

"It's French," I told him in English. My Grandmother looked at me like I'd lost my damn mind.

"Oh," he said, then bit into a piece of toast.

My Grandmother put on her walking shoes then said, "Allez-y (c'mon)," to my son as she prepared for her morning walk around the neighborhood.

"Today you learn French!" she told him, then kissed the top of his head as they went out the door. I stood on the porch and watched as they disappeared around the corner talking happily.

"Hey Tyson," Mrs. P. said as she pulled up in her yellow school bus.

"Tyson?" I asked confused.

"Yeah, you knocked my ass out last night," she said with a giggle.

"Best jab in the business!" I said feeling myself a little too much. "Round two tonight?" I asked feeling my dick get hard at the thought.

"No, I can't. Danny's sister is coming over tonight.

"Too bad," I said showing her my dick.

"Damn boy you like a robot, ever do it on a school bus?" she asked smiling.

"Nope."

"Maybe tonight," she said laughing, then pulled off with a wave and air kiss. I blew her a kiss back then turned my attention to the ruined daycare center. Only the rear of the frame remained intact. Everything else was gone. Now all I had to do was dig up the three stairs of the porch and I'd have the money. Finally, I thought the Feds would be watching, but if they let me burn down a building, I figured they couldn't be watching that closely.

As the day rolled on, my son continued his French lesson with his Great Grandmother. I sat and waited for the sun to go down. When it did, I fed and showered my son, then let him call his mother before he went to bed. He told her about how much fun he was having and about how much he loved his Great Gram'. This obviously got on her nerves because when she asked to talk to me her attitude was stiff. I hung up. I had too much to do and didn't have time to play on the phone. When my son was safely tucked into bed I sat and watched the ten o'clock news while my Grandmother read her beat-up old bible and sipped her tea.

"We're moving when I get that money," I told my Grandmother in an adult voice.

"Oui, ou? (Yeah where?)"

"To the nice side of the city."

"D'accord (ok)."

"I'm serious, Memom"

"Je sais (I know)."

And that was the end of our first adult conversation.

At 12:30 that night, my shovel hit my Grandfather's suitcase; I smiled as I pulled it out of the ground. I dragged the money laden suitcase into my Grandmother's garage and sat on the side of my Uncles Camry staring at the piles of money in a daze.

"Combien? (How much?)" My Grandmother asked, I jumped at the sound of her voice and hit my head on a bucket of paint that was hanging in the corner.

"Enough to make things easier," I said rubbing the knot that was forming on the back of my head.

"Attention (be careful)," she warned, then kissed the top of my head and went back in the house. Things were about to change. Quickly. I had five years and four months to come up with the perfect plan. Now, I had the means to put it into action.

Chapter Eighteen

Westchester California 2002

"Kevon, wake up! Keevonnn…" I opened my eyes not remembering exactly where I was, then Fifi started licking my face and I heard Simone's voice.

"Get off me fat ass!" I joked in a sleepy voice.

"I'm not fat, asshole!" She said as she continued to lay on my back.

"I love this tattoo," she said as she traced her finger tips across the ink on my back.

"What time is it?"

"You don't wanna know."

"For real, Simone."

"Four thirty."

"What!" I screamed trying to sit up too fast.

"Ow ow shit!" I yelled as pain shot through my arm and shoulder.

"Be careful," she said laughing.

"Ha ha," I mocked. "I have a joke of my own. What do you call the Creole girl that needs to take her ass to work?"

No answer.

"Well?"

No answer.

"Puppy you gotta go open up the shop and check on things."

"I'm not leaving you!"

"I'm fine."

"Kevon..."

"I'm not asking Simone," I said firmly.

"You're not my father!"

"Not yet…"

"I hate you!" she said getting up and heading for the bedroom, but not before throwing a pillow at my head. "You need Jesus," I said laughing as the phone began to ring.

"Hello?"

"Mr. Dumas, it'sparole agent Smith. I got your message and I'll be out to see you at your home in about an hour."

"Okay, I'll be here."

"Good bye."

Click.

"I'm only opening the shop for a few hours," Simone said as she grabbed her purse and keys.

"Yeah, yeah," I said pulling her into my arms and palming her booty.

"I love you." I whispered

"I know but I'm scared…"

"Of what?"

"What you're gonna do."

"I have a plan ma."

"Your last plan got me ten years and you eight"

"HA! fucking ha!"

I kissed her eyes and the top of her head, then walked her to the elevator. We kissed again as she stepped on then the doors closed and she was gone. "She's pretty," a voice said behind me. When I turned around, my neighbor was standing in her doorway, drinking a bottle of water.

"Girlfriend?"

"Nahh, we're close though."

"So, are we still going out?"

"Can't, Ihad an accident," I said pointing to my bandages.

"Does your cock still work?" she asked taking a long swig from her water bottle.

"Yeah, he's fine"

"Come over around seven, we'll play doctor."

"I'll be there. Are you a doctor or a naughty nurse?" I asked enjoying the game.

"Me? I'm a brain surgeon," she said, then stuck more than half of the water bottle into her mouth.

"Daaamn!" I said pleasantly surprised at her talent.

"See you in a few," she said, then closed the door. When I walked passed her door I could've sworn I heard two pairs of giggles, but maybe it was the pills. While I sat patiently waiting for my dick-head parole officer to come by I decided to make the rest of my phone calls, and something to eat. When I dialed Boomer's cell phone number he answered on the first ring cautiously, with the password.

"Boy and man," he said with his heavy Cambodian accent.

"Koi and dragon," I responded giving him the other half of the password.

"Wah sup, neega?" he said happily at the sound of my voice. I laughed out loud because even though Boomer was full blooded Cambodian, he swore he was Black. Most of his homies from the 'Tiny Rascals Gang' in Long Beach were the same way.

"What's up, you fried rice eating mothafucka?"

"Fuck you, neega. I eat dog and noodles," he said and I laughed even harder.

"I need some hammers." I said in my business tone.

"I jus' gay you a shipment."

"I know. I need some heavy shit, I got shot up."

"What, The Crips?"

"Naw the Mexicans, T-Flats I think."

"Ok, come to the fish sto,' ten o'clock. Bring Samoan too," he said laughing.

"You mean *Simone* fool," I said laughing. "Simone is bigger than your smurf ass. She'll hurt you."

"I know," he said laughing, then we hung up.

I took a long breath as I sat down and ate my grilled cheese sandwiches, then I picked up the phone to call my son.

"Daddy?" he answered in a scared voice. At that second I knew his stupid ass moma had told him what happened. "Yeah kid what's up?"

"My moma said somebody shot you."

"Yeah, they did. I'm ok though."

"Did you shoot them back?"

"No, I called the police," I lied.

"Did they catch'em?"

"Nahh, not yet. You know how the police are."

"Yeah. I hate the police."

"You know I can't make it to Parent-Teacher night." I said feeling like shit.

"I know, it's ok Dad."

"And you know you can't talk about what happened. Family business, remember?"

"I know."

"I love you boy, you know that?"

"I love you too. My moma said I gotta go."

"Okay, call me before you go to bed."

"Ok, bye Dad."

"Bye kiddo." When I hung up, I felt even worse. I just sat there playing with the crust of my toast. When the doorbell rang, Fiona bolted out of the bedroom and began to bark frantically.

I said, "Hold on," and took her down the hallway to my bedroom. I grabbed a burgundy Stanford University T-shirt to cover my bandages, then opened the door.

"Come in."

“Where’s that dog?” He looked around nervously and fingered his holster.

“Don’t do that.” I said a little too sharply, but I didn’t care. Nobody made threats in my house.

“Is that mutt secured?” he asked in a sarcastic tone.

I just gritted my teeth and nodded.

Pointing at the burgundy T-shirt, he said,“I see you’re flying your colors today huh?”

“I see you’re flying yours too,” I said pointing at the pink and yellow tie he was wearing. Thenwatched as he turned bright red.

“I also see the haircut business is doing well,” he said looking around the apartment.

“Yep.” I said dryly.

“Are you sure it’s just haircuts you’re selling?” he asked, picking up the bottle of oxycontin.

“Are you sure it’s not?” I asked in the smartest tone I could muster.

“No, but I only have you on my caseload for six more months so I could care less if you cut hair or kilos of cocaine,” he smiled.

“You can search my condo if you want, but be careful when you open the bedroom doorbecause there’s a $1,500 trained attack dog that you called a mutt and I think she heard you” I smiled.

“No, we’re done here.”

“It’s been a pleasure,” I said then walked him to the door, not bothering to walk him to the elevator. Six months and I’d really be free.

After I put the dishes in the dishwasher I grabbed Fifi’s chewed up pink Frisbee and leash and decided to take her for a walk and some exercise at Westchester Park. “Fiona” I screamed as I made my way down the hallway. She responded immediately by barking on the other side of the door.

"Nous allons dehors! (We're going out)," I told her. "Assiez-vous! (Sit!)," I said, then opened the door. Like I expected she was sitting like she was trained. I had the Frisbee and leash hidden behind my back, and when I showed her, she jumped on top of me knocking me back. "You're hard headed, I said sit," I said through my laughter then clipped the leash to her harness and walked her out.

When we exited the elevator in the garage, a cute Black girl was headed in our direction. She stopped dead in her tracks when she saw the huge pit-bull blocking her path.

"Does he bite?" she asked in a preppy valley-girl tone.

"Oui, elle mordre," I said in French deciding to have some fun.

She cocked her head and said, "Parlez-vous Francais (do you speak French?)," with a bad accent.

"Oui, et vous? (yes, do you?)"

"Oui, une petite peu (Yes a little bit)."

Then I dropped the leash. "Assiez-vous," I told Fifi. She sat, then I told the girl, "Allez! (Go ahead)"

She took a few steps towards Fifi then as she got close to the elevator I said, "Viens! (Come here!)" The girl screamed but Fifi looked at her annoyed and walked by her like she wasn't even there.

"That was mean," the girl said with a nervous smile.

"Oui (yep)." I said, then fished in my Burberry pajamas for a doggie treat to give to Fifi. We stared at each other until the elevator doors closed, then Fiona and I made the short walk to the park.

I ran, walked, and exercised Fiona for an hour, then bought us both a bottle of water from the ice cream truck. Then, we headed home. When I got in I called KD about the meeting with Boomer.

I took a quick shower making sure to cut my finger nails and shave. The clock read 6:40 as I sprayed Curve cologne in all the right places, then lotioned up and headed out. All I was wearing was some old Polo sweats and a tank top so she would have easy access to whatever she wanted.

When I knocked on the door, nobody answered. Then when I was about to walk away she opened it and said, "You're early" with a devious little smile. She was wearing a wife beater and some red and white boy shorts I noticed as I stepped into her apartment. It was pleasantly furnished in beige and brown and had tasteful decorations. "Damn you smell good" she said as she hugged me, then pushed my back against the wall kinda aggressively.

"Kinda rough aren't you," I asked as she pulled her shirt over her head.

"You have no idea," she said, as the Black girl from the garage came outta the bathroom then pressed her lips against mine. She let her tongue explore the inside of my mouth while I squeezed and massaged her massive titties.

"Yeah, pinch my nipples," she said as she ripped my tank top open and started planting kisses on my chest. I moaned as she flicked her tongue over my nipples, then bit me. Not hard, but just enough to make my dick jump when she grabbed it.

We went at it like that until almost nine o'clock, then I got up on wobbly legs while the girls slept quietly on the couch.

My phone was ringing when I entered my apartment but I was too slow to catch it. The message was from KD. He said he'd be at my apartment in twenty minutes and that he had the tape.

Chapter Nineteen

Long Beach California 2002

As we rode on the 710 freeway on our way to Long Beach, I told KD about my adventure with my neighbors and the faggot–ass parole officer.

"Wait a minute, you took it out of the White girl's ass and stuck it in the Black girl's mouth?" he asked still not believing the shit I told him.

"On Piiiiru nigga, that shit was crazy!"

"Yeah, I'm definitely going over there to borrow some sugar when we get back" he said laughing. A few minutes later we exited on P.C.H. (Pacific Coast Highway) and pulled into Boomer's exotic fish store. Most of the front lights were off, but as we approached the glass doors a girl greeted us and opened the door.

"Hilo," the girl said with a heavy Cambodian accent as we passed her in the doorway. She was young, maybe sixteen at the most. The fact that she was dressed in a Catholic school girl's uniform didn't enhance her age. What *did* make her look older was the gun she picked up and started to clean.

"What's that?" KD whispered as we stood and watched the young girl reassemble the gun like a trained Navy S.E.A.L.

"Damn," I said as she clicked the black sub-machine gun back together in a bored fashion."Is that what I think it is," I asked as Boomer arrived from the back of the store.

"Where's Samoan?" He asked as he hugged me and KD.

"She's working fool," I said, then pointed to the girl and the big ass gun on the counter.

"Oh her? Das ma bitch!" He said pinching the girl's small booty. She smiled and shook her pony-tailed head.

"Boomer, how old is she?"

"Fiteen" he said smiling, then kissed the girl on the mouth.

"You nasty," I said, then followed him to the back of the store.

"Sup kay gee?" he said instantly annoying KD.

"Kay Dee, mothafucka, get it right!"

I laughed as we entered the back of the store. I stopped when Boomer clapped his hands and the lights came on. There were guns everywhere. Stacks of wooden crates, hanging neatly on all four walls, there were AK's, SK's and other large assault rifles in trashcans. There was also twenty-thirty milk crates filled with pistols and handguns. "You're sooo gay, you have the clapper?" I joked as KD walked off like a kid in a candy store.

"I no gay, ask yo sistah" Boomer said pulling up his blue khaki shorts.

"Fuck you!"

"No, I tol' you I no gay!" he laughed as his echo filled the small room.

"What's this I asked pulling a machine-gun off the wall?

"MP5," he said taking the gun from me and unfolding the stock. "Fifty percent plastic," he said handing it back to me.

"Damn it's light," I said testing the weight.

"Not with eighty bullets, be'lee me."

"I found what I want," KD said coming towards us with a big ass Kool-Aid smile on his face.

"That?" I asked, pointing at the Sub-Thompson machine he was carrying like a small child.

"What? I always wanted one of these," he said looking at the gun adoringly.

"Pizza shit!" Boomer spat, then walked over to a blue wooden crate and came back carrying two flat boxes the size of computer keyboards.

"Look this," he said, then opened the boxes. "Calico M-110 masheen gun. Shoot 100 bullets in thirty seconds. Clip on top, neva jam"

"Fuck that Star Trek shit! I'm old school nigga," KD said actually kissing the Tommy gun. I shook my head and laughed at the shit that made him happy.

"Gimme two Calico's, the Tommy gun, and a silencer for my Beretta."

"Better get Simone something," KD reminded me.

"And one of those Tech- 380's," I said wrapping up my order. "Oh wait, I need a phone too."

"Who I look like, AT&T mufucka?" Boomer asked.

"Naw, Samsung asshole, gimme a phone." We laughed, then walked to the front of the store with our purchases. The girl was still sitting at the counter, only now she had a plate of food in front of her that smelled good as hell.

"What's that?" I asked as we headed towards the door.

"'Member that puppy you gay me?" he said with a thin smile. Then it clicked.

"Sick bastard!" I said holding my stomach.

"Ugh," KD barked, then we loaded the stuff in the Tahoe and got back on the freeway.

"Cuzz really ate that puppy you gave him?"

"Probly' ain't no telling with Boomer." I said as we pulled into the Tam's on Central and Rosecrans Ave. I ordered my usual, Chili cheese fries covered with pastrami, and a large Orange Bang. I almost spit soda all over the dashboard when KD ordered Tuna on rye and bottled water, instead of his usual colossal Burger combo, with a side of chili.

"Don't say shit!" he said as he finished talking to the girl at the window. I just held up my Styrofoam cup and took a sip. We both knew Dana was the reason he was eating right. While we sat and waited for our food, two youngsters walked up to the Drive-thru window and started to flirt with the girl working there. The shorter kid tapped his friend on the shoulder, then pointed at KD's 24" rims.

"Looks like we're about to get carjacked," I joked as the taller kid pulled a blue rag out of his pocket and wrapped it around his knuckles.

"He is too cute," KD said in an amused voice as I handed him one of the fully loaded Calico's.

"What'd Boomer say? Thirty seconds."

"Yeah somethin' like that," KD said, then got out of the truck.

"What nigga?" he said quickly approaching the kid with the rag. I rolled down my window and calmly stuck the toy looking Calico out of the window.

"Come 'ere stupid!" I said to the other guy while KD smacked the tall kid upside the head.

"Sit down" I told my hostage as we watched KD continually smack his victim upside the head. "You see the Laker's game?" I asked, pointing the gun at his scared face.

"Yu- yeah."

"Say yes, nigga, I'm somebody's daddy."

"Yes."

"Kobe still hurt?"

"No, he played," he told me as KD took the blue rag and the gun out of the kid's waistband.

"Gimme this!" he said snatching the rag. Then he emptied the bullets out of the kid's .380 and handed them back to him with the empty gun.

"There's Mexicans out here killing us and you trippin' off some rims?" He said smacking the kid on the side of the head.

"Make'em pay for the food!" I yelled laughing. Then, told my hostage, "Go get my food before I shoot you in the booty!" he got up slowly and brought the bags back, then sat back on the cold ground of the parking lot. "Where you from?" I asked just making conversation.

"Nowhere," he stuttered

"Stop lyin' nigga, you a Crip? Don't lie."

"Yeah."

"Crip's suck," I told him.

"But your friend's a Crip," he said while I watched KD still slapping the kid with the gun in his hand. Now he was crying.

"You a Blood?" the kid asked me.

"Nahh, I'm just bandana racist." I turned the red beam on making shapes on the kid's dark forehead.

When KD got back in the truck he was agitated, which made me laugh even more. "If you shoot that gun at us when we pull off, I'll turn this mothafucka around. You got six shots, we got two hundred. Don't fuck around! Oh, I'm KD from Neighborhood Forty Crip if y'all wanna' come looking for me." After that, we pulled off. When we passed the kid sitting on the ground I leaned out the window, poured my soda on his head and rolled up the window. "You a asshole," KD said, still in a bad mood.

"Yeah," I agreed as we pulled up at the light on Rosecrans and Dwight. When we pulled up at the shop Simone's truck was still there along with two other cars and a Jeep Cherokee.

"Late night?" KD asked as we parked and got out of the Tahoe.

"Shit!"

"What?"

"I didn't get her nothing to eat."

"Yo ass is dead"

"Shit, I ain't scared of her!"

"Yes you are." he said sipping his water. When we got to the front door the smell of weed invaded my nostrils and my senses automatically told me there was something wrong. Everybody knows I don't allow smoking of any kind at my shop. KD caught on immediately and came back with the two Calicos.

"Let's go through the back," I said leading the way around the corner and into the alley. When I reached the back gate to my patio my dogs began to bark viciously until I opened the gate and they saw me and KD. I threw my food on the ground instantly losing my appetite, then opened the locks and entered the dark hallway.

"Lemme go first." KD said taking the lead spot then stopping when we heard soft music where the hallway ends.

"Kevon come here," was all he said. And my stomach dropped to my feet. KD only called me Kevon when something was very wrong.

When I came and stood next to him I couldn't believe what I was seeing. Simone was sitting with a client between her legs while two other girls sat on the floor passing a blunt back and forth. The guy sitting super close to Simone was whispering in her ear and had a hand on her exposed knee. I grimaced and watched as he continually tried to kiss her and she rejected his advances.

I could feel seething anger wash over my body as KD and I stepped from the dark hallway and into the light of the shop. Simone jumped first, kneeing the hood-rat in the head as she hurried to straighten her clothes. One of the girls screamed when KD pointed the Calico at her, then backed into a corner.

The guy, dressed in slacks and a dress shirt just sat on the couch with his hands in the air like he was being robbed. "Put your hands down you look stupid!" I told him as I picked up the blunt that was slowly burning a hole in my new carpet.

"Kevon I …" Simone started to say but I fixed her with a look and watched the words die in her mouth.

"Come 'ere!" I told the girl that was shaking in the corner. "Can you read?" I asked the scared woman.

"Yeah"

"Read that sign!"

"No smoking."

"What!"

"No smoking!"

"You burned a hole in my fuckin' carpet!" I said grabbing the girl hard by the jaws.

"I'll pay for…" Simone stated to say but I pointed the Calico at her and shook my head

"Y'all are trespassing!" I said in a calm voice, "I can shoot every one of you mothafucka's and not go to jail." I said and watched as KD left and came back with the Duke. I passed my gun to KD and took the pit-bull from him. "Sit!" I told him, then let him go and walked up to Mr. Wall Street Journal. "Who are you?" I asked making sure spit flew into his face.

"My name's Daniel," he said wiping sweat from his face. The dog barked angrily when he did.

"I wouldn't make any more moves like that if I was you," I said while the dog watched intently.

"You fuckin' her?" I asked pointing at Simone.

"No we just met," he stuttered nervously.

"Do you know who I am?"

"No are you her husband?" he asked and I instantly became more pissed off; remembering how not long ago, Simone and I sat on that same couch and decided to get married.

"Nahh, I'd never marry a bitch like that!" I said letting the words burn into Simone. She made a gurgling sound in her throat, then began to cry. Hard racking sobs.

"I'm sorry, please Kevon," but her words fell on deaf ears.

"Don't come to my shop again unless you want a hair cut or you wanna die" I told him. Then fixed his tie for him and said, "Bye!" He didn't move he just stared at the dog. "Go 'head" I said and watched as he took cautious steps towards the door. When he left I picked up the two girl's purses and emptied them on the table. They had $102.00 between the both of them. "This is for my carpet" I said, then handed them their purses. "Bye!" I said in a bored fashion, then walked down the dark hallway to my office. KD and the Duke followed.

When we got in my office I told KD to lock the door, then I sat at my desk and massaged my throbbing temples. Nobody said anything for a while. We just sat there. Me, KD, and the dog.

"You believe that shit?" I said finally able to speak.

"What?" KD asked ripping the crust off of his sandwich.

"Whatchu' mean what?" I asked not believing his attitude. "She had a nigga in the shop like it was cool, and bitches smoking pot!" I said not believing his calmness.

"So?" he said biting his sandwich, "Are you jealous?" I wanted to jump across the desk and strangle his ass. "You're kidding right?"

"Nope," he said dryly. "The way I see it, y'all aren't together so she can have a boy toy if she wants. Shit, you just had a fuckin' orgy earlier." He said landing back to back true punches.

"That's different." I said weakly.

"Why?"

"It just is..."

"Yeah I know," he said in his I got your ass voice, then handed the rest of his sandwich to the dog. Next he passed me the DVD and took the guns and the dog back outside. I loaded the disc into my computer and watched as the Mexicans shot my truck up and Simone saved my life. None of that mattered now. I copied the license plate number of the Caprice down and was interrupted by light knocking at the door.

"Come in!" I said knowing it was Simone.

"Can we talk?"

"Maybe, when you get back.

"Huh? From where?" she asked in a scared voice.

"You're going on vacation," I told her, not looking up from the scene on the computer.

"Where?"

"Anywhere away from me."

"I wasn't doing anything."

"Bye Simone."

"Can I at least explain my side?"

"You don't have a side."

"Please, Kevon."

"Don't come to the shop for three weeks."

"Fine!" She said through her tears. "You called me a bitch and pointed a gun at me!"

"My bad."

"Can this ever be fixed?" she asked through her sniffles.

"No." I said feeling more hurt than anything else. She left as KD came back into the office.

"Y'all straight?"

"Yep."

"What'd you do?"

"Nuthin."

"Man, you're stupid," he said, then took off after Simone as she cried her way down the hallway.

When he came back we watched the video together a few more times, then he took me home. I sat at home for the next two weeks felling lost and confused. I kept seeing ol boy touching Simone and hearing KD's words. The only thing that kept me from going crazy was the visits and phone calls from my son and Grandmother. I'd also been spending a lot of time with Misty, the girl I met at the bank. In the beginning of the fourth week I finally got the phone call I was waiting for.

"Hello?"

"Sup Puto?"

"You got my damn cars Jose?"

"Fuck you Tyrone!" he said and I laughed my ass off.

"Where you at?" I asked.

"Down stairs."

"I'm on my way down."

"When I got down stairs Ernie and his wife were standing at the elevator to greet me. After hugs and kisses were exchanged we walked over to my parking spots and all I could do was smile. The 2003 Cayenne Porsche SUV was a brownish color with matching Louis Vuitton interior. Even the wood on the dashboard had the Louis Vuitton logo engraved in it. When he hit the automatic start button on the key ring nothing happened.

"Turn it on," I said anxiously.

He mumbled "Baboso," under his breath then said, "It *is* on."

I noticed he was right when I put my hand on the hood."Damn it's quiet." I said smiling, then the four headrests came on and Mariachi music came blasting out of the two 15" MTX competition speakers.

He smiled and told me to get in. I felt stupid when I reached for the door handle and realized there weren't any."Ha ha mothafucka," I said as he pushed another button on the key and the doors popped open. After he explained all the features of the truck he handed me the fold-out key and we walked over to the Viper.

"Nice huh?" Ernie said sounding like a proud father. When I ran my hands over the roof he said, "That comes off." I just looked at him confused. He looked back at me irritated then opened the door. When he sat in the driver's seat he popped a few latches, then got out and removed the roof with a grunt. "Hard top convertible," he said.

I smiled and turned the key. What happened next scared the shit out of me. "Boom-boom-boom, boom boom," the speakers blared as 'Whoa' by Black Rob played on the sound system way too loud. “Damn nigga, what’s the volume on, ten?” I asked, looking for the button to lower it.

“Four,” he said laughing, handing me the small silver remote. When I turned the music down several off the parked cars’ alarms will still going off. The Viper was clean. Canary yellow with black interior. Lamborghini doors, 22” Niche Bella’s. It looked like a Hot Wheels toy.

“You did good Paisa,” I said giving him another hug.

“Yeah, yeah pay me!” he said walking over to his burgundy Aston Martin.

“I’ll come by tomorrow.” I said as he and Maria prepared to leave. “Is noon good?”

“Yeah, I’ll be there. No food stamps.” he said laughing. Then he pulled out of the garage and into traffic.

“Nice wheels,” Brandy said as she and Amber walked over to a Honda Accord.

“Thanks, I just got’em.”

“Really, are you a drug dealer?” Brandy asked.

I laughed, mostly because I had just gotten racial profiled by a *Black* girl. “Nahh, I sell insurance,” I said, hoping I sounded clever.

“You need to sell that!” Amber said, pointing at my crotch and giving Brandy a high five.

“Come by later, I’ll show you the premium package.” I said grabbing my dick.

“We’re going to get a bite, want us to bring you something back?”

“Where y’all going?”

“California Pizza Kitchen, then Jamba Juice.”

“Yeah, get me a slice of Spinach and Goat cheese pizza, and a Mango smoothie. Oh and some condoms.”

“Condoms? For what, we both swallow.” Amber said with another high five with Brandy, then they pulled out of the garage. I played with the cars for twenty more minutes then decided to go upstairs and finally return Simone's phone calls. She'd called at least a hundred times since I put her on vacation.

When I picked up the phone it rang immediately."Sup bruh? This yo boy Mess"

"Oh what's up fool where you at?"

"On my way down there."

"Fa real?"

"Yeah, I got some business in L.A."

"Come to the shop Saturday night. I'm having one of my Madden Tournaments."

"Yeah?"

"Nigga, you scared?"

"Naw, I'll be there but I gotta be back in Palo Alto by Sunday."

"Fa sho.'"

"Aiight, nigga."

One. I love Mess. He was one of the few dudes I stayed in contact with from the Bay Area. He had a good heart and a fucked up attitude, just like I liked my friends.

I decided I needed a shower before I called Simone. I needed to make sure I had my thoughts together and didn't speak out of anger or hurt. After my shower I half dried off, then called her cell phone expecting a confrontation. Instead, I got her voice mail. The message was simple: "Stop fuckin' calling me!" I hung up smiling a little, then called her apartment in Bellflower. The phone just rang. Now, I was juggling a mixture of anger and paranoia, then I thought 'fuck it' and hung up. I tried. I plopped down on the sofa and watched Sports Center, and decided to invite my Grandmother over for dinner. When Simone answered my Grandmother's phone, I knew they'd been talking about me.

"Hello?"

"Memom?"

"No, it's me."

"Oh, umm, what are you doing there?"

"I took Madame Dumas to the Spa."

"The what … why?"

"We both needed a break."

"Oh."

"You ready to talk?"

"No, but I'm ready to listen."

"Can I come over?"

"Nahh, I'm on my way over there."

"On the bike?"

"Nahh, I went to see Ernie."

"Oh, okay. How long?"

"Thirty minutes."

"I'll be here."

"Okay."

"Bye."

"Bye." I got dressed and put on my holster, then rushed out of the door and towards the elevator. Before I got on I ran smack into Amber and Brandy.

"Those are illegal,"Brandy said pointing at the half exposed gun that was hanging under my arm.

"What is?" I said quickly closing my Avirex jacket.

"Those fully automatic Beretta's," she said knowing exactly what I was carrying.

I took the food and drink she was holding out to me then asked, "What, are you a cop or something?"

"No, not really…" she said as we stood eye to eye.

"Well?" I asked.

"She works for the D.E.A, I'm the cop." Amber chimed in. My mouth hit the floor.

"You're shittin' me."

"Nope."

"Guess I'm busted huh?"

"Nahh, I think we can cut you a deal."

"Yeah? What kind of deal?" I asked as Brandy let the doors close and pushed the emergency stop button.

"You have the right to remain silent," she said grabbing my zipper and pulling out my dick. "Anything you say…" Slurp… By the time they let me off the elevator my knees were weak and my vision was blurred.

"You forgot the handcuffs." I told Amber as I exited the elevator.

"Next time," she said, then the doors closed.

I got in the Viper. It was thirty minutes laterwhen I pulled up in front of my Grandmother's house. Simone was sitting like a little girl on the porch, and I could tell that she'd been there since our first phone call.

"What happed to your neck?" she asked touching the spot where two pairs of lips had just been.

"I fell."

"On someone's mouth?"

"This isn't about me."

"It never is."

"You wanna argue? Cause we can."

"No."

"Good." The next hour was spent going over what happened and how I felt. In the end, it was cool. She agreed that she was out of line for what she did and I apologized for disrespecting her.

"So what now?"Simone asked.

"I have trust issues."

"Do you still love me?"

"Of course, even when I was mad."

"Enough to marry me?"

"Yeah, come here," I said as she fell into my arms. But even as she did, I knew things would never be the same between us.

"Cute car, did you get a truck too?"

"Cute? Vipers aren't cute! And yes, I got the new Porsche truck."

"How much?"

"Thirty."

"Oh." We spent a few more hours together just getting back use to each other.

My Grandmother took my pizza and fed us a full three course dinner. I told her that she'd be in charge of the shop for a while and that after the tournament on Saturday the killing would start.

"How much killing?"

"Til I feel satisfied."

"We should go to Mass."

"Church?"

"Yes."

"Okay, Sunday. Memom's gonna freak." I said thinking about my Grandmother's reaction to me showing up at Catholic Mass on Sunday.

I spent the rest of the day at the shop. I cleaned up, then cut a few heads and prepared the shop for the tournament. My Madden tournaments were the most popular in Southern California. The grand prize was no less than $3,500 depending on how many people showed up. Getting in was $250.00 per person and $500.00 per team. All of my closest associates and a few of my friends showed up.

KD was in charge of security and keeping niggas in line. In the two year history of the event, there had only been one incident where blood was drawn. Besides that, it was a friendly gathering in the spirit of competition.

Chapter Twenty

Westchester California 2002

On Saturday morning I woke up in a strange bed, and in a tangle of arms and legs. Amber, Brandy, and I had been going at it like wild rabbits ever since I'd gotten back from the shop. I stared at their sleepy little bodies while I stood and got dressed. I thought, 'I'm fucking two cops. Not one but two.' After I dressed and returned to the bathroom, I grabbed my keys and kissed Amber's nipple as it pushed through her tank top.

"You leaving already?" she asked as she stretched.

"Yeah I have a long day"

"What's on your schedule?"

"Mostly errands and the tournament."

"Boys and their toys."

"What's on *your* schedule?"

"I'm taking Brandy to the airport, she's due back in Miami on Monday."

"That sucks," I said as I looked at Brandy's sleeping form.

"I'm gonna miss her."

"Me too," she said, then turned on her side and got in the spoon position with the Black girl.

I let myself out, and made the small trip down the hallway to my apartment. After I fed Fifi and put her on the treadmill for a while I called all the players in the tournament and confirmed or denied if they would be there. Everybody except Black Zeek from Athen's Park and Jay-Ru from West Side Piru was supposed to show up. Shack from two P's was in jail in Pacoima so he probably wouldn't make it either.

After the phone calls were made, I grabbed my holster and hit the road to run my errands. First I had to stop at the Liquor Bank on Crenshaw to buy the case of Moet that I always served at the tournament. After that I stopped at Costco to buy the hot wings and fries. When I turned up the canned foods aisle I saw Misty and her little boy. "Hey Moma" I said as I crept up on her.

"Oh, hey what're you doing here?"

"Shopping, 'sup Jermaine?"

"You didn't call me last night."

"I got tied up."

"I bet," she said eyeing me suspiciously. "Can you come over tonight?"

"Yeah, I'll be late though. Miss me?"

"A little," she said giggling, then her phone rang. She looked at the caller I.D then stuffed the ringing device back into her huge Gucci purse.

"Answer it," I said not knowing what else to say.

"It's nobody," she said, but the color rising in her cheeks gave her away.

"Kevon can we go to the park again?" Jermaine asked breaking the awkward silence.

"Yep, me, you and, Fifi okay?"

"Cool!"

We spent a little more time together, then I paid for my groceries and headed for the bank on Crenshaw and Jefferson. When I took my withdrawal form to the empty teller, the lady looked at me, then asked, "Excuse me is this a mistake?"

"Huh?"

"The amount Sir, is it a mistake?"

I couldn't help it; I burst into laughter as I looked at the nervous Black girl holding my slip.

"Ava, is that your name?"

"Yes."

"Well Ava, no honey that's not a mistake. I have two accounts here. A savings account that has $186,000, and my Merchant account that has over $200,000 in it."

She laughed nervously, giving me her best smile then said, "I have to get my manager to approve a withdrawal of this size."

I hunched my shoulders and made a 'go ahead' motion with my hands. Five minutes later she returned with an older Hispanic man with a bad comb over. My transaction was immediately taken care of.

"How would you like your money?"

"In two dollar bills," I said, deciding to have some fun.

"Really? Because…"

"I'm just playing." I said cutting into the explanation she was about to give.

"Hundreds please," I said as she eyed me suspiciously and put three stacks of banded $10,000 pre-counted money on the counter.

"Are you a rapper?"

"Nahh, I rob banks."

"Really?"

"Yup."

"Oh." She said.

I put the money in my hoodie and laughed. I could still see the small 'O' she made with her mouth as I walked out of the bank.

When I pulled up to Ernie's shop it was 11:46 and I was early. I parked the Cayenne next to Ernie's Aston Martin and walked towards the side entrance.

"No go in dere!" One of Ernie's workers told me, looking up from the hood of an old Ford Explorer. As I turned to go through the side entrance, I saw why the old Mexican guy didn't want me to go through the side entrance. Ernie had Maria bent over the trunk of an all Shelby Mustang, and was ramming into her from behind. I watched as his fat dimply ass pushed forward into the round ass cheeks of his wife. When I backed out of the garage, the old guy said, "Tol' you" and smiled, exposing a mouthful of silver teeth.

"How long?" I asked.

"Tin minute" he said holding up seven greasy fingers. I laughed again, then walked around to the front and waited for them to finish. To my surprise, when I walked to the front they were both present and arguing as usual.

"Stupid Bitch!"

"Your Moma," they bickered as I walked in the shop. "Hey Travieso," Maria said in her cute voice as I walked over to her desk.

"Bad day?"

"No, he wants to fuck my ass, I say no," she said picking up her lipstick.

"Oh, uh can you tell'em I'm here?" Before I could prepare myself she screamed, "Kevin is here!" Then smiled and put a stick of gum into her bright red mouth.

"Come in!" Ernie said through the door. When I walked in his office I wanted to laugh. He was sitting under the fan and drinking Gatorade like he'd just played nine games of basketball.

"Sup fat boy? Tired?"

"Yeah, it's hot today."

"Here," I said throwing the stacks of money on his messy desk.

"Bout time, you're late." He said pointing at the Dodger's wall clock.

I ignored him then asked, "You get it?" he gave me an insulted look, then passed me a folded up piece of paper.

"That cost'd me a pair of dubs, with tires." He said irritated.

"You'll get over it," I said heading for the door.

"Be careful!" He said to my back as I walked out of his office. Maria was bent over, picking up spilled sunflower seeds when I entered the front lobby.

"Damn Maria, nice ass." I said as I admired the curves of her hips.

"You like it?" she said a little too sexy. "You should see it for real," she said, then smacked herself on the ass.

I smiled, then said, "I did, I saw y'all in the garage," and made my exit.

When I looked back she was standing in the doorway, smiling and pointing her finger at me. I'd never sleep with an associate's wife, but flirting was a natural thing. When I pulled up at the light on Exposition I took the piece of paper Ernie gave me out of my pocket and looked at it. I recognized the logo for the California Department of Motor Vehicles right away. The thing that shocked me the most was the address on the print out. 492 West Magnolia, Compton, California 90221. Damn, that's not even ten minutes from the shop.

I didn't know if this made the job easier or harder. When I finally made it to the shop the parking lot was full and my parking spot had a chrome and pink Harley Davidson Soft tail parked in it. I pulled around to the alley and entered the shop from the rear. As soon as I walked in the front I saw who the bike belonged to. Jackie.

"Hey Rowdy," she said as she looked up from the couch where she was getting her hair braided.

"Hey lady," I said, then told Dannie to help me unload the truck. After we did I opened my chair and cut a few heads, then went back to my office to do paper work.

For a while I just sat at my desk and looked at the pictures of my Grandmother. Me and KD posing in Folsom, Pascal's baby pictures, me and Simone in Jamaica, me and Damion at Knott's

Berry-Farm. All good memories, but they all had one thing in common; I wasn't smiling in any of the pictures. It kinda made me sad.

"Kevon some dude's here to see you," Simone said bursting into the office and snatching me out of my daze.

"Who is it?"

"Ness or Mess, or something like that."

"Send'em back here." When Mess came in my office he looked like money. Brown Parasuco jeans, white Saint Laurent dress shirt with a brown Prada sweater vest, beige and brown Hermes boat shoes. "Nigga you sure you're a dope dealer?" I asked as we hugged.

"Me? I don't sell dope. I help people get to sleep, or stay up. They're choice." He said in his usual quiet tone.

"You look like a cute ass Prada model," I said laughing.

"Don't hate, that's ugly," he said, then introduced the guy he had with him.

"This my nigga, Short. from Brookfield."

"Sup folks?"

"Sup."

"You early. The tournament ain't til seven."

"I know, I was in the area."

"What're you drivin', the Vette?"

"Nahh, my old school. It's nasty…."

"Lemme see," I said as we walked out of the office. When we got outside I saw he wasn't lying. The 1972 Chevy Monte Carlo was one of the cleanest cars I'd ever seen. It was dark purple with light purple flakes and had so much candy on it; it could give a nigga sugar diabetes. "Damn nigga, how many coats of clear you got on there? Three or four?"

"Twelve."

"What?" I said more surprised at how calm he was. "Are those Irocs?"

"Yep, twenty sixes."

"Son of a bitch. Wanna sell it?"

"No."

"You sure," I asked excitedly

"Nahh, bruh I'm good."

"Hater," I said through my laughter.

"I'll be back at eight," he said, then started the Chevy. It sounded like a dinosaur roared.

"Damn what's under there?" I asked pointing at the hood. He just smiled and shook his head. I gave him some dap and watched as he pulled into traffic on Rosecrans. When I got back to my office Simone was sitting in my chair and holding my phone.

"Who's Misty?"

"Where'd you hear that name?"

"She called you."

"You answered my phone?"

"Yes, is that a problem?"

"No, just curious."

"Who is she?" she asked a little too aggressively.

"A friend."

"That all?"

"Yeah."

"Fine!" she said slapping the phone into my palm and storming out of the office.

"Mannnn," I said, then laughed at myself because I sounded like my son. As seven o'clock quickly approached, G-Rick called to tell me he couldn't make it. That left me without a partner. I decided to sit out this tournament anyway. Instead, I would film the whole thing and put it on the internet. At a quarter to seven KD rolled up and came into the office.

"You ready?"

"I'm not playing tonight."

"I ain't talking about that."

"Oh yeah. I'm ready."

"You still mad?"

"Nahh."

"Good, never shoot at a nigga when you're mad. You'll miss."

"Alright."

Chapter Twenty One

Compton California 2002

"I thought you didn't like those," I said pointing at the Calico he had hanging around his neck. "I don't, Dana took my Glock to work."

"Aww, y'all even share guns… how cute."

"Fuck yourself," he said as I followed him out of the office. While he went to check the food, I went over to the sitting area and set up the T.V. My 80" plasma had a lot of features, but the most impressive was I could split the screen in half and play two games at once. I set it up and waited for the players to arrive.

The first to arrive were my homies Fat-Rat and Junk Man. I greeted them lightly, then gave them a bottle of Moet and took their entry fee. They played as a team. 'Sherm Alley' was the name of their team. After they showed up Stretch and Spider showed up drunk.

"Sup Blood?"

"Man how much y'all drink already?"

"I dunno," Stretch said, then handed me too much money. I took five one hundred dollar bills and gave him the rest back.

"What name y'all using tonight?" I asked Spider who was more sober.

"Bottomsville Blood!" he said almost screaming, then they walked off with their bottles.

Capone from 89 East Coast showed up next and was talking shit before he even got in the door. "Where's the rest of the victims?"

"What, you been practicing?"

"Very funny nigga. Get my money ready. What's the prize tonight?"

"Like 2,500."

"Oh I need that. I needs that!"

"How's Julie?" I said asking about his mom.

"She cool she, said to tell you hi."

"Give her my love."

"Aiight. Where's the wings? I'm starving like a mothafucka!"

"KD's in the kitchen," I said as he walked in the direction of the food. The next two arrivals were the only two that I hoped *wouldn't* show up; Little Slim and Baby Slim from Inglewood NHP. Baby Slim wasn't that bad, I knew him from the Y.A. days. But Lil Slim was 100% asshole. The only incident I ever had involved these two, KD, and a lot of shots fired. "Blood you dirty?" I asked Lil Slim as soon as they gave me their money.

"Nahh we good," Lil Slim said instantly spotting KD. They locked eyes.

"Blood, if you on some bullshit tonight take yo money, grab a bottle and bounce."

"Nahh, Rowdy I'm straight."

"Bang it!" I said making him give me his word as a Blood.

"On Piru I ain't tripping."

"You too, nigga!"

"Blood I'm here for all that free money and the belt." Baby Slim said referring to the Championship belt I had made for the winner. They each took a bottle, then walked over to the Street Fighter game by the door.

"Cuzz trippin?" KD came over and asked, hoping he'd get to shoot first this time.

"No he ain't trippin', but if you gone call everybody, Cuzz all damn night, some shit might start." I said passing him the video camera and walking over to greet Pot and his brother Sean from the Trees.

"Sup with you niggas?"

"That belt. That money," they both said at the same time.

I laughed and said, "Y'all got y'all hands full tonight. The champ ain't even here yet."

Sean the usually quiet one of the two said, "Before the night's over, we need to talk. I have some information you might need."

"Good or Bad?"

"Good I guess. I'm not sure." He said in a cryptic way that made me nervous. By now the shop was alive and full of energy and conversation. A few non-players showed up to spectate: O.G.Cuicide from Lantana, Pineapple from Luedars Park, and Short Dogg from Sho'line all came to the tournaments to trash talk and side bet. Mess and Short came at about eight and blended right in.

"Where's Tiny and Tony Bogart from the P.J's?" Capone asked, inquiring about the champs from the last tournament.

"They'll be here," I said as I started to put names in a hat to see who played who. I went to the bathroom to take a piss and when I walked up the hallway I stopped. Tiny had the belt slung over his shoulder like The Rock off WWF and was talking shit to the video camera. Tony Bogart wasn't with him though. Instead, he had a youngster with him. I recognized the kid immediately as the guy from Jordan's café a few months prior. I crept back down the hallway and called Tiny from the office, deciding to have some fun.

"Hello?" Tiny barked into the phone

"Tiny it's me."

"Oh hey Loc, what's up?"

"Who's the kid you got with you?"

"This my nephew, he playing cause TB got the blue."

"The what?"

"He sick."

"You mean the flu?"

"Yeah, whatever."

"I'm gone have some fun with yo nephew, just play along."

"Why what he do?"

"Just play along nigga, damn!"

"Aiight."

Click… After I hung up with Tiny I called KD and said two of his favorite words, "Blanket Party."

"Who?" he asked and I could see him smiling into the phone.

"The kid, Tiny's partner."

"Tiny know?"

"Yeah, I just called him."

"C'mon!" I grabbed my Centennial High School beanie and walked back to the sitting room. I winked at Tiny as KD crept up behind the youngster and I pulled the beanie over his head, down to his chin, then KD grabbed him in a choke hold and dragged him down the dark hallway.

Somebody screamed, "Oh shit look," but by then, I was already on my way back to my office. When I entered the office KD had the kid sitting in the chair across from mine. He looked like one of those Iraqi hostages with the beanie pulled over his head and the calico pressed firmly against his temple. I sat on the edge of my desk close to the kid, then asked KD, "Tu es prêt? (You ready)."

"Oui (yeah)."

"Tu veux tuer? (wanna kill him?)."

"Oui (yep)."

"Il est tres peur, oui? (He's hella scared huh?)."

"Oui." This all made the kid hella nervous, but he was tough though. Until KD cocked the Calico.

"I'm sorry," he said in a scared voice. "I don't know Spanish, don't kill me."

Tiny came in the office a few minutes later. I put a finger to my lips in a 'shhh' manner, then told KD to take the beanie off the kid's head.

"Sup homie?" I said with a big ass smile.

His eyes bulged out of his head as I waited for his memory to defog. "The Restaurant?"

"Yep"

"I gave you a pass" he pleaded.

"I had a gun," I shrugged.

He looked over at his uncle, but his uncle pointed back to me and said, "This my nigga, I've known him for a long ass time. Whatever you did or said, apologize for it. Now!"

He apologized then we talked for a while, then went back to the front to start the tournament. I gave my little speech about respecting me, my shop, and each other. After that, I told everybody the rules and offered them their money back for the last time. With that done I hung the belt on a wall hook and pulled the first two names out of the hat. 500 Degrees vs. Sherm Alley was the first match up. Bay View vs. Sag Low was the second.

When the games had officially started, I grabbed Sean and walked back down the hallway to my office. He closed the door when he came in which automatically told me this was going to be big.

"Kevon I know you, you not finna let that shit go. The streets is watching. And talking. A war is coming. If I can give you the shot caller for the T-Flats will you just kill blood and leave it alone, or are you finna go on one?"

"How do you know that's who shot me?" I asked curiously.

"Everybody knows."

"How?"

"They just do, people talk."

"Look blood, if you can give me ol' boy, I'll keep it low and quiet. That's all I'll promise."

"No Gang war?"

"Nahh, I want revenge not fame."

"And when you go, can I come?"

"Why?"

"He's my connect. I might as well re-up for the last time."

"KD gets half."

"The Crip nigga?"

"That's my Bro'."

"Aiight, but no money, just dope."

"That's fine."

"Bang it!"

"On Tree's blood." We sat and talked for a while longer, then went back to the tournament and watched as the Bay View team easily knocked off team after team. It came down to them and Sherm Alley. After two over times, Bay View won 38-35. It was easily the best tournament I ever had.

"It's the water man," Mess said popping his collar as I passed him the $2,500 and the belt. "Keep that" he said handing me the belt back as we walked out to the parking lot.

"You good?"

"Yeah, I gotta' get on the way-way."

"Call me so I'll know you made it."

"Fa sho."

"Aiight then, Kell"

"Aiight bruh." Then they were gone.

The shop was a disaster area. There were cups, bottles, and plates everywhere. "Just leave it" I told KD when he started to clean up."That's why I pay Dannie and them," I said, passing KD the $775 that was left over.

"What's this for?"

"For the Peaches' deal. I forgot to pay you."

"I know!"

"Shut up fool…"

I locked up the filthy shop, then we stood in the parking lot and I told KD about my conversation with Sean.

"You trust him?"

"No but I trust you," I said as I looked into his face.

"I got you," he said.

"I know."

We hugged like brother's, then got in our trucks.

"Wanna race?" he asked as we pulled up to the light on Wilmington and Rosecrans.

"On green," I said, but he hit the gas and vanished into the fog and traffic.

Bastard!

Chapter Twenty Two

Compton California 2002

My ride home was kinda peaceful… Aside from a few phoneinterruptions from adrunkenKelis, I rode on the freeway alone. Just like I liked it.

When I exited the 105 freeway on Sepulveda there was virtually no traffic. The light was taking way too long so I said, 'fuck it' and ran the red light. What I didn't see was the damn Highway Patrol car tucked behind the Airport Marina car lot. They immediately got behind me and hit their lights and siren.

Pulling over to the curb I felt stupid. These were the kind of small mistakes that could easily turn into a life sentence. If I had taken the Calico instead of letting KD keep it, I'd probably be in a high speed chase right now, or on America's Dumbest Criminals. For a while the officer just sat in his car and allowed his spotlight to burn through the back of my window. I assumed he was back there running my plates and was pissed off when they came back clean. The situation was perfect for racial profiling of some kind, young Black man, sixty thousand dollar truck, etc. There had to be a gun, or some drugs somewhere.

After what seemed like forever, the cop finally got out of his patrol car and approached my driver's side door. I already knew the procedure so I rolled my window down half way and stuck my license, registration, and proof of insurance out of the window. Instead of taking the paper work out of my hand, the cop stuck his hand inside the Porsche window and I felt the cold steel of a revolver press against my forehead. I didn't jerk or make any sudden moves, because if this was one of *those*cops, I was probably dead any way. I kept my left hand on the steering wheel and my right frozen in the position it was in as the cop opened the truck door and sat in my lap.

"Hey baby doll," Amber said giggling like a school girl.

"Are you crazy?" I asked pushing the gun away from my face. "Girl you scared the shit out of me!"

She handed me her gun and began to plant kisses all over my face and neck. "My shift's over in an hour, can you come over?"

"Are you gonna' give me a ticket?"

"No, just a warning."

"Okay, just knock on my door when you get off."

"Okay."

"Okay," I said trying to squeeze one of her huge breasts and getting nothing but bullet proof vest. "Wear that uniform too, it's kinda' sexy" I said, swatting her hard on the ass as she walked back to her patrol car.

When I finally made it into my apartment Fifi didn't greet me at the door in her usual excited fashion. Instead, she looked up from her spot on the couch and yawned like she was bored. "Fuck you too!" I said giving her the finger on my way to the kitchen. After I grabbed two Lunchables and a juice box that was left over from my son's last visit, I checked my messages. Misty, Mess, and Simone. Simone's message was dry and clear, "Don't forget we have church tomorrow. I'll pick you up at nine." I returned everybody's call except Simones, then took a quick shower.

After my shower I sat on the couch to watch Saturday Night Live and wait for Amber to come by so I could Rodney King her with this dick. She did at about 12:15; we went over to her place to play cops and robbers.

Morning came fast, but time flies when you're having fun. And to be honest, after the nasty shit I'd just did with this White girl, I needed to go to church. I walked out of Amber's apartment at 9:15a.m rubbing my wrist from the handcuffs she had used on me. When I got into my own apartment, Simone was dressed and waiting for me.

"You're late!"

"You're early!" I said as I walked by her, avoiding her gaze. I don't know why I felt guilty. But, I did. We rode to St. Peter's Cathedral in difficult silence. In a way, I knew things had changed and I didn't even care.

"Are we okay?" Simone asked.

"Yeah I guess, why?"

"You seem different."

"A lot of drama lately."

"The shooting?"

"That too," I said and she knew exactly what I was talking about. The church service was good. The sermon was about the true hearts of men. It seemed like the Catholic priest was looking directly at me every time he said the words *evil* or *demon.* I wanted to ask him if he'd humped any ten year old boys lately. My Grandmother would have killed me if I had though. After the service I caught up with my Grandmother and Aunt Janet to chat, then asked Simone to take me home. When we got to my floor and exited the elevator, Amber was in full uniform and headed right towards us.

"Hey Tiger."

"Hey Ma. Off to fight crime huh?"

"Yeah, it's a job, Have a nice day."

"You too," I said and as the elevator doors closed I could feel Simone looking at Amber.

"Oh my God, a fucking White girl!" She said as she turned around.

"What?"

"Don't what me! I saw the way she looked at you."

"Yeah, how?"

"Like you fucked her."

"Man you're trippin'!"

"Like I said before, you're gonna lose me."

"Don't threaten me Simone."

"I'm not."

"Look," I said changing the subject. "I won't be in the shop for a while, just take care of everything and do the bank runs. Ten percent of everything goes into Pascal's account. Can you handle that?"

"I'm not stupid."

"I'll take that as a yes," I said going into my apartment.

"I love you Kevon," she said instantly going from tough to soft.

"I love you too." I said it more out of obligation than emotion.

"Call me later, please?"

"I will puppy, I promise." I said as she headed towards the elevator. When I got in, I called KD and told him my plan, then ate the last Lunchable and layed down in my church clothes. Tomorrow, the killing started…

"You look cute," I told KD as he came in my apartment in his best suit.

"Whatever nigga." He passed me his backpack, rushing to the bathroom.

"Damn, what's in here?" I asked opening the black backpack. He had two of everything: two Tazers, two Halloween masks, two pairs of gloves, and two handguns. His Glock, and my Berreta equipped with the silencer. He emerged from the bathroom carrying a water bottle filled with what looked like piss. "What the hell?" I asked pointing at the bottle.

"How do most niggas get caught shooting?"

"Powder burns, duhhh!"

"And what's the one liquid that prevents powder burns?"

"Oh," I said, then went to look for a water bottle for myself.

"You can use some of mine!" KD said laughing at his own sick joke.

"Nahh, I'm good nasty ass!" I screamed from the bathroom. After I made my own pit stop we got on the elevator and got on the road. "Where'd you get this shit box?" I asked as I looked around the Toyota we were riding in. "It's Dana's."

"Dana's big ass be riding in…" I started to say until he looked at me crazy. "Nice car I mean."

As we went over the plan again I explained to him that we were Jehova's Witnesses until we got in the house. Then once we got in, it's whatever.

"You get the bibles?"

"I forgot."

"Jackass!"

We pulled up at the house on Magnolia and just sat in the car. It was about 10:00 in the morning so all the kids, if there were any should be at school. The house was typical for a poor Hispanic family in Compton. Junk cars, and chickens in the front yard. A sagging chain linked fence, and a lawn full of Budweiser cans.

After we'd sat for a while KD asked, "You ready?" then got out of the car before I could answer. When I caught up with him on the porch I saw the primer'd up front end of a Chevrolet Caprice. The license plate matched the one on the video. After a few knocks on the door, an old lady finally answered. "Hi we're here to spread the gospel of Jesus—."ZZZZZZAP. I jumped as KD pushed his tazer into the old lady's sagging breasts and fried her night gown. I caught her, mostly by her thinning hair, then we pushed into the house and closed the door.

I pulled my Berretta out and pointed it at the old man sitting in the old ripped up Lazy Boy chair. He had half a bottle of Jose Cuervo in front of him and was fast asleep with his chin on his chest. KD raised his gun to shoot, but I slapped his wrist and pointed at the picture on the DMV print out. Instead, he walked over and gently lifted the man's chin and stuck the tazer on his sore, bloated lips. The old body jerked and spasmed as the ten thousand volts woke him up and then knocked him back out again. The smoke coming from his mouth made me gag as I pushed quickly through the back of the house, opening all the closed doors on my way.

The house was cleared except for the back room. I figured from the smell of PCP, and the oldies blasting, the people we wanted were in there.

Then the bathroom door opened. I reached it too late. KD was already emptying his gun into the girl's small body. Each bullet jerked her body a different way as huge red blotches appeared on her N'SYNC t-shirt. When she collapsed into the bath tub I closed the door but not before noticing her age. No more than 15-16.

I crouched low and waited for the bedroom door to open. It didn't. I knew somebody had heard the 14 shots KD fired. I thought, 'fuck it' and opened the door. When I did, I saw the guy from the DMV print out and a friend of his sitting in separate corners. Both *stuck.* Stuck is the term for high off of PCP. A person that's stuck is usually like a living mannequin. They can't move or talk. And, a lot of the time, don't know where they are.

KD put in a fresh clip and casually walked up and shot the first guy in the middle of the chest. He jerked once and fell backwards into the walk-in closet. The shot obviously gave the other guy some awareness because he screamed "Hey!" before KD blew the noodles of his brains and pieces of his skull all over the blinds and a picture of an Aztec guy holding a dead lady that was hanging on the wall.

"C'mon!" said closing the door, then we walked back through the house and out the front door. The atmosphere outside was the same. Only the chickens seemed to notice that something was different because they were all under the house.

I loosened my tie as KD turned on Alondra and headed towards the rendezvous. When we stopped on Alondra and Central I finally broke the silence. "She was just a kid. A kid."

"How many innocent kids they kill? Plus, you know the rules, ain't no rules."

"Still dog," I said as a gray Lincoln Town-Car pulled up next to us.

"It's a war Kevon. No prisoners!" as he said that I looked out the window at the car full of Ese's, then I looked passed them at a little girl crossing the street. She had the dead girls face.

"What the fuck you looking at Ese?" The back seat passenger of the Town-Car asked me as I snapped out of my daze.

I said, "Nothing, sorry man." Then the light turned green and we rode to the next light. When they pulled up next to us again, I smiled, then leaned all the way out of the window and emptied the whole twenty one round clip into the car, hitting everybody and leaving the driver lying against the horn dead.

"Plan B?" I said feeling the power of busting a gun surge through my body. Plan B was always the same. Park the car and get on the bus. We parked on 169th and Avalon, then got on bus number 446 headed to Rosecrans.

"Feels good huh?" KD asked as we rode on the back of the bus.

"Yeah," I said smiling. This was the best alibi in the world. All people would remember was two guys in business suits and carrying a backpack. I got off on Rosecrans and KD stayed on.

"Two weeks?"

"Two weeks."

"Call me." I said and watched the bus until I couldn't see it anymore, then called a cab to take me home. As I sat with the mixture of students and workers waiting for the bus I watched the helicopter circle over the area where I'd just killed three or four people. The cab ride home was quiet on the outside, but in my head, guns were going off and people were dying. I paid the cabbie, then got on the elevator happy to finally be home. Before the elevator doors could close a black boot was forced between them and was followed by a Highway patrol uniform.

"How ya doin?" the older cop said as he un-tucked his uniform shirt and took a deep breath. I wasn't in the mood to talk, especially to a cop so I put on my best confused face and goofy smile and said, "Eh?"

"How-are-you?" the cop said slowly and deliberately making sure I understood.

"Je ne comprehend pas"

"What? Oh…" the cop laughed embarrassed. "Habla Espanol?"

I smiled, this time for real. The double gold bars on his shoulders made him a captain, but I didn't understand how when he couldn't tell the difference between Spanish and French.

Luckily, the doors opened on my floor so our time together was over. As we walked down the hallway it didn't dawn on me where he was going until she opened her apartment door almost naked. He picked her up in a huge bear hug and I fumbled for my keys while he palmed her ass with a loud smack and kissed her on the neck. She stared at me over his shoulder as my lock finally cooperated. I shook my head in disgust, then walked into the depths of my dark apartment.

Fifi was herself today and jumped into me as soon as I made it in. It's funny how all *bitches* were two faced. Even my damn dog. After I reloaded her automatic feeder and changed her water I walked out onto the small patio and prepared my BBQ grill. After I made sure the clothes caught fire I closed the top and went to take a long hot shower. I couldn't shake the image of the little girl, it just kept playing in my head.

As I toweled my body I knew I needed some company to get my mind off of the day's events but I didn't feel like being bothered. And, as a rule, I never let anybody know where I lived. I put on some basketball shorts and walked to the kitchen to find something to eat. There was nothing there which really pissed me off because I was almost starving. Angrily I grabbed a bottle of Aquafina and a row of Ritz crackers then, sat down at my computer and logged onto Pink Dot.com. This was the only site on the internet where you could order all of your groceries and have them delivered. While I browsed up and down the virtual aisles I decided to give Misty a call.

"Hello?"

"Hey Ma."

"Oh, so you *are* alive."

"Don't be like that Misty."

"Do you answer your phone, or is it just me?"

"Is this our first argument?" I asked, laughing at how genuinely upset she sounded.

"Yes."

"Okay, you win."

"You're not getting off that easy!"

"Whatchu doing, where's Jermaine?"

"With the sperm donor."

"Oh, how long?"

"A few days."

"Wanna get kidnapped?"

"Yes."

"Okay. I'll be over there in an hour."

"How long am I being kidnapped for?"

"Til Jesus comes back."

"That's a long time."

"Yeah, you better pack some extra thongs."

"Okay. See you in a minute."

"Bye."

"Bye."

After I ordered and paid for my groceries, I lotioned my ashy body and grabbed the keys to the Viper. When I pulled up in front of Misty's complex and she came out, I noticed that I was really happy to see her. Almost excited.

"Nice car, 2000 right?"

"Yeah, how do you know that?"

"I know everything," she said leaning over and giving me a nice long kiss.

"I needed that."

"Is that all you need?"

"No."

"What else do you need?"

"Some of your big juicy…"

"My big juicy what?"

"Cooking," I said as she punched me in the shoulder. "I missed you," I told her, actually meaning it. "I couldn't tell."

"I'm busy ma."

"Doing what exactly? You own a Range Rover and a Viper. I'm almost scared to ask what you do."

"Then don't."

"Drugs?"

"Hell no! Stop racial profiling me!" I said and we laughed for a while.

"You park these cars in Watts?"

"Huh?"

"You told me you lived in Watts."

"Oh yeah, I moved." For a while we rode in comfortable silence, then I did something that I'd never done before. I reached out and took her hand. It was warm and it fit perfectly into mine. When my phone rang, I was actually pissed off.

"Yo!"

"Hey Blood, this Sean."

"Oh hey, wassup folks?" I said trying hard to hide my gang affiliation.

"Was that you?"

"Whatchu talkin about?"

"Those four bodies on Magnolia," as he said that I counted the bodies we left in the house. There was only supposed to be three. "Four?"

"Yeah, two dudes, a girl, and an old lady"

'Shit'—"Nahh, that wasn't me dog."

"C'mon Rowdy don't lie."

"For real dog."

"Bang it!"

"On P's, but why do you care? And why do you want me to admit some shit like that on the phone."

"Cause blood ain't fucking with me now."

"Who?"

"My connect, he cut me off."

"It wasn't me. I swear." Yep, I was lying my ass off, but *technically* I wasn't. KD did all the shooting on Magnolia so I was telling the truth.

"Alright, when do we go?"

"Two weeks."

"Aiight, Su Whoop."

"Bye"

The look Misty had on her face said everything she was thinking, and so I answered her question before she could ask it. "You *don't* wanna know, trust me."

The next three days were the most pleasant and erotic I'd ever had. We didn't just fuck. We explored each other from the inside out. She asked all the right questions, and if she didn't like the answer, she told me that too. We laughed, joked, cuddled, had sex, and made love. When I had to take her home it made me sad.

"So, this is it?" I asked as we pulled up to her apartment complex.

"For now," she said biting my bottom lip gently."Yeah, there's a good chance."

"Yes!" I said like a happy kid. This made her laugh, that made me smile. "Bye Misty."

"Bye Kevon," she said using my real name for the first time.

For the next five days, I learned the habits of Sean's connect. I followed him, his wife, and his other girlfriend all over L.A. He lived with his wife and ten year old son in a gated community in Signal Hill. His son went to Leapwood Elementary in Carson. His wife dropped their son off and picked him up from school. She didn't work and enjoyed the pampered life of a drug king pin's wife. At least that's what the 600 Mercedes said.

He had a fetish for old muscle cars and owned a fleet of Mustangs, Corvettes, and, GTO's. He never went anywhere alone and only spent the hours of 10-12 at the dope house.The dope house was in a quiet section of Paramount. From the amount of traffic at the spot, and the quality of the vehicles coming and going, he was making a killing. Security at the house was minimal. Aside from two Rottweiler's and a high gate, security was non-existent. He probably figured he didn't need a bunch of dudes running around with guns in a neighborhood like this.

I continued to watch and continued to take notes until I had his patterns down pat. The following Saturday I tracked the wife to an address not on my list. When we arrived at the cheap little duplex in Lynwood and Sean opened the door and grabbed her in a

Lover's embrace; I almost shit on myself. I crouched low in therented Taurus and watched in awe as she retrieved a small Victoria's Secret bag from her Benz and disappeared inside Sean's Apartment.

"He's fuckin her!" I told KD when he picked up his phone.

"Huh? Who's fucking who?" he asked through a yawn.

"Sean. He's fucking the connects wife."

"No!"

"Yeah."

"So where does that put us?"

"I don't know dog. I need to sit and think."

"How'd you find out?"

"I followed her to his house."

"Damn!"

"Let me bounce this around in my head, then imma' call you tomorrow."

"So we still on schedule?"

"Yep, two days but we might end up going alone."

"Let me know…."

"Aiight."

"One."

Chapter Twenty Three

Compton California 2002

As I drove down Imperial Hwy on my way home I went over all the angles that Sean could possibly be trying to work. None of them made sense, except one. He was thinking with his dick. That one thing helped me put together a new plan with the only tool a person needed to win a war. The element of surprise.

I know it sounds like one of those chapters out of the 'Art of War' or '48 Laws of Power', but hey, whatever works… I turned onto Wilmington Ave and decided to pick up an Ox tails dinner, and flirt with Pam at Jordan's Café. As soon as I walked through the glass door she was on my case.

"Boy where you been?"

"Why, you miss me?"

"Yeah, come'ere and gimme a hug." When we hugged I kissed her on the cheek sensually and squeezed her booty through her thin dress.

"You are a mess," she said still holding onto my lower back.

"What scent are you wearing?"

"Chanel. You like it?"

"Yeah, it's making me hungry," I said as she slowly pulled away, and out of our embrace.

"Good, order something," she said becoming a business owner again.

"Give me an Ox tail dinner"

"Okay," she said writing my order down, then switching her ass on purpose as she walked away.

While I sat and waited for the food I called my Grandmother, my son, and Simone. The last call was stiff and formal. She filled me in on how well the shop was doing, then told me she had a date. I laughed and said, "Congratulations!" Avoiding the argument she was trying to start.

When we hung up I took my food and got on the freeway. As I neared the 105-110 interchange I decided to surprise Misty at work.

As I pulled up at the Kaiser building on LaCienega and Cadillac, I instantly became claustrophobic. I hate hospitals! Both of my parents died in one. When I got to Misty's floor I didn't see her but I did notice the lady's name tag at the Nurses Station. It was Devereaux. A name that was definitely French. My guess was right. It turned out that she was Louisiana Creole, but learned to speak French in college. I had fun speaking to her and didn't notice when Misty walked up beside me.

"Oh my God, you speak French?"

"Oh hey ma, I brought you dinner"

"Oh how sweet, where'd you learn how to speak French?"

"My family is French"

"I didn't know that," Misty said, giving me a small kiss appropriate for the work place. "Say something in French"

"Vous aimez quand je te fesse,"

"That sounds pretty, what does it mean?"

"You like it when I spank your booty."

"Oh my God!" she said smacking me on the arm.

"Well, it's true," I said defending myself. This made her laugh even more because she did like to be spanked during sex.

"What did you bring me for dinner?"

"Some good soul food," I said passing her the tray.

"Ooh, I love ox tails. How do you say thank you in French?"

"Merci..."

"Okay, Merci."

"De rien" (you're welcome). "Well imma go ma. I just wanted to surprise you and bring you dinner."

"Ok, let me walk you to the elevators." As we walked hand in hand to the elevators she stopped and looked me in the eyes and asked, "How do you say I love you in French?"

"Why?"

"Just tell me," she said in a tone I hadn't heard before. It was soft yet demanding.

"Love is messy."

"Tell me, please..."

"Je t'adore." I said as I pulled out of our hug and stepped onto the elevator.

"Kevon."

"Huh?"

"Je t'adore," Misty whispered as the doors closed.

I pushed all the buttons trying to get the doors open. She loved me. That's crazy... it made me feel warm and fuzzy inside, and at the same time, it worried me. I tucked this all in a slot in my mental 'deal with later' file.

I punched KD's number into my phone. He answered again sounding irritated.

"What!"

"I got it."

"You got what?"

"The new plan."

"Okay what?"

"We go tomorrow night."

"Huh. That's a day early."

"Exactly. If we do it this way Sean doesn't have the element of surprise, *we* do. Especially when we show up at his house unannounced.

"Can we kill him?"

"Naw fool! For what?"

"Just asking. I thought you said ol boy only goes to the dope house between the hours of 10-12. If we go at night, he ain't even gone be there."

"I know, bring a sleeping bag," I said laughing at the potentially volatile situation.

"Home invasion?"

"Nahh, let's call it a slumber party."

"You're a dumb-ass!"

"Thanks."

"So what time do we move?"

"We'll surprise Sean at like 9 or 10am, then push to ol boy's spot a little later. I'll take the tools tonight. We don't wanna be riding around Paramount at night, three deep with pistols.

"Should I bring the precious?"

"The what?"

"The precious, my Tommy gun."

"You *named* that thing?"

"Yep."

"Something's seriously wrong with you."

"Whatever, call me in the morning."

"One…"

"One."

I had to stop at Chris Burger to get some food since I had given Misty my food. I loved riding on Crenshaw Blvd at night. Even though it wasn't Sunday night; the day when the 'Shaw cracked, it was still filled with the sights and sounds of a possible party. When I made it to KD's house on 41st, he met me at the gate and passed me the backpack.

"Got company?" I asked pointing at Dana's car.

"Ha ha, nigga. The Calicos are in there, I'll keep the nines."

"Dana take your Glock again?" I asked laughing.

"Yeah," he said in a little boy voice that made me laugh even harder.

"I still have *your* nine though," he said reminding me.

"Alright alright," I said heading back to the rental car.

"Nice car!" he said to my back.

Walking away, I gave him the finger, then watched the huge silhouette of Dana 'the bully' Banks came into view. "Hey Dana."

"Hey Pumpkin!" she said with a wave as I pulled away from the curb. When I got to Paramount I hid the backpack in the neighbor's trashcan and headed home. When I got off the elevator Amber was dressed in her gym clothes and headed in my direction.

"Hey baby doll!"

"You're such a ho'," I barked at her as I walked passed.

"No I'm not! Don't say things like that!"

"I'm going to the Doctor to get checked for H.I.V."

"That's mean Kevon," she froze in the hallway, almost about to cry.

I didn't care and kept walking."Are you trying to fuck your way to the top or do you just fuck *any* and *everybody?"*

"Oh my God, that's so messed up."

"Bye Amber, I'll send you my results," I said as I stepped inside my apartment and closed the door. I knew she was still standing there because I could hear the elevator go back down to the garage.

True, that was some real fucked up shit to say but I didn't give a fuck. She *was* a whore. I sat down on my sofa and ate my dinner with Fifi. After dinner I put her on the treadmill and I did ten sets with my curl bar. After our work out I changed the plastic kiddie pool that served as her litter box and took a shower. I did the triple S as Kelis would call it, then hopped in the bed and fell directly to sleep.

Chapter Twenty Four

Compton California 2002

I awoke the next morning to the sound of someone beating on my fucking door at 6:00 a.m.

Fifi was barking and scratching, trying to get to whoever was on the other side.

"Assiez-vous!" (Sit) I told Fifi, then opened the door. Parole Agent Smith, and another man were at my door. Guns drawn and ready. "Can I help you?" I asked in my 'I just got up voice'.

"Put the dog away, we need to talk."

"Hold on."When I put Fiona on the balcony the two parole agents came in and immediately started searching the apartment. I stood with my arms crossed as the two stupid bastards tore my living room and kitchen apart. "Looking for something in particular?" I asked as irritation began to spread over my whole body. The fact that they ignored me made it even worse.

When the search came up empty, the short Asian man asked if I had a problem giving a urine sample. I told him no, then demanded that they both follow me to the bathroom. Mr. Smith quickly asked why.

"So nothing gets planted and so nothing mysteriously happens to my dog. The truth was I wanted them both to see my dick and be uncomfortable. "Here you go," I said handing the small bottle of piss to Mr. Smith who wasn't wearing any gloves.

"Whoa! Be careful with that!" he said as piss sloshed around in the container. I tried my hardest to fart, but I couldn't. I would have loved to contaminate the air in the small space we were sharing. Instead, Parole Agent Smith said I had 90 days left on his caseload and that he'd be on my ass every hour of it.

When they left I let my dog in and decided to get dressed and go into down town L.A. to pick up a fake passport and other documents for my trip to Haiti. It was illegal for parolees to leave the country so I had to have all my ducks in a row before I left.

I parked the rented Altima at the McDonald's on 5th and Alvarado, and casually walked up and down the busy street. There were clusters of illegal Mexican immigrants that specialized in fake I.D's, Driver's licenses, and passports. If you knew what to look for you could easily spot them quietly tucked into donut shops and parked cars. Some would actually approach you and solicit their products. I had a guy; well my family had a guy that they'd been using for years. These were the same people I assumed, that produced Simone's birth certificate and social security card. I stopped at a hot dog vendor in Macarthur Park and bought an orange Fanta.

"I need a passport," I told the guy that was wearing way too much gold to be pushing just hot dogs.

He looked me up and down. "I'm sorry, no English."

"I'm not a cop."

"I'm sorry no English."

"I'll pay five hundred dollars for a good one."

"Meet me at Taco Bell in an hour," he said miraculously in English that sounded better than mine. I walked back to McDonald's to make sure nobody had stolen the rental car, then walked down to Taco Bell and sat at a back table. Thirty minutes later the hotdog vendor now dressed in Gucci from head to toe approached my table and took a seat.

"You sure you're not a cop?"

"I hate Niggers and Beaners."

"Huh?"

"Could I say that if I was a cop?"

"Ok, ok."

"I need a passport. Today."

"Those are expensive …"

"No they're not," I told the guy. "A guy just offered me one for eighty bucks so don't play yourself." I let him know I couldn't be bluffed.

"Ok, ok my friend. Six hundred."

"My price is five. And I want two copies."

"Huh?"

"Never mind," I said getting up to leave.

"Wait my friend! Today I do this special deal for you," he said giving me his prize winning smile.

"Thanks, I feel so special."

"Come with me." When I followed him back into the afternoon sun, we stopped at a pearl white Cadillac Escalade on gold 26's. A cute fat girl in a matching Fendi skirt and jacket took my picture with an expensive looking digital camera, then looked over and asked her husband if I was a cop in Spanish.

I answered, "If I was a cop could I do this?" and grabbed two handfuls of her big titties.

She smiled. "If you poliss, you bad poliss!" She closed the passenger's side door, still smiling and adjusting her blouse.

"Twenty minutes," the vendor told me, then pulled out of the parking lot in rapid fashion. Ten minutes later the fat woman came into the Taco Bell and sat closely next to me.

"For you," she said putting two small leather booklets on the table. I inspected the passports and immediately gave her my approval. She smiled, then leaned in close and put her chubby hand on my crotch. I laughed as I felt my dick harden and her smile widened.

"Muy grande …."

"Gracias," I told her as she softly caressed my dick through the thin material of my basketball shorts.

When the husband entered we quickly parted and I began counting out the fee for the passports.

"Pretty good, huh?"

"Yeah, I'm impressed," I said handing him the money. "Gimme your number we might do a lot more business," I said looking at the chubby lady with the magic fingers. He wrote his number out on a napkin, then we all got up to leave.

"Hey, what's your name my friend?" he asked as he got in the driver's seat of the Escalade.

I looked at his wife and said, "Muy Grande," then, turned and walked back in the direction that the Altima was parked. When I got on the 110 freeway I decided I'd hang out at the shop for a while and check on things.

When I pulled up at the shop Simone, and the guy from before, Mr. Wall Street, were standing at the front door arguing. I just sat in the Altima and watched as he grabbed her by the shoulder and she knocked his hand away. My feelings went through the obvious phases of anger and jealousy. Finally they settled on amusement. I got out of the Altima to both of their surprise.

"He hasn't been inside!"

"I didn't go inside!" they both started to say but I waved them off and walked passed them and into the shop. I knew from the smell of fried foods that my Aunt had decided to come to work. I went to hug her on my way to my office.

I made a few quick phone calls, checked all my accounts and the bills. Then I went on the patio to spend some time with my puppy. At 7:00 the last customer walked out of the shop and Simone finally made her way to my office. She sat quietly while I spoke on the phone with KD who was en route to the shop. When I finished my call she just sat on the couch and looked at me.

Finally she asked the question I'd been expecting, "Who is she?"

"Who is who, Simone?"

"Who is the reason you look like that," she crossed her arms over her chest and leaned back.

"Like what?"

"You look happy, Kevon."

"I'm not happy. I'm hungry, horny, and tired."

She leaned forward. "I can help you with that."

"Nahh, I'm sure the suit wouldn't like that."

"Fuck him!"

"I'm sure you already did …."

Silence… At that exact moment KD entered the office, and my Aunt poked her head in to tell me she was leaving.

"Y'all alright?"

"Yeah."

"No!"

Silence… I asked Simone if I could talk to KD alone and after she stalked out of the office we got down to business. KD told me he had just came from Sean's apartment, and that his car was there. After going over the plan again he told me Dana was already parked outside the dope house in Paramount and that she'd be there the whole mission as a look out. Me and KD both knew she was mostly there to make sure nothing happened to him. When we walked out to the front KD walked over to Dana's Corolla and picked up a new backpack before he jumped in the car with me. "What's that?"

"Handcuffs, duct tape, pills and a sleeping bag…"

"You dirty?"

"Yeah, but if the pigs get behind us imma' jump out."

"Alright, let's do this."

When we pulled up at Sean's complex I grabbed KD's backpack and threw it in the back seat. He jumped and screamed,

"Don't do that!" I looked at him crazy and continued to eyeball him as we walked up the stairs to Sean's door.

Before I knocked, KD pulled out his Glock and cocked it. I made a 'put that away' motion and continued to knock on the door. Sean answered on the third knock and opened the door wearing his too little boxers.

"Get dressed!"

"Huh? How do you know where I live?"Sean was standing in the doorwayrubbing his eyes.

"A little bird told me. Get dressed." I told him as I pushed passed him and into the apartment. He went to his bedroom and came back dressed like he was going to a club.

"Change!"

"Huh?"

"We're going to kill people, not goin' to fuckin' Sky Sushi, Blood go change!" When he came back in an all black khaki suit we went out the door and headed to Paramount.

"How'd you find out where I live?"Sean asked again after we got on the freeway.

"I told you."

"That's some bullshit!"

"Yeah. A lot of bullshit is going on," I said as I watched KD in the rear view mirror.

"What's that supposed to mean?" KD looked up at me from the back seat.

Silence…

"What are you carryin'?"

"My fo-five why?"

"How many shots?"

"Thirteen why?"

Silence…

When we finally pulled up to the house, I spotted Dana in KD's Tahoe parked a few house down.

"Here's the plan, gimme your gun."

"Huh? Helllll naw!"Sean protested.

"You afraid of somethin'?"

"No."

"You up to something?"

"Of course not, come on dog…"

"Okay, well gimme your gun because they gone search you before they let you in. Then once you get in, open the bathroom window for me in exactly five minutes."

"That's it? Ol' boy ain't here, you know that right?"

"All you want is the dope and money," I said to Sean. "Let me and KD worry about ol boy." I was still holding my hand out for his gun.

When Sean approached the gate the Rottweilers started barking which automatically made a huge Ese in Dickies' shorts and a tank-top come out and see what was causing the noise. After he shushed the dogs he searched Sean, then let him in the house and closed the door.

"I forgot about the dogs."I said looking back at KD.

"I didn't," KD handed me a Ziploc bag filled with four huge raw hamburger balls.

"What's this?"

"Just give it to them," he said giving me my silenced Beretta. I got out of the car and walked over to the neighbor's trashcans to retrieve the backpack I had stashed there last night. The dogs immediately came over to where I was. I put on the backpack, then threw all of the hamburger balls over the gate. They each attacked one and stopped barking the minute they got it in their mouths. I quickly jumped the gate and tazered the female dog. The male charged me, but stopped and couldn't open his mouth. I recovered from my initial fear and tazered the shit out of the other dog. I made my way to the opened bathroom window.

Then climbed into the bathroom making way too much noise, then settled quietly on the cold tile floor

After I tucked the Beretta, I pulled out both Calico's and made my way up the carpeted hallway. As I approached I could hear the older Ese telling Sean he had fucked up by coming over here without Nico's permission. Sean tried to speak, but a younger Ese socked him in his mouth.

Sean was about to get socked again before I stepped into the living room and said, "Feliz Navidad!" a Calico pointed at each of them. The girl sitting on the couch looked up shocked, then put her hands up like everybody else. Sean immediately jumped up and socked the young Ese in the face knocking him unconscious.

"Shoot this mothafucka, Blood!" Sean said, angrily wiping blood from his mouth.

"Sit down," I told the older guy as I walked over to the front door. When I did, the doorbell rang. I peeked through the peep hole and saw KD and the precious. I let him in, closed the door, and started the party. "Get him up" I told Sean and watched as he picked up the skinny guy that socked him.

"Let's kill these mothafuckas!"

"No."

"Huh? Why not?"

"What if Nico calls. Then what?"

"Oh yeah."

"Let me run this ok? Do you mind?"

"No."

After KD cuffed everybody I relaxed a little, watched in awe as KD went to the kitchen and got an apple. Making sure to wash it off in the sink.

"What now? Sean asked sounding worried.

"We talk"

"Huh?"

I told KD to take the two guys in the back, but asked him not to kill them

"Why not?"

"They're not my enemies," I told him; then walked up over and asked the older guy what set he was from. "Paramount Varrio Dog Patch!" he said loud and proud.

"Take'em in the back," I told KD. When he did, I told the girl to stand up. When she did I pulled up her skirt and slowly pulled her panties down. She looked at me unafraid, almost like she enjoyed it. I held the sexy red thong in front of her and asked her, "Am I going to have to stick these in your mouth and tape it shut?" she smiled and said no, then sat back down.

KD came from the back room and grabbed one of the backpacks, but not before asking me if my phone had a camera on it. I told him it did and watched as he and my phone disappeared down the dark hallway. We all sat tensely in the living room for a while; then KD came back to the living room with the two guys naked and taped together belly to belly, face to face.

The girl let out a little giggle, I laughed and asked, "What the hell is wrong with you?"

He looked innocent and said, "What?" Then, threw me my phone. The girl was red in the face from laughing and pointing at the guys' little weenies.

While the guys stood like a naked statue, Sean said, "I'm going to look for the money."

I gave KD a Calico and said, "Go with him, no accidents!" They vanished towards the back of the house. The girl and I sat on the couch and watched "Coming to America," for a while and then with a loud smack the two Ese's collapsed on the kitchen floor. Ironically the big guy was between the little guys legs. "Oh my God!" the girl said pointing her handcuffed hands.

"They aiight," I said figuring KD had something to do with their present condition.

Picking up the girl's thong and shooting it across the room like a rubber band, I asked her,"You ever been a hostage before?"

"No, it's pretty cool though." she said smiling and shaking a piece of hair out of her face. A few moments later Sean and KD returned carrying a suit case apiece.

"What'd you find?"

"Twenty keys, and *my* money!" Sean said a little too aggressively.

"Nigga, what you mean *your* money?" KD asked in that voice that was usually followed by violence of some kind.

"Can I talk you in private?" I asked KD, heading towards the kitchen. "First, what was the deal? That is his money and you know it. You get half of the dope. Ten kilos is a lot."

"I hate his ass!"

"I can see that, but a deal is a deal right?"

"Yeah, fuck it"

"Secondly, what'd you do to them?" I asked pointing to the obscene pile of flesh on the tiled floor.

"Pills."

"Shit. How many?"

"Five… Each."

"Damn, will that kill them?"

"Nahh, just fuck up they memory."

"You sure?"

"Scouts honor," he said as the girl screamed, "Stop it!"

When we got back to the living room Sean was standing and trying to force his dick into the girl's mouth. "Stop, Blood. Knock that shit off," I told him as he laughed and put his equipment away.

He told the girl, "Bitch I'm finna be ballin'. You know you wanna fuck wit a nigga like me" After that he picked up his suit case and prepared to leave.

"How long you been fuckin' her?" I asked him as he headed towards the door. He stopped instantly and dropped the bag.

"Fuckin' who?"

"Don't play games Sean, games are dangerous."

"We're in love," he said, and I watched as he tightened his grip on the handle of his gun.

"Don't do that, guns make me nervous." For a while he didn't move, then finally he dropped the gun on the suitcase and sat on the single step near the door.

"How'd you know?"

"That doesn't matter, but I do have a question that does. Is ol boy really from T-Flats?"

"No."

"So you used us to rob and kill him?"

"No."

"Fuck you mean no!" KD said charging towards him before I grabbed him.

"So, what now?"

"I don't know, but we'll spend the night here like one big happy felony family."

We slept in shifts. KD mostly stayed up talking on the phoneto Dana and picking his toes with a big ass Rambo knife. When the sun came up through the blinds, I woke up from an unexpectedly good sleep. When I opened my eyes, KD was standing over Sean's sleeping body, holding the precious in one hand.

"Maybe later," I said as I got up to rinse my mouth out.

"Excuse me, I gotta pee," the girl told me. I looked at KD who vigorously shook his head. This meant I had to take the girl to the bathroom.

When she finished she said, "You have to wipe me" and smiled like she knew I would be grossed out. I pulled what seemed like half a roll of toilet tissue off the roll and clumsily wiped her cleanly shaved pussy too roughly. "You did good," she said as we walked back to the living room.

Sean and KD were on opposite sides of the room. Then, the phone rang. For a minute nobody moved. We all just kinda looked at it, then the girl said, "I'll answer it. I promise not to try anything." I looked at KD who hunched his shoulders, then picked up the phone and pressed it to the girl's ear. She spoke cordially as if she were speaking to her boss and said, "Okay, bye," and pulled her ear away signaling to hang up. When I did she said, "He's on his way here."

"Now?"

"Yeah, he says he'll be busy between ten and twelve." KD picked up the now drowsy, but fully awake Ese's and herded them into a back room. I called Dana and told her to be on the lookout.

Peeking out the window I saw the two Rottweilers patrolling the yard again.I asked KD what was in those hamburger balls I'd given them. He smiled and said, "*Choosey moms choose Jif!*" using his White lady accent. If I wasn't so tense I probably would've laughed.

When Dana called and told us Nico was pulling into the garage, I put Sean and KD in the first two bedrooms, on opposite sides. I figured,if they really wanted to shoot each other, now they would have their chance. The girl I gagged and put in the bath tub in the Master bedroom.

A pair of strong voices made their way up the hall to where I was standing. I heard doors swing open, and KD yell, "Get down!" I entered the hallway where KD had the Tommy gun pointed at shoulder's length, across the hall at both of the entrants. And Sean. Sean in turn had his .45 pointed in the opposite direction.

The older guy I assumed to be Nico called Sean a backstabbing nigger before I tazered his ass unconscious. The other big guy just smiled, then didthe stupidest thing he could've done. He head butted Sean knocking him against the wall, making him drop his gun. He was on top of Sean before either one of us could get a shot off. The knife he had seemingly came out of nowhere. As they fell into the open bedroom on the left, I fired a burst from the Calico into his expensive looking dress shirt. Sean quickly escaped from under his dead body and frantically wiped blood from his arms and neck.

"Let's go!" I said lifting Nico's unconscious body and dragging him into the garage. Sean went to get his suitcase and KD did the same. After I put Nico's body into the trunk of a '68 Pontiac they returned with their bags. I dumped the full clip of the Beretta into his unconscious body and closed the trunk. Next I went and got the girl and found KD and Sean at the front door.

"No good!" I said as I pointed out the window to the big ass dogs. We all ran frantically back towards the garage. KD pulled out a weird looking alarm clock with dynamite taped to it out of his backpack, then rushed back into the house. While I waited for KD, Sean jumped into a gold '66 mustang and started the engine. When KD came back we jumped into a Grand National with the girl, then we all pulled out of the garage with a squeal of tires. The male Rottweiler bounced off the door of the Grand National as we headed down Somerset followed by Dana and Sean.

The sirens were drowned out by the sound of the explosion. As we went down alleys and back streets, I stole a glance at KD who was grinning like a maniac. "What?" he asked as I reached in the back seat to remove the girls gag.

"You okay?"

"Yeah."

"I didn't wanna do that."

"I know," she said as she sat back and put her seatbelt on. When we turned off McKenzieStreet, Sean shot passed us continuing on his own. We took Somerset until it turned into Compton Blvd, then slowed our speed and drove like a normal person would.

"Gimme some money."

"Huh?"

"C'mon man, I don't sleep that hard.," I told KD letting him know I was up when he went in Sean's bag and took one of the Ziploc bags filled with 50's and 100's.

"Fuckin' party pooper!" he said throwing me the back pack.

"No more bombs?" I asked scared to open the backpack.

"Nahh," he said laughing, then we entered downtown Compton. I took two huge stacks of money and gave it to the girl. "This is for you. Yesterday and today never happened, and, if it did, you don't know anything. This is 'thank you for your cooperation money'. But, it's also hush money. You got relatives out of state?"

"Yes, in Arizona."

"Good, go and visit them for a while." Next I showed her the I.D card that I had taken out of her purse back at the house. In a firm tone I said, "Don't make us come to this address. If we have to, I'll make sure your whole family gets closer to God. And as you can tell, even when I tell him not to kill people, he does it anyway."

"Today never happened."

"Good girl."

When we pulled into the shopping center and parked in front of the Superior super market, I told the girl to go across the street and get on the Metro Rail. As she slowly eased out of the back seat, KD got out and began to unload our gear into the Tahoe. We watched as the girl walked across Willowbrook Ave and passed the Sheriffs car that was stationed there. She smiled and waved when her train arrived, then stepped on clutching her bulging purse to her small breasts.

"You think that was smart?"

"I don't know. I figure, she took some money so she's as guilty as we are," KD and I hopped in the Tahoe. When we were safely on the 105 freeway and out of harm's way, I slapped KD on the back of the head as hard as I could.

"A bomb? A got damn real bomb! Are you outta' your mind?" I asked him laughing as he rubbed the spot where I smacked him. "Where'd you get a fuckin' bomb from anyway?"

When Dana smiled and raised her hand, I said, "I shoulda' known." We rode the rest of the way back to my house in silence. At my complex KD got out and walked me to the elevators.

"So, you really going huh?"

"Tomorrow."

"How long you gone be gone?"

"Depends, I'll call you."

"And you're really taking the Viper with you?"

"Hell yeah! Have you seen the cars in Haiti?"

"Who knows you're leaving?"

"You, Simone and Misty. I'll tell my Grandmother in the morning. My flight leaves at ten.

"Want me to see you off?"

"Nahh, just keep an eye on everything and take care of Fiona."

"Aiight fool, I got you."

"Oh and stay out of jail."

"I'll try."

We hugged hard, but warmly. He turned and walked back towards the Tahoe.

"Leave Sean alone!" I said to his retreating back. He gave me a peace sign, got in the Tahoe and pulled into traffic. When the elevator dinged and opened on my floor, I let out another one of those breaths I didn't know I was holding. I showered, then ate a whole extra-large Digiorno's pizza with Fifi. After dinner I decided to take her across the street to the park for some much needed exercise. During the middle of one of our games of Frisbee my phone began to ring, and to my delight it was my son. "Hey kid, what's up?"

"Dad can I come and live with you?"

"What's wrong?"

"He hit her. He hit my mom again." He said breaking into tears.

"Huh? Where's your mom now?"

"We're at my Grandma's house. She's scared to go home"

"Did you see him hit her?"

"Yes, I'm the one that ran over Uncle Paul's house and called the police."

"Put your mom on the phone!"

"Hu, Hello?"

"Your problems are you problems. But if my son see's or hears that shit again, ol boy disappears. You understand?"

"Yes."

"Good! I'm going O.T. for a while. When I get back, we gone talk."

"Okay."

"Put Pascal on the phone."

After I consoled my son I decided to go home and pack. I was ready to go after checking my accounts and paying a few bills on-line. I set my alarm clock and my phone for 6:00 a.m., then jumped in bed and fell instantly asleep. The dreams came right away. The bank, Damion dying, Holding Solo's bloody body... they all came in a rush. In the last dream, there was only a dove. A snow white dove. Seconds before my alarm clock erupted with Radio Free KJLH 102.3, the beautiful dove was splashed with blood.

I jerked out of my sleep and shook off the remnants of the dream, dismissing it as a mind trick. After I showered and shaved I loaded my bags in my arms and told Fifi to be a good girl. Dressed only in black jean shorts, a pair of red/black and white #4 Jordan's, and a red Brett Favre Atlanta Falcons jersey over my Kevlar vest, I hopped in the Viper and headed to my Grandmother's house. The dash board clock read 7:26 which meant my Grandmother had been up for a while. She was sitting in the kitchen having her morning coffee when I walked through the side door.

"Eh, bonjour Minouche" (good morning my, love), she told me hugging me tightly, then pulling away and knocking on my bullet proof vest.

"Trouble?"

"Non, J'ai un surprise" (no, I have a surprise).

"Quel surprise?" (What surprise?).She asked looking at me skeptically over her coffee cup. I smiled, then pushed my plane ticket and passport across the table to her.

"Oh, mon petit!" She cried happily, then grabbed me and held me tightly. We chatted excitedly for a few more minutes, then I gave her a $10,000 cashier's check. After that I got on the freeway and headed for L.A.X.

Since I was taking the Viper to Haiti with me, I had to go through the commercial section of the Airport first. After going through a million gates and check points, I entered the loading zone and saw the huge airplane that the Viper would be loaded on. The Tech in charge of the loading told me five minutes so I sat in the warm cock pit of the Viper against the morning cold. When my phone began to ring I started to ignore it and take my vest of since I'd have to take it off anyway in a minute.

"Hello?"

"Hey, what's up? Are you in the air yet?"

"No, not for another hour."

"Good. Are you sitting down?"

"Yeah, why? You sound funny Misty."

"I do? It's probably because of this baby of yours I'm carrying."

I sat up to say, for real? When the passenger's side door opened, I barely had time to notice. All I heard was the first shot and Misty scream my name into the phone. It was ahead shot, I knew for sure. The rest of the bullets hit my vest or landed in the side panels of the car. I remember being pushed out of the driver's seat and into the passenger's side. I figured that much out. Before the loading hatch and my eyes closed, I saw it, or at least I think I saw it. The same white dove....

EPILOGUE

The Creation and Life of 'Just Like Compton'

Growing up, both of my parents were on drugs and both died on parole. See, like most kids whose parents were victims/participants of drugs and Reaganomics I was raised by my Grandmother, and she tried to steer me out of where I was headed, but I wouldn't listen to her.

After she died, I landed in the foster care system. And soon after that, all of the other systems soon followed. I spent a total of thirteen and a half (13.5) years in ***"systems".***

I learned that the Foster care system is a preparatory system for the Juvenile Hall system.The Juvenile Hall system is a preparatory system for the Youth Authorities. The Youth Authorities are a preparatory system for the Prison System.

I learned during and after prison that you have to be tired enough to change.You have to be sick and tired of being sick and tired to really want to change. People, particularly men who continue to go to Jail, Juvenile Hall, Youth Authorities and then Prison over and over do so because they aren't tired. In the end, you have to get tired, I did.

I learned you have to hit rock bottom before you can begin to make the changes that will improve your life. I had two (2) strikes as a juvenile, and I got nailed on a three (3) strikes case. My rock bottom was hearing a judge tell me he planned to sentence me to 150 years in prison with no plea bargain.Those where rough words.

The opportunity for me to write came when my friends and I had a "disagreement" with the Correctional Officers. Because of this “disagreement” we were ordered to go to the “Hole” which is called Administrative Segregation. In this unit there are a total of thirty (30) cells, and I was placed in unit number nine (9).

I had an excellent lawyer who gave me very good advice. Now having time to sit down and focus my thoughts,I used my time in prison to read and study and further my education. The novel came easily to me. Once I started thinking about the story and remembering certain events from my past, it began coming to me in my dreams. I picked up the structure of the novel from books I had read.

I’ve read my competiton in the genre of urban novels and instead of making the mistakes they made; I chose to write the personal stories of living my life in Los Angeles... my hood, Compton.

While writing the first chapter of the book I didn’t know if it was going to be a good, bad, or okay job. So, when I completed the first chapter I passed it to the cell next door, once they finished reading it they gave me their thoughts, then they passed it to the cell next door to them until all thirty (30) cell units read the first chapter. When we had an opportunity to go to the “recreation yard,” a place where all inmates go to exercise, everyone was talking about the chapter. They give their positive reviews like it was real book and treated the characters like real people.

I was then inspired to write the second chapter of the book. With so much postive feedback and inspiration the second chapter was completedquickly and I began to circulate that chapter just like I did the first chapter. However, when it came to writing the third chapter I ran out of paper. In a California penitentiary, they only issue inmates four (4) pieces of paper a week. Unless you are lucky and have friends, loved ones, or family looking out for you.

Knowing I needed to complete my writing I would trade food off my tray during breakfast and or lunch. Items such as cookies, apple juice etc. In return, I would receive the writing paper I needed to continue building "Just Like Compton." As a result, I had began a barter system that allowed me to produce my manuscript and breathe life into ***Just Like Compton*** the novel.

In April 2010, I was released from prison I had this 386 page handwritten novel and the next obstacle was getting it published. I went to lots of different publishing websites and eventually I found Amazon's Create Space publishing program. I liked the deal I got from them so I went with them. Then I used guerilla marketing by going to various bookstores, barbershops, and beauty supply stores, selling over 1200 copies myself with little to no promotion.

I went from a level-IV prison yard to standing in an ice cream line next to a lady with my book in her hand. It just shows you that anything is possible and you can turn your life around if you're committed to the idea and don't give up.

When you see someone who is wrapped up in the criminal lifestyle, you are only seeing the outside--what he/she wants to project. But inside there is a person (not a prison) who has real feelings, and maybe has something he/she wants to do that would be good for him and good for society. One thing I heard all my life was"you can't do that." I heard that often enough that I was determined not to use my misfortune, bad decision making, or Society's ills as a crutch any longer.

My whole life is different. I'm definitely not "Rowdy" anymore.

SHOUT OUTS

FOR MY HOMIES DOING LIFE, HOLD YOUR HEAD.
FOR ALL MY HOMIES RESTING, YOU LIVE FOREVER IN THESE PAGES …

AKILI-BHW, ARTURO-TTP, BABY DAVE-ICG,
B.G AWOL-KPCC, BANG-APG, BIG JUNE-DLB,
BIG TWEET-MSB, BIG OOS-PVCC,
B-KRAZY-PPB, BLACC-CUZZ -WCC, BLACK-FLAG-VNG, BOXER-62-ECC, C-LOONEY3-VSLC, CAPONE-89ECC,CASPER-CPF,
CEREAL-PPB, CHICO3-NH60'S, CHINA DOGG-LPP,
CHUCKSTONE-BPS O.G.CUICIDE-LBCC,
D-DOG-APB, DE-DOGG-FDCC, EVIL-PDL, *FATRAT*-FTP, G-SEX-DLB,
G-ROCK, TTP, GODDFATHER4-PDL, HANGOUT-DLB,
ICEE-TRG, IDI-AMIN-BPS, INCH-TTP,
J-RU-WSP, JACKIE-FTP, *JUNKMAN*-FTP,
JUNIOR-FRESNO BULLDOGS,KD-NH40'S, KABOOBY-69 VILLAGE,
MUSCLES-TTP, *KRE-KRE*-APB, *LUMBERJACK*-BWB, LK-OPB,
LOONEY-NH60'S, M-ROCK2-BPS, MESS-EPA, *MOMO*-FTP, MOON4-ICG, BABY SOLO-77SWANS, , MOOSE-CPP, MOTOR-CBP,
NELLARU-CPP, LIL MAN-FTP, OAKPARK-MARK-OPB, OTTO-LNX13,
PEACHES-CPCC, PINEAPPLE-LPP, PUKA-RU-FTP, POTT-TTP,
CHILLY DUB-FTP, *ROOSTER*-FTP, SCROOGE-WBLC, SkREWY LOUIE-DLB, SHACK-PPB, SHADEY GRADY-ESP, SHORT DOGG-VSLC,
SHORT-BROOKFIELD, SILENT-CMG, SLIM2&3-NHP, SLUG-TTP,
SNAKE-NHB, SOLO2-OL20'S,*SPIDER*-CMG, SQUEAK-CAC,
SQUIRT-R20'S, STEEL TOE-FTB, *STRAWDOG*-83HCG, STRETCH-CMG,
TONY BOGART-PJW, *TINY*-PJW, TOOCHIE-FTP, VDOG-PVCC,
WOODY-PDL, ZEEK-APB…

IF I FORGOT ABOUT YOU I'LL GET YOU IN PART 2.

ACKNOWLEDGEMENTS

Sean, I didn't mean to make you a bad guy dog, it just happened like that. I know you in heaven mad at me. LOL. June, I didn't forget about you Comrade it's just taking longer than I expected.

Love and respect, Taco, Rowdy, Kevon....

On another note, this book is dedicated to the Memory of some very special people.

Willie-Mae Bender, my Grandmother, the lady that came to get me when I was living in an abandoned Project unit alone. All she said when she pulled up was, "C'mon baby let's go." I can still smell the faded perfume she was wearing as I hugged her tight and cried all the way to Compton. Grandma I love you and I thank you so very much for doing the best job you could raising your kid's kids.

To Billy Ray Scott, I did it big rellie! I know you're up there proud of me and yep, I still remember what you said...

And finally, to Floyd Kenneth Smith Jr. What can I say they don't even make dudes like you no more Lil Bro. You stayed with me through court even when they were trying to give me 150 years to life. And you were at the gate to pick me up 7 years later. I Love You lil bro and I'll spend the rest of my life trying to pay you back for everything you did. You kept your word when everybody else lied and left me for dead. God bless you and Thank you. To my Parents. Y'all were wrong about me... I love you. I hope you're proud. Ultimately, to God... I didn't forget the promise I made to you as I kneeled in the middle of that cold prison cell. Imma do it, just give me a little time.

Ganguage/Glossary

13:(x3) The number signifying all *Southern* Hispanic gangs. (South Siders) i.e; MS13, F13. Etc. “13” is the biggest gang in the world stretching all the way to Mexico and Central America.

14:(x4) the number signifying all the Hispanic gangs in *Northern* California. (Nortenos)

190: One of the various factions of the Crip gang **East Coast**.(ECC) i.e; 69 East Coast Crips, 76 East Coast Crips. The number signifies the street the neighborhood began on. In this case 190th Street in Carson California.

2P’s: An abbreviation for the Blood’s gang Pacoima Piru’s. in Pacoima California.

456:A Blood’s gang located in Pomona California, and Dallas Texas.

.32: A caliber of hand gun

.38: A caliber of hand gun

.380: A caliber of hand gun

.9mm: A caliber of hand gun (the most popular and most accessible in the gang culture)

40NHC: A faction of the massive gang Neighborhood Crips, or “Rollin.” Some of the other factions are the 20’s, 30’s, and 60’s. These gangs boast popular celebrity members like the rappers **Kurupt**, **Nipssey Hussle**, and **Snoop Dogg**. All are located in West Los Angeles except the 20’s which are located in Long Beach California.

69 Village: A neighborhood in East Oakland California, and home to now deceased millionaire drug kingpin Felix Mitchell.

A.R.: An abbreviation for the assault rifle A.R.15.

Aiight: A slang variation of “alright”

Avenue Piru Gang: (APG) A known Blood gang in Inglewood California

Athens Park: (APB) A public park and recreation centerand known Blood gang in South Central Los Angeles

B.I.P.: Blood In Peace. The Bloods version of R.I.P. (Rest In Peace)

B.M.: (baby’s moma) the mother of a child who is no longer in a relationship with the father.

B.P.S.: (Black Peace Stones) a known Blood gang in West Los Angeles and one of the biggest. Originally started in South Chicago it now spans many states in the USA. It’s two main factions are the City (bity) Stones and the infamous “Jungles” made famous in the movie Training Day, starring Denzel Washington.

Badonka Donk: a slang term for a large posterior, butt, booty.

“Bang It”: A gang members way of saying “Give me your word.” i.e “I’m going to pay you on Tuesday.” I don’t believe you, *Bang it*!”

Bay: (The Bay) any area located near the coast of Northern California. Particularly including Oakland, San Francisco, Vallejo, and Richmond.

Beef: a slang term for animosity. i.e “Hey Charles, do NHC and BPS have *beef*?”

“Bickin’ it”:A Blood’s gang-member way of saying “kickin’ it” which is slang for hanging out with friends, alone, or with a loved one. i.e “Hey Charles wassup?” “*Bickin* it with my Dad”

Bloods: The **Bloods/Pirus** are a street gang founded in Los Angeles, California.in 1969 The gang is widely known for its rivalry with the Crips. They are identified by the red color worn by their members and by particular gang symbols, including distinctive hand signs. The Bloods are made up of various sub-groups known as "sets" between which significant differences exist such as colors, clothing, and operations, and political ideas which may be in open conflict with each other. Since their creation, the Blood gangs have branched out throughout the United States.

Bloods have been documented in the U.S. military, found in both U.S. and overseas bases.

Gangs in some European countries including, England, Holland and France pledge their allegiance to the bloods but they are not thought to be directly linked to sets in the USA. The bloods now have a host of famous members including but not limited to NBA professionals **Paul Pierce**, and **Baron Davis.** Rappers**, Lil Wayne, The Game**, Waka Flocka Flame,**and Mack10**.

"Blood rack": A prison bed claimed by the Bloods"

Books: an inmate's Prison/Jail checking account.

"Bool": A Blood's gang-member way of saying the word 'cool'. i.e " Hey Charles you ok?" "Yeah, I'm *bool*"

Bompton: A Blood's gang-member way of saying the word Compton

"Brazy": A Blood's gang-member way of saying the word Crazy

Campanella Park (CPP): A public park and recreation center, known Bloods gang in Compton California

Carver Park (CPCC):A public park and recreation center, known Crips gang in Compton California

C.O.: an abbreviation for Correctional Officer. (Prison Guard)

Compton Avenue (CAC): A known Crips gang in Watts California

Connect: The Person one purchases his Drugs, Guns, Cars from.

C.T.Q.: Confined To Quarters. “Locked in a cell”

Cheese Toast: A term of disrespect for the East Coast Crips.

Chow: A prison meal

Crab: A term of disrespect for the Crips. Also included are, ricket, ericket, and crosstown

Crenshaw Mafia (CMGB): A known Bloods gang in Inglewood California

Crip(s): The **Crips** are a primarily, but not exclusively, African American gang. They were founded in Los Angeles, California, in 1969 mainly by Raymond Washington and Stanley “Tookie” Williams. What was once a single alliance between two autonomous gangs is now a loosely connected network of individual *sets*, often engaged in open warfare with one another.

The Crips are one of the largest and most violent associations of street gangs in the United States, with an estimated 130,000 to 135,000 members. The gang is known to be involved in murders, robberies, and drug dealing, among many other criminal pursuits. The gang is known for its gang members' use of the color blue in their clothing. However, this practice has waned due to police crackdowns on gang members.

Crips are publicly known to have an intense and bitter rivalry with the Bloods and lesser feuds with some Chicano gangs. Crips have been documented in the U.S. military found in bases in the United States and abroad

Crip Walk: a dance created by and for the Crips:

Cuzz: A term of endearment the Crip gang members call eachother.

CV: (Compton Varrio) All Hispanic gangs in Compton begin with these initials. i.e CVTF, CV70's, CVL36. Etc

D.A.: District Attorney.

D.P.: (Discipline) an act in which your friends kick and punch you to correct an infraction of some kind. Some D.P's can lead to death

Damu: The Swahili word for Blood, and second name for the Bloods gang

Daytons: Popular car rims for gang members during the 80's and 90's

Dear John: A letter in which your girlfriend/wife tells you that she's leaving you.

Del Amo: a section of Carson California

Die-ru: A disrespectful term for Pirus

Dinga Lings: A disrespectful term for Denver Lanes

Dirty: slang term for being in possession of contraband. i.e "Hey Charles you *dirty*?"

DLB: (Denver Lanes) A known Bloods gang in Los Angeles, and Pasadena California.

Dopefiend: Sucker punch

ECC: East Coast Crips. A known Crips gang located on the east side of Los Angeles, Carson, and the Inland Empire.

ESP: (East Side Pain) A known Bloods gang in Wilmington, California.

Ex-Con: Ex-convict

Fish: A new arrival at a correctional facility, Prison

F13: (Florencia) A known Hispanic Gang in Los Angeles

FTB: (Fruit Town Brims) A known Bloods Gang in Los Angeles, California

FTP: (Fruit Town Pirus) A known Bloods Gang in Compton, California

G-Ride: a slang term for "Stolen vehicle"

Gear Gang: A known Crip Gang in Los Angeles

Grape Street Watts:(WBLC): A known Crip Gang in Watts, California

Guerrillas:(BGF) Black Guerrilla Family A known Prison Gang in the California Penal System. Deeply rooted in African Culture, History, Politics.

Hard white: A slang term for rock cocaine

Hating (hatin'): A slang term for exhibiting jealousy openly

Hawthorne Piru:(HPG) A known Bloods Gang in Hawthorne California

Heat: A slang term for a weapon of some kind usually a knife or gun.

Hood: A slang term for neighborhood

Hoodrat: An extremely promiscuous female

Homes: A term of endearment used by all Hispanic gang members.

Hot one: a slang term for Murder, penal code 187.

Jama: the Swahili word for *family*

Juneteenth:**Juneteenth is the oldest known celebration commemorating the ending of slavery in the United States.** Dating back to 1865, it was on **June 19th** that the Union soldiers, led by **Major General Gordon Granger**, landed at **Galveston, Texas** with news that the war had ended and that the **enslaved were now free**. Note that this was **two and a half years after** President Lincoln's **Emancipation Proclamation** - which had **become official January 1, 1863**. The Emancipation Proclamation had little impact on the Texans due to the minimal number of Union troops to enforce the new **Executive Order**. However, with the **surrender of General Lee in April of 1865**, and the **arrival of General Granger's regiment,** the **forces** were finally strong enough to **influence** and **overcome the resistance.**

Kiwe: the *alleged* Swahili word for Crip

KO'd: "knocked out"

Kumi: A known Prison Gang in the California Penal System. Deeply rooted in African Culture, History, Politics. A division of the Black Guerilla Family

Kutt: A member of a known Prison Gang.

L36: (CVL36) A known Hispanic gang in Compton, California

Lantana: (LBCC) A known Crip Gang in Compton California

Luedars Park:(LPP) A public park and recreation center, known Bloods Gang in Compton California

Level: I, II, III, or IV: Different levels of security in California State Prisons, IV being the highest and most dangerous

Loc: a term of endearment used amongst the Crips

Long Beach Insane: (ICG) A known Crip Gang in Long Beach California

Mash: a slang term for a violent assault. i.e "Let's mash his ass"

Mad dog: A menacing stare

Mini 14: The standard issued assault rifle used in California Prisons

Mona Park: (MPCC) A public park and recreation center, known Crip Gang in Compton California

Nachos: A disrespectful term for 190 East Coast Crips

NHB: (Neighborhood Bloods) A known Bloods gang in South Central Los Angeles

NHP: (Neighborhood Pirus) A known Bloods Gang in both Inglewood and Compton California.

Nickerson Gardens: A Housing Project, and home of the **Bounty Hunter Bloods** Gang in Watts California.

Nuttys:(NBCC) A known Crips Gang In Compton, California

O'Farell Park: A public park and recreation center, known Bloods gang in San Diego California

Oak Park: a known Bloods Gang in Sacramento California

Outlaw 20's: a known Bloods Gang in Los Angeles California

P.C.P.: As a recreational drug whose main ingredient is embalming fluid. PCP may be ingested, smoked, or snorted.

PDL: (Pasadena Denver Lanes) A known Bloods Gang in Pasadena California, A faction of the Denver Lanes originally started in Los Angeles

P.Funk: A term of endearment used amongst Pirus

Paisa: a Mexican national living in the United States

Park Village: (PVCC) A known Crip Gang in Compton California

Piru: The **Pirus** are a Compton,California area street gang alliance (under the larger alliance, Bloods) based out of Compton which spread to Carson, Inglewood, and Watts,San Diego, as far as Japan.

Project Watts: (PJW) a known Crip Gang in Watts California

Playboy Gangsters: (PBGC) a known Crip Gang in Los Angeles

R&R: Receiving and Release. A section of the California State Prison System

Raza: The neo-Chicano word for the Mexican race.

Ru Ryda: A term of endearment used amongst Pirus

Santana Block: (SBCC) a known Crip Gang in Compton California

Shot Caller: A high ranking gang member responsible for all decision making duties

Skyline: (ESP) A known Blood Gang in San Diego California

Sky Sushi: A popular nite club and restaurant during the late 1990's and early 2000's

Slob: A term of disrespect for any Blood gang member

South Sider: A moniker for any Southern California Hispanic gang member

Strikes: any and all violent or serious felonies in the California Penal code handbook. Associated with the *3 strikes and you're out* law enacted in the mid 1990's.

SubThompson Machine Gun: (Tommy Gun) A machine gun made popular by the Italian Mafia during the Early 1940's

Su Whoop: A call to arms, and acknowledgment for all Blood gang members.

Swans: (MSB,FSB) A known Blood Gang in South Central Los Angeles California

T. Flats: (CVTF) Tortilla Flats. A known Hispanic Gang in Compton California

Tree Top Piru: (TTP) A known Blood Gang in Compton California

Tiny Rascals Gang: (TRG) A known Asian Gang in Long Beach California. Loosely allied with the Crips.

"**Trippin":** a slang term usually used as a verb. In most cases the term is used for one who isn't behaving properly. But sometimes it can be used in other forms.

"**Twenty G's**": an abbreviated slang term for twenty grand. Or $20,000

Venice13:(V13) A known Hispanic gang in Venice California.

Venice Sho' Line:(VSLC) A known Crip Gang in Venice California

West Coast 30's, 80's:(WCC) A known Crip gang in San Diego, Long Beach California

Young Gangsta: (Y.G.) a title of Blood gang members

Youth Authority: (Y.A.) A form of prison for juvenile offenders in California

Sociology 104: Social Problems - JLC Reference Grid

Chapter 1 Family Relationships The “babymoma” culture Economics	Chapter 2 Creole culture, Gang culture Crime/Legal system Relationships Family Economics	Chapter 3 Crime/Legal system Relationships Economics	Chapter 4 Creole culture, Gang culture Family Relationships Crime/Legal system Economics
Chapter 5 Crime/Legal system Gang culture Relationships Family Economics	Chapter 6 Crime/Legal system Gang culture Relationships Economics	Chapter 7 Crime/Legal system Relationships Gang culture, Creole culture Economics	Chapter 8 Relationships Crime/Legal system Family Economics
Chapter 9 Relationships Family Creole culture, Gang culture Crime/Legal system Economics	Chapter 10 Relationships Family Creole culture, Gang culture Economics	Chapter 11 Crime/Legal system Relationships CreoleculturePrison culture Economics	Chapter 12 Relationships Crime/Legal system Gang culture, Prison culture Family Economics
Chapter 13 Gang culture, Prison culture Crime/Legal system Relationships Economics	Chapter 14 Gang culture, Prison culture Relationships Economics	Chapter 15 Gang culture, Prison culture Relationships Economics	Chapter 16 Relationships Creole culture, Cougar culture Family Economics
Chapter 17 Gang culture, Creole culture Family Relationships Crime/Legal system	Chapter 18 Relationships Crime/Legal system Economics	Chapter 19 Crime/Legal system Culture Relationships [double standard] Economics	Chapter 20 Relationships Economics
Chapter 21 Crime/Legal system Relationships Gang culture Economics	Chapter 22 Crime/Legal system Relationships Economics	Chapter 23 Creole culture, Cougar culture Relationships Economics	Chapter 24 Gang culture, Creole culture Crime/Legal system Family Relationships Economics

RED=CRIME/LEGALSYSTEM VIOLET=CULTURE YELLOW=RELATIONSHIPS BLUE=FAMILY

ECONOMICS=GREEN